DEATH IS NO SPORTSMAN

DEATH IS NO SPORTSMAN

CYRIL HARE

PERENNIAL LIBRARY

Harper & Row, Publishers

New York, Cambridge, Philadelphia, San Francisco

London, Mexico City, São Paulo, Sydney

This work was originally published in England by Faber & Faber Limited. It is here reprinted by arrangement.

First PERENNIAL LIBRARY edition published 1981.

ISBN: 0-06-080555-2

81 82 83 84 85 10 9 8 7 6 5 4 3 2 1

DEATH IS NO SPORTSMAN

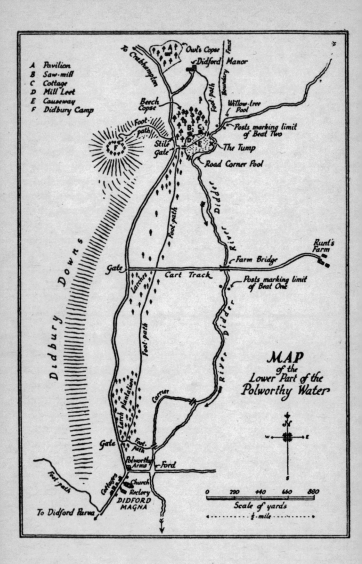

A Pavilion
B Saw-mill
C Cottage
D Mill Leet
E Causeway
F Didbury Camp

To Crabhampton

Owl's Copse

Didford Manor

Beech Copse

Foot-path

Boundary Fence

Willow-tree Pool

Posts marking limit of Beat Two

The Tump

Road Corner Pool

Foot-path

Stile Gate

Didbury Downs

Foot-path

River Didder

Runt's Farm

Gate

Cart Track

Larches

Farm Bridge

Posts marking limit of Beat One

Foot-path

New River Didder

Foot-path

Corner

Larch Plantation

MAP
of the
Lower Part of the
Polworthy Water

N
W   E
S

Gate

Foot-path

Polworthy Arms

Ford

Cottages

Church

Rectory

DIDFORD MAGNA

To Didford Parva

Foot-path

0   220   440   660   880

Scale of yards
¼ mile

CHAPTER ONE

The 'Polworthy Arms'

SHORTLY after the signature of the Treaty of Versailles, four business men, who had made enough money during the war to be able at last to attend to the really important things in life, formed a syndicate among themselves and bought the fishing rights of a reach of the River Didder. They were fortunate, for fishing on that famous chalk-stream is, as all the world knows, hard to come by and the properties along its banks are tightly held. From the village of Didford Parva down to the estuary it is reputed that few below the standing of a millionaire can afford to cast a fly upon those limpid waters. None of the four who composed the syndicate was a millionaire, or anything approaching it, and they counted themselves lucky to be able to secure the little-known stretch that goes with the Polworthy property, upstream from Didford Magna.

Didford Magna, as its name implies to anyone familiar with English topography, is a very small place. An eighteenth-century Act of Parliament, empowering certain turnpike trustees to build a road bridge across the river at Didford Parva, six miles lower down, effectually diverted thither the traffic and the trade of the valley, and the only relics of Magna's old superiority are its name, its vast church – which is the despair of the Rector – and its tithes – which are (or, until the recent legislation, were) his consolation. Apart from the Rectory itself and Didford Manor, nearly two miles away, the whole village comprises no more than two farms, a dozen labourers' cottages, the post office, and the 'Polworthy Arms'. This last, standing at the corner of the lane that leads down through lush water-meadows to the old ford, became the unofficial headquarters of the syndicate. For seven months of the year an undistinguished and not very prosperous public-house, it blossomed out in the summer, and at week-ends in particular, into the semblance of a fishing hotel. Two things it had in common with all such establishments – a pervasive smell of damp waders, and an extreme irregularity as to mealtimes. The landlady had in all probability never even noticed the first, and had certainly learned in the course of time to accept philosophically the second.

At about a quarter to ten on a warm Friday evening in June, when the murmur of voices from the bar was rising to a throaty *crescendo*, two fishermen were just sitting down to their supper in the parlour. Neither was an original member of the syndicate. Since its formation death had claimed one member and the crisis of 1931 another. A third, crippled with rheumatism, had resigned his membership only when his fingers could no longer be forced to tie a fly. Their places had been filled. The first newcomer was Stephen Smithers, who now sat at the head of the table. His bland, round face concealed a lively intelligence and a particularly crusty temper. He had used the former to advantage in his profession of a solicitor, and it was common knowledge that only an unwise display of the latter had prevented him from having been long since elected president of the Law Society. This evening, with a brace of two-pound trout to his credit, he was, for him, in an agreeable mood.

'Did I ever tell you, Wrigley-Bell,' he said to his companion, 'how I came to be a member of this outfit?'

'No,' said the other, 'I don't think you ever did.'

'You'd have remembered it if I had. It was when old Lord Polworthy died and the executors sold the Manor to your friend Peter Packer.'

'He's not my friend,' Wrigley-Bell put in emphatically. His heavy brows came down in a frown as he spoke.

'I apologize. Your business rival, Sir Peter Packer, baronet, I should have said. The estate was split up, you may remember. The farming tenants – poor devils – bought the freehold of their farms, and Peter took the house and demesne land only. Well, the farmers gave no trouble, but the purchaser of the

8

Manor claimed that the fishing rights were not a covenant running with the land, but merely an easement terminable with the death of the grantor, if you can understand that – '

'Put into plain English, you mean that Packer claimed he had bought the fishing with the estate?'

'For a business man you show unusual intelligence. That is just what I do mean. His property only affects a bit of our water, of course, from the road corner to the willow tree pool, but it's the very heart of the fishing, and naturally if he established his claim, the other owners might have done the same, and there would be an end of the syndicate. Matheson, who was then as now the secretary of the syndicate, came to see me about it. The fellow who drew up the original agreement, like more than half of my profession, hadn't known his business, and it looked as if Packer had a case. I examined the papers and said to Matheson, "I can get you out of this difficulty, but my fee will be the next available vacancy in the syndicate." I'd wanted to fish the Didder all my life, you see, and I knew Hornsby was due to go bankrupt, so I shouldn't have to wait long.'

'And Matheson agreed?'

'He had to. I told him that if he didn't like my terms he could go elsewhere, and he didn't care to take the risk.'

Wrigley-Bell laughed.

'And I always thought you liked the old guv'nor,' he said.

'I do,' answered Smithers unexpectedly. 'Unfortunately, he doesn't like me. Why, I can't for the life of me imagine.'

The other found it prudent to make no comment. He helped himself largely to potatoes and then endeavoured to change the subject.

'I wonder why Packer has set up that sawmill by the road corner?' he remarked.

'Because he's the kind of beast who can't resist the temptation of spoiling anything he gets his hands on,' was the reply. 'Because he's so rich that he must take the chance of making a little money out of the estate wherever he sees it. Because he knows that the road corner is the best bit of our water and he hates us like poison for having it. By putting up the sawmill he manages three things at once – he destroys the prettiest beech copse in the country, makes a little profit for himself, and makes life a hell for the unfortunate who happens to be trying to fish the road corner pool.'

'It's easy to see that you don't like Packer,' said Wrigley-Bell with a smile. He was much given to smiling, and unfortunately his smiles were not attractive. They began and ended with the lips, and were invariably coupled with a quick glance upwards from beneath his thick brows. The effect was oddly disturbing, a mixture of humility and defiance. It was a kind of propitiatory snarl.

Smithers looked at him as though he were seeing him for the first time.

'Like him?' he repeated. 'No. No more than anybody likes him, so far as I know. I could forgive him if he were a self-made man, as his father was, but he isn't even that. For Sir Peter Packer, second baronet, I have no use at all. Why, even you are no friend of his. You've just said so.'

'Good gracious no! Not a friend,' Wrigley-Bell protested. 'But in business, you know, one has to keep on decent terms.' He smiled again. 'I certainly don't feel any better disposed towards him after suffering from that sawmill today.'

'Yes. It has spoilt the second beat altogether. You'll be happier tomorrow in the peace and quiet of beat three. The guv'nor will be the sufferer tomorrow.'

'Only in the morning. I suppose they knock off work at midday on Saturdays.'

'Then you suppose wrong. Our beloved Peter is so anxious to make the most of the fine weather that he is paying overtime to keep the men on all day.'

Wrigley-Bell spluttered in indignation.

'Really, that is most – most inconsiderate,' he exclaimed. 'Are you sure?'

'Perfectly. Jimmy Rendel said so, and he ought to know.'

'I don't see that Rendel knows any more about it than the rest of us.'

'Don't you? Really, even for a business man you are remarkably obtuse. Hasn't it occurred to you that Jimmy and Marian Packer are – shall we say – somewhat closely acquainted?'

'Rendel and Lady Packer? You astonish me, Smithers, you really do!'

'Well, don't be so old-maidish about it. You can ask him about it tomorrow when he comes, if you like. Let us hope Peter is as slow on the uptake as you are.'

'But Rendel!' Wrigley-Bell protested. 'Why, he's only a boy!'

'I agree. Just the age for a romantic and hopeless love. Hopeless it is, mind you. I fancy that Marian Packer has her head screwed on the right way. But it can be no joke being married to Peter, and I expect she gets some fun out of Jimmy's attachment.'

'Certainly, now I come to think of it, Rendel has been behaving rather strangely lately. He has scarcely caught a fish this season.'

'As to catching anything, he's a rank bad fisherman. What can you expect from a lad of his age? The Didder is no place to learn the game on. We had to let him in, of course, because old Rendel had paid his shot before he crocked up, and Matheson insisted that he had a right to name his successor. But he's too young. This isn't a place for boys – or for women either. And talking of women,' he added, as quick footsteps sounded in the passage outside, 'that must be the fair Euphemia.'

CHAPTER TWO

Birds and Fishes

EUPHEMIA MATHESON was a woman of thirty-five or so, who, without being in the least degree stout, contrived to give a general and decidedly pleasing impression of roundness. Her cheeks were plump, her lips full and delicately curved, her brown eyes large and liquid, and she walked with a spring that was just not a bounce. Though dressed for the country in tweeds that admirably set off her really beautiful figure, she scarcely seemed to belong to the dingy inn parlour. Her careful make-up and reddened finger-nails contrasted too sharply with the untidy paraphernalia of rods, nets, and fly-boxes that encumbered it, and with the shabbily attired men at the table.

'Good evening!' she exclaimed in her rich contralto.

'Good evening, Mrs Matheson,' said Wrigley-Bell. 'Are you coming to join us?'

'Good heavens, no! I had my dinner at a Christian hour, ages ago. I've been out for a walk. It's such a delicious evening. What I came to ask for was news of my truant husband.'

'Your husband is still flogging the unresponsive waters of beat one, so far as I know,' said Smithers.

'The poor lamb! He'll be dead when he comes in! Why are you such brutes to him? It's the worst beat on the whole river. Couldn't one of you have changed with him?'

Smithers grinned, and rising, walked over to the mantelpiece, above which hung a green baize notice board. On the board was displayed a large card, setting out the names of the members of the syndicate and the beats that were assigned to them throughout the fishing season, in strict rotation. With great solemnity, he consulted a pocket calendar.

'Friday the 17th of June,' he announced, and studied the card. The relevant part of it was to this effect:

	17th June	18th June	19th June
R. MATHESON	1	2	3
T. WRIGLEY-BELL	2	3	4
S. F. SMITHERS	3	4	1
J. RENDEL	4	1	2

'I find that your husband was fishing on beat one according to the rules,' he said, going back to his chair. 'They are somewhat Draconian, I agree, but after all, he made them, so he should be the last to complain. Every man has to take each beat in turn, and it's as much as our lives are worth to try to change them. Now, for instance, I was on beat three today, and beat four, at the top of the water, was empty. There was a good fish rising fifty yards above the boundary post, but do you think I could have come home and confessed to him that I had caught one outside my beat? I shouldn't have dared.'

Mrs Matheson shrugged her shoulders.

'I think men are perfectly ridiculous,' she said with an adorable pout. 'You simply make rules for the sake of rules. Why should you take so much trouble to spoil your own pleasures?'

'Women are lawless cattle by nature,' observed Smithers. 'Our ancestors were sensible enough to recognize it. The ridiculous modern idea that they can be treated like reasonable beings – '

Mrs Matheson, who was looking out of the window, paid no attention.

'It's pitch dark outside,' she declared. 'The rise must have been over ages ago. What can he be doing?'

'I shouldn't worry,' said Wrigley-Bell. 'He's probably investigating the domestic habits of a brown owl, or something of the kind.'

'Now then, Wriggles, you're not to laugh at my dear old man.'

'Oh, but I wasn't, Mrs Matheson, I assure you, I wasn't. I think his enthusiasm is wonderful, at his age. I only wish I had it.'

'Thank you, Wriggles. You don't mind my calling you Wriggles, do you?'

'Not in the least.'

'Your husband is very lucky,' observed Smithers, 'to have ornithology to fall back upon when fishing fails. We less fortunate ones, when we have a blank day, are unable to plead what American boxers – inaccurately – call an alibi. If I don't catch anything, it is obvious that it was because I couldn't. He always has the excuse that he was so busy looking at a three-toed flycatcher that he forgot to put up his rod. I've noticed that the excuse grows on him with advancing years.'

'You are a jealous brute, Smithkins. You know that he is still the best fisherman of the lot of you. He can catch as many fish as he wants to, any time.'

'Even on beat one, Mrs Matheson?'

'Even on beat one, Smithkins. You don't mind my calling you Smithkins, do you?'

'I do, very much indeed. I think I have said so before.'

Euphemia grinned at him without a trace of malice.

'Sweet Smithkins, I really believe you have,' she said, and then, at the sound of the front door opening and closing behind an incomer, ran from the room. The two men heard her voice in the passage raised in affectionate remonstrance: 'Robert, you're to change your socks before you do anything else! No, never mind about drying your line, that can wait. Come upstairs at once, you bad old man!'

'She is a wonderful wife to him, is she not?' said Wrigley-Bell. His smile seemed at once to apologize for her and his own temerity in defending her.

'Wonderful is the word, no doubt,' grunted the other. 'I never cease to wonder that any woman should marry a man old enough to be her own father. But it continues to happen.'

'I didn't mean it in that sense exactly. I only meant that she is such a splendid wife for him, looks after him, makes such a success of marriage, and so on.'

'As to the marriage being a success, I have only outward appearances to go on, and they are apt to be deceptive, in my experience. But that doesn't concern me. Whether he likes it or not, whether she adores him or finds life a hell, is their affair, unless and until they get to the point of calling me in professionally. What does concern me, and what I do wonder at is the fact that for the last year or two she should have insisted on coming down here with him. She doesn't fish – thank God! She doesn't even care for the river. She has nothing to do down here except moon about the countryside and incidentally spoil what used to be a very agreeable bachelor party with her feminine imbecilities. What does she want to do it for?'

'But that's just my point,' protested Wrigley-Bell, 'it's just because she's such a wonderful wife to him. Obviously she comes down to look after the old fellow, see that he doesn't get over-tired or wet through, for instance.'

'Rubbish! The guv'nor is as strong as a horse. He doesn't need any looking after. And if she really wanted to do it, she'd be out on the water with him, making sure he came home in good time, instead of going for long walks by herself after dinner.'

'Then what do you think is the reason?'

'I haven't got one. It's not my business to find reasons for other people's behaviour. But if I were asked for an explanation, I should be tempted to say – '

His explanation, whatever it was, was cut short by the reappearance of Mrs Matheson, accompanied by her husband.

Robert Matheson, everybody who knew him agreed, was a remarkable man for his age. How remarkable might be judged from the fact that it was only within the last few years that his age had come into consideration at all when he was being discussed. His lean, erect form had seemed to ignore the passage of time, his movements had remained as vigorous, his voice as firm as those of a man in the prime of life. When, twelve years previously, already well over sixty, he had married a young woman, nobody had seen in it anything extraordinary, or been moved to make the usual comments which the alliance of age and youth provoke. But nature cannot be defied for ever. Long days of hard exercise had begun to take their toll, and those who knew him best and studied him most closely could see that the tremendous nervous energy which had sustained him so long was beginning to droop. Just now, as he came through the door, a heavy fishing bag in one hand and a rod case in the other, he looked an old, tired man, and the contrast between him and his vivid, vital wife was only too evident.

Matheson dropped into a chair with a sigh of relief, and, rummaging in the bag, produced a reel.

'Well, well!' he exclaimed. 'It's been a long day. I shall be glad of something to eat.'

'They are just heating up some soup for you, darling,' put in his wife.

'Good.' He began pulling the line off the reel. 'Well,' he went on, turning to the other two, 'and how did you get on? There was quite a useful hatch of fly this evening, wasn't there?'

'I didn't do too badly,' answered Smithers. 'I got two and a grayling, and returned two.'

'Splendid! Where did you get them? In the Alder Pool?'

'One in the Alder Pool and the other just below the weed-rack. Did you –?'

'Just below the weed-rack, eh? Excellent! I always said there would be good lying for a fish there once we had the bottom muddied out. That proves I'm right.'

'It certainly does. And did you catch anything?'

Matheson did not hear, or at all events did not answer, the question. Instead, he said to Wrigley-Bell:

'Did you do any good on your water?'

'Not very much,' grimaced the other. 'I got one just above the bridge, one pound six ounces, and then at the road corner I hooked a big fish. He got me into the weeds and broke me.'

'Hard lines! Very hard lines! What was the fly, by the way?'

'The little hackle blue I told you about the other day.'

'I wish you'd let me have one or two. It seems to be a very taking fly.'

'I only wish I could, Matheson. But unfortunately that was my last. I shall have to write for some more.'

'A pity. It's always the fly you most want that you run short of, isn't it?'

'You haven't told us yet what luck you had on beat one,' Smithers pointed out, somewhat aggressively.

'Oh, everybody knows what beat one is like,' put in Wrigley-Bell, with a propitiatory smirk. 'Nobody expects much there.'

At this moment a diversion was effected by the entrance of the dishevelled maid of all work, carrying a steaming plate of soup.

'Ah, thank you, Dora!' said Matheson, settling himself at the table. 'Beat one?' he went on, spooning the soup into his mouth. 'It's not so bad as all that, you know. There are some good fish there, though they take some getting.'

'Did you get any of them this evening?' asked Smithers.

'Oh, I wasn't fishing. As a matter of fact I –'

'But I noticed you were drying your line just now,' the solicitor persisted. 'Why was that, if you hadn't been fishing?'

'I took a cast or two early on in the evening,' Matheson admitted in some confusion. 'But that isn't what I meant to tell you about. It's really most interesting, and I've had a delightful evening. Listen. You know that tree-creeper that is always about on the elms by the bottom of the lane?'

'I know that you have often mentioned it,' said Smithers. 'I can't say that I have the pleasure of the bird's acquaintance. I don't even know what a tree-creeper looks like, for that matter.'

'My dear Smithers! What on earth do you do with your eyes? I see that tree-creeper every time I go down to the river. But what has always puzzled me till this evening has been, *where does the bird roost?*'

Matheson delivered the question with profound emphasis. In the enthusiasm of the subject, he looked almost young again. His eyes sparkled, his cheeks glowed, and his spoon swung forgotten in mid-air.

'Robert, dear,' cooed his wife. 'Your soup is getting quite cold.'

'Thank you, I've had all I want. Perhaps if you would cut me a little ham.... Thank you. You see the importance of the question,' he went on. 'It is well established now that the tree-creeper prefers to roost in the trunk of some soft-barked tree, such as the sequoia, digging himself into the bark for shelter. Now there are no sequoias near here except up at the Manor. (I wish Packer would let me go up there and examine his trees, by the way.) So this evening I made a careful examination with my torch of every place that seemed likely, and where do you think I found him?'

'Where, darling?' asked Euphemia from the sofa in the corner. Neither of the other two seemed in the least interested. Wrigley-Bell was staring up at the ceiling from under his eyebrows, Smithers was ostentatiously fluttering the pages of the *Fishing Gazette*.

'In a holm-oak!' cried Matheson triumphantly. 'It is most interesting – probably unique! I shall send word to the editor of *British Birds* about it. I'm quite sure it has never – but am I boring you?'

'Not a bit, darling,' exclaimed Euphemia before Smithers could open his mouth. 'Do go on.'

He went on.

CHAPTER THREE

Dr Latymer

A LARGE and shabby grey saloon car drew up outside the inn with a squeaking of uncared-for brakes. The driver descended and after glancing up at the lighted parlour window opened the front door. The light in the hall revealed a cheerful, florid face surmounted by a mass of thick grey hair. He was of medium height, thick-set, and noticeably quiet and quick in his movements. Dora met him in the passage and he nodded to her cheerfully.

'Good evening, Doctor,' she said.

'Good evening, Dora. How are you?'

'Quite well, thank you, Doctor.'

'No more coughs?'

'No thank you, Doctor.'

'That's good.' He jerked his thumb at the parlour door. 'They're still up, are they?'

'Yes, Doctor. Only just finishing supper.'

'Good. I'll join them.'

'Please, Doctor –'

'Yes?'

'How is Susan, please, Doctor?'

'She hasn't had her baby yet. I'm expecting it any time now. She'll be all right, don't you worry. But don't you go following her example, either.'

'Oh, Doctor!'

He laughed at her horrified expression and walked into the parlour. 'May I come in?' he said. 'Dora told me you were still up, and –'

'Latymer!' exclaimed Smithers. 'Come in, my dear fellow. You're just in time. The guv'nor's been giving us a lecture on the habits of woodpeckers, and you're lucky to be in for the dénouement. What on earth are you doing out at this hour of the night?'

'Tree-creepers, I said, not woodpeckers,' said Matheson crossly.

'Oh, aren't they the same thing? I thought they were.'

'Really, Smithers!' Matheson seemed suddenly deflated. The fire which his recital had kindled in him had gone out, and he looked older and more exhausted than ever. His eyes seemed to follow with envy the alert figure that was now crossing the room.

Latymer, meanwhile, was nodding his greetings in every direction. He ignored the little passage at arms between the two men, and answered Smithers' question.

'If you had my job, you wouldn't be surprised at my being out at this hour, or any hour,' he answered. 'Susan Bavin, in the cottage just up the road, has elected to have a baby tonight.'

'Without benefit of clergy?' Smithers grunted.

'So I gather. I don't know what the Rector and Mrs Large will have to say about it. I'm only concerned with the physical side of the affair, thank goodness. I leave the spiritual aspects of it to them.'

'But how thrilling!' exclaimed Euphemia. 'Is it a boy or a girl?'

'That I can't say at present. I give it another two hours at least. I've been sent for too early as usual. And meanwhile –'

'Meanwhile, you thought you'd scrounge a drink, is that it?'

Dr Latymer knew Smithers too well to take offence.

'That is exactly it,' he answered. 'Thanks, that's quite enough. Whoa, whoa! You'll be making me see twins where none are, if you're not careful.'

He looked round for a seat.

'May I sit beside you?' he said to Euphemia.

Without speaking or even looking at him, she made room for him beside her. A moment later, on the excuse of filling her husband's glass, she got up, and sat down again, not on the sofa but on a hard chair at the head of the table with her back directly turned to him. The snub could hardly have been more crude, but the doctor appeared quite unimpressed. He lolled in his corner, a glass between his large hirsute hands, looking entirely pleased with himself and his company.

'What is the news in Didford, Doctor?' asked Wrigley-Bell, after a pause.

'Miss Bavin's baby is the news of the moment,' was the answer. 'There is no news in places like this, in your sense of the word, at least.'

'Why on earth,' asked Smithers impatiently, 'did an intelligent man like you come and bury yourself in this dead-alive neighbourhood? It seems unnatural.'

'Ah, it puzzles you, eh?' said Latymer.

'Yes. I used to think that you must have done something pretty shady in the past, so that you couldn't show your face in London. But I made inquiries and I found that it was not so, much to my surprise.'

The doctor laughed. 'Thanks,' he said, and taking out a pipe, began to fill it. 'I came down to these parts,' he went on, 'to see life.'

'What on earth do you mean?'

'Just that. Life and, incidentally, death – and especially death, I might say – are highly interesting phenomena. There are one or two others in the world worth looking at – birth, growth, decay, and the rotation of crops, for example. If you can tell me of any better place to see them than this, I'll go there.'

He stopped and lighted his pipe.

'I think I should find it very dull,' said Wrigley-Bell.

'I dare say you would.'

'But of course it takes all sorts to make a world.'

'Yes, I believe that to be the fact.'

'Do your studies of life,' inquired Smithers, 'include the life of tree-crawlers?'

'Smithkins!' exclaimed Mrs Matheson, breaking what was for her a long silence, 'you are not to tease Robert any more.'

The doctor looked hard at Matheson, across the room. He was leaning back in his chair, his eyes half-closed, and his face looked pinched and drawn. He seemed oblivious to what was going on around him. Latymer's expression became suddenly serious. In a few strides he came up to the table, and looked down at the old man intently.

'You've been overdoing it, haven't you?' he said quietly. 'You look done up.'

'Nonsense,' protested Matheson, pulling himself together. 'I'm perfectly fit. Just a little tired, that's all.'

'You wouldn't like to take a day off tomorrow?' suggested Smithers in a more kindly tone than usual. 'Or just potter about on beat one for half the day near home? Rendel could take beat two.'

'Yes,' put in Wrigley-Bell eagerly. 'That's a splendid idea. Why don't you take an easy day tomorrow on beat one? After all, Mrs Matheson was saying only just now, these rules are rather absurdly strict – in a party of friends like us. Why not make a change, just for once?'

'No, no,' said the old man stubbornly. 'Rules are rules. I shall fish beat two tomorrow, I tell you.'

Euphemia said nothing, standing behind her husband's chair, a faint flush on her full cheeks.

'But you don't realize,' Wrigley-Bell persisted, 'how anxious I am – we all are, about you! I assure you – '

'Nonsense! I shall be all right, I tell you – perfectly all right.'

The discussion was suddenly interrupted by the entrance of Dora, breathing heavily as was her wont.

'If you please,' she said, 'there's a telephone call – from the Manor.'

Euphemia looked up suddenly and her lips parted. The doctor took a step towards the door. But Dora went on:

'For Mr Bell, it is.'

'For me? Oh, excuse me!' Wrigley-Bell smirked his way hastily out of the room.

'Well,' said Latymer, when he had gone, 'you must please yourself, I suppose. You're tough enough, but – you've heard of the pitcher and the well. Anyhow, Mrs Matheson, if you can persuade your husband to take a tonic – '

He took a sheet of paper from a side table and jotted down a prescription. Then, after a pause for thought, he took another and wrote upon that. Folding them up, he handed them separately to her.

'The chemist at Parva can make this up for you,' he said. 'And this is just a suggested course of treatment which may be useful.'

She took them from his hand without any acknowledgement beyond a nod.

'I think you had better come to bed, Robert,' she said to her husband. 'It's very late.'

Matheson obediently rose to his feet, just as Wrigley-Bell returned into the room.

'Well?' said the latter. 'Have you settled to take the day off tomorrow?'

'Certainly not. I shall fish as usual.'

'Oh ... perhaps you're wise. One is nearly certain to get a fish on beat two, anyhow, and after your blank day today it will do you a lot more good than medicine.'

'Wriggles, really, I'm surprised at you!' exclaimed Mrs Matheson, and indeed his tone was very different from his usual ingratiating manner.

'I've already explained,' said Matheson, annoyance bringing him back to full vigour at once, 'that I was not fishing this evening.'

'Ah, well – the fish are very dour on beat one, aren't they?'

'What do you mean?'

'Oh, nothing.'

'Robert, you're tired. Come to bed.'

'Don't interrupt, Euphemia. Are you suggesting that I can't catch fish on beat one?'

'Well, *I* certainly did the last time I tried it.'

'Now listen to me. Given ordinary conditions, I can get a fish on any beat in this water whenever I please.'

Wrigley-Bell shrugged his shoulders.

'You don't believe me?'

'I'm prepared to bet you a fiver that you won't get a brace of fish out of the water you were on today,' he said defiantly.

'A brace? I'll get two!'

'You'll bet on it?' Wrigley-Bell was grinning triumphantly, as though the money was in his pocket already.

'Of course I'll bet on it. I shall have those fish tomorrow!'

'On beat one?'

'On beat one, I said.'

'What about the rules?' cried Smithers.

'Damn the rules! Come along, Euphemia!' said Matheson, and stumped off to bed.

'Now why on earth has our wriggly worm turned so violently?' inquired Smithers sardonically.

The other did not reply for a moment. He stood looking at the ground, with a heavier frown than usual drawing down his ugly eyebrows.

'Silly of me, perhaps,' he muttered at last. 'Wrong way to do things, I dare say, but sometimes one feels – ' He stopped abruptly, and then looking up, said in quite a different tone of voice: 'By the way, Smithers, do you happen to know when young Rendel is coming down tomorrow?'

'About midday, Matheson told me. Why?'

'Nothing – oh, nothing. Only, I suppose someone ought to let him know of the change in the arrangements.'

'I'll do that,' said the solicitor, and sitting at the desk wrote a note in his neat, precise hand, which he pinned to the notice board.

'He is sure to look at that when he comes,' he observed. 'I have only stated the facts. I shall leave the discreditable explanation of them to you.'

'I'm going to bed,' said Wrigley-Bell violently. 'Good night!'

He threw open the door to find Euphemia on the threshold.

It was an embarrassing moment. Wrigley-Bell began hastily a stumbling form of apology. Before he had got out more than two words, Euphemia interrupted him with a well-directed smack on the face, delivered with the full force of her arm. Then, with faintly flushed cheeks and a hard glitter in her eyes, she strode across the room.

'I left my bag on the sofa,' she said. 'Will you please give it to me, Dr Latymer?'

She took the bag from the doctor's outstretched hand and, without another word being spoken, swept out of the room, from which the wretched Wrigley-Bell had already fled.

'H'm,' said Latymer, after the door had closed behind her. 'A very pretty piece of feminine psychology. I'm thankful their physiology is less complex. Which reminds me, it's about time I went to attend to my unmarried mother. Thanks for the drink, Smithers. I've enjoyed my evening immensely.'

After he had gone, the solicitor remained for some time, meditatively smoking a pipe. Finally he rose, shook his head with a quiet smile, knocked out the ashes from his bowl and left the room.

The 'Polworthy Arms' was quiet in the scented summer night.

CHAPTER FOUR

Jimmy Rendel

JIMMY RENDEL's hands trembled a little as he put up his rod in the inn yard. He was excited and at the same time ashamed of his excitement. At his mature age – he was twenty-two and looked every day of it – it was ridiculous that he should be worked up into such a state at the mere prospect of a weekend's fishing. He ought by this time to have been able to emulate the composure of the men he had heard speaking of 'running down to the Test' or 'putting in a couple of days on the Itchen', as though fishing were an everyday occupation, no more exciting than a game of tennis. If he could only control the nervous joy that the mere feel of a rod in his hands gave him, he might become as efficient an angler as some of the bloodless old men. But he could not help it, any more than he had been able to help his voice going into absurd uncontrolled waverings when he tried to tell Marian Packer . . . Damn! Jimmy blushed a hot red while his fingers clumsily pushed the end of the line through the rings. He was *not* going to worry about Marian – he was not even going to think about her. He ran out twenty yards of line (twice as much, at least, as he could ever manage to cast) and greased it carefully. He was glad, he told himself as he did so, that it was his turn for beat one today, even though everybody knew it was the worst of the four. Because to get to any of the other beats one had to go past the grounds of the Manor, and there was always the chance of meeting her on the bank. He reeled up his line again, while his heart thumped in spite of himself as he remembered occasions when they had met.

Well, that was over now, quite definitely over. She had made it plain enough, and he had accepted the position. It had been a noble renunciation, he told himself, conveniently forgetting that he had had absolutely no choice in the matter.

Of course, it meant that the only important thing in life had gone out of it, and that the years that might remain to him would be a miserable anti-climax. That went without saying. What were those lines of Swinburne he had read?

> I shall go my ways, tread out my measure,
> Fill the days of my daily breath
> With fugitive things not good to treasure,
> Do as the world doth, say as it saith —

He managed to achieve quite a melancholy gait as he tramped down the lane, but something told him, even while he repeated the verse to himself, that he didn't feel in the least like that. Nobody could, for that matter – not on the Didder in June, with the wind in the south. And this time, he determined, resolutely putting aside memories of blank weekends and lost flies, he really was going to catch a basketful – if only he could remember, when the monster rose at his fly, not to strike too soon or too hard!

Near the end of the lane, he climbed a fence on his left and made his way quickly down to the post on the river bank which marked the boundary of the Polworthy water. He had walked fast and he stood for a moment or two by the water's edge to collect his breath. As he did so, he looked around him. He saw as fair a scene as any that England could offer. Many pens have striven to describe the spell that has from generation to generation drawn men's hearts in love towards this chalk-stream valley. Many more, no doubt, will in their turn seek to capture that placid, changeful charm in a net of words. Jimmy, like most of his kind, was inarticulate in the face of beauty; but he was conscious, nonetheless, of the deep feeling of content that now descended upon him, while he gazed and gazed, wordless. After the turmoil of the morning – the rush to catch the train, the noisy journey in a crowded, smoky third-class carriage, the jolting of the hired car that had brought him from the station, the scrambled haste to change from city clothes into patched and comfortable tweeds, to assemble rod, reel, net, flies, casts – he felt that he had stepped into another world, a world of peace and permanence, where the face of things moved gently and deliberately, in time to the even-flowing stream.

Before long, two practical considerations obtruded themselves upon his thoughts. The first was, that the afternoon sun was very hot – too hot, by far, for any reasonable chance of success in the lower reach of the beat, which is shadeless, and where the stream runs straight and comparatively fast; shallowing and broadening as it approaches the ford. His best chance would be higher up, and not on the main stream at all, but on the slow deep water of the carrier, which had been dug roughly parallel to its course to supply water to the meadows. His second, as he began to walk in that direction, was that against all precedent, somebody else was fishing his beat. Two hundred yards away, he could distinctly see the flash of sunlight on a varnished top-joint above the rushes as it went to and fro. A little nearer, and an unmistakable grey-green clad figure revealed itself. Jimmy was puzzled. He knew that he could not have mistaken his beat. True, he had not looked at the card which hung all the season in the parlour, setting out each member's fate from April to October, but that was an unnecessary precaution for one who beguiled each weary day in London with elaborate calculations of just where he would have been on the river at that moment if the gods had only been kinder. It flashed across his mind that if he was not to fish this beat, he might perhaps see Marian after all. The thought vanished almost as quickly as it had come, but it left an uncomfortable feeling behind it, whether of hope or fear he could not say.

Quietly he approached the angler, who was far too absorbed to hear his coming. He was casting towards a little bay of reeds on the farther side of the carrier. As Jimmy watched, the fish rose, a tiny circle of ripples barely breaking the smooth surface of the water. The line shot out, the gut gleamed for an instant in the light and the fly pitched (a trifle heavily, was Jimmy's private criticism) just on the upper edge of the ripple, fairly in the semicircle of reeds. It floated there for a few seconds that seemed an hour, scarcely moving in the almost stagnant stream. Then the quiet water stirred beneath it. The rod-point rose sharply. There was a plunge from the unseen trout. 'He's been too quick. He's missed it,' thought Jimmy. But at the next instant he saw the line go taut, heard the harsh scream of the reel as the fish darted upstream.

It was a long struggle. Time and again the fish was brought under the rod-point, apparently ready for the net which Jimmy had there. Time and again with renewed strength it plunged irresistibly away. Twice it sought shelter in a bank of weeds, twice it was patiently coaxed out into clear water. Matheson's face shone with excitement, and the sweat poured down his face.

'A heavy fish!' he remarked. It was the first word spoken between them since Jimmy's arrival.

Jimmy was not so sure.

'I think he's foul hooked,' he said.

'Foul hooked! Nonsense, my boy. He took it beautifully – a head and tail rise!'

But Jimmy was right, as he proved a moment later or two when he slipped the net beneath a trout of only moderate size. The hook was fast in the back fin, and the fish's prolonged fight had obviously been due to the greater freedom which this had afforded it. He smiled to himself. So the old man *had* struck too quickly after all! It was the merest chance that he had not missed altogether. Decidedly he was not the impeccable fisherman that he used to be.

Matheson fairly snatched the fish from Jimmy's hand as he extracted it from the net. He was breathing hard, like a man in a hurry.

'Thanks, my dear boy, thanks!' he gasped. 'You were right after all. Not a big fish, but worth keeping. But you will want to be getting along now. The best of the day's nearly over. I thought you were catching the train that gets in at twelve?'

'So did I,' said Jimmy, bitterly. 'It's my free Saturday, by all rights. But those swine in the office took it into their heads that my presence was wanted there this morning. I was in the

City till nearly one. I only caught the afternoon train by the skin of my teeth, and then it was ten minutes late this end. But look here, sir, I thought you – '

'Bad luck! I wondered what had become of you. I've been expecting to see you ever since half past twelve. Now you must make up for lost time.'

'But surely, sir, it's your day for beat two, and I ought to be fishing here?'

'Didn't you look at the notice board, then?'

'No, I didn't bother. I was in a hurry, and I was sure it was my turn for this beat.'

'Well, we've decided to make a change for once. I – I've a special reason for coming here today. I'll tell you about it later. There's no time now. I thought you wouldn't mind. You'll have a much better chance up there on a day like this.'

'That awfully good of you, sir.'

'Not a bit, not a bit! Though, mind you, this beat isn't as bad as it's painted. Look here!'

From his bag he drew out two magnificent trout, tenderly wrapped in butter muslin.

'There's life in the old 'un yet, isn't there?' he said complacently in answer to the young man's envious congratulations. 'But we mustn't waste time talking. There's a good fish waiting for you at the corner road, with one of Bell's flies in it.'

'Perhaps I'd better go there first,' said Jimmy. 'I can cut up through the copse. The bank is a bit soggy.'

From where they stood, a cattle track led to a gate on to the road. On its way it passed through a plantation of young larches, where it was joined on the right by a path running roughly parallel to the river. This offered a drier and more direct route to the upper reaches, and was regularly used by the syndicate.

Matheson did not answer. Jimmy looked at him, and saw that he was gazing absorbedly through the field-glasses which he always carried ready slung about his neck, at something high above the level of their heads.

'Cross-bills!' he said in an excited tone. 'Right in the top of those larches! Remarkable! What?' he turned suddenly to Jimmy. 'Go through the copse? Certainly not! I mean – those birds – I don't want them disturbed at any cost. You understand, don't you?'

'Of course,' said Jimmy. 'Of course. I'll walk up the bank.'

'Good lad! I'll come with you a bit of the way.'

'Oh really, sir, you needn't bother – '

But the old man, his rod laid down, was already walking briskly upstream beside him.

'I can get a much better view of those birds from a little higher up,' he explained. 'They were moving up the trees in the hedge by the road. Didn't you notice?'

'I'm afraid I didn't see them,' said Jimmy. 'That is – what does a cross-bill look like, exactly?'

'My dear boy! Fancy your not knowing that! Why at your age, I – '

And for the next few minutes he poured out such a stream of theories, facts, and reminiscences on the subject of cross-bills, that Jimmy began to think it highly inconsiderate of the Almighty ever to have created the species. It was a not infrequent experience for those who were rash enough to ask Matheson a question about birds.

Just above the boundary post dividing beat one from beat two, Matheson stopped abruptly. So did his flow of talk. Out came the field-glasses once more. They ranged hither and thither for a moment or two, then settled steadily on one objective. Matheson gave vent to a heartfelt 'Ah!' of satisfaction, so utterly disproportionate to the importance of the subject-matter that Jimmy, for all his respect for his senior, had difficulty in suppressing his amusement. He waited for a moment, but no further words came. The old man remained quite motionless, his whole attention utterly given over to the far-off vision in his glasses.

'Perhaps I'd better be getting on, sir,' he said at last.

Matheson returned to earth with a start.

'Good heavens, my boy, are you still there?' he said. 'Go

along and don't let me waste any of your time. I – ' the last words were breathed with an almost lover-like devotion into the distance, as the glasses went back to his eyes '– I shall stay here till they move.'

Jimmy walked on, only too glad to be free of his company. With the tolerant wisdom of his years he treated his senior's passion for birds with pity, not untinged with envy. It must be wonderful, he thought, to have attained such an age that you could grow excited over things that didn't really matter in the least. Instead of the heartache, the anxieties and pains that preyed upon him, Jimmy, to be preoccupied by nothing more violent than an affection for willow warblers or ring-ousels! And yet how pitiful it must be to have reached a state when life had no more to give one than such petty enthusiasms – strangely enough, it never occurred to Jimmy that fishing could be ranked by anyone as a subject for petty enthusiasm – to be indulged in only at the risk of the utter boredom of one's acquaintance! Privately, from the height of great experience of life, Jimmy decided that it must be very difficult to be as old as that and not to be a bore. Not that his recognition of the fact prevented him from liking the old guv'nor. All things considered, he reflected, he was a very decent fellow; and it had been particularly decent of him today to let him have the better beat. Knowing nothing of the events of the night before, he wondered what had prompted the unheard-of departure from the rules. Was it possible that Matheson knew of his, Jimmy's, devotion to Marian, and wanted to give him a chance of seeing her? Like every lover, he was morbidly self-conscious, and imagined that everyone was thinking of his affairs. How little they understood his feelings! As if, just now, he wanted anything more in the world than to be alone!

He rounded a bend in the stream and let himself through a gate in the hedge which divided the water-meadows at this point, only to realize with a sickening feeling of disgust that he was not to be alone much longer. Fifty yards above, a moss-grown stone bridge carried the farm track which connected Runt's Farm with the main road. On the bridge, her back towards him, stood a tall gaunt figure in a rusty black coat and skirt. There was no mistaking that ramrod back, that out-of-date straw hat perched insecurely on the wispy, mouse-coloured hair. It was Mrs Large, and Mrs Large, he told himself with a groan, was a busybody, a chatterer, a Nosey Parker, a – his thoughts ran on regrettable, zoological similes.

To say that Mrs Large was the wife of the Rector of Did-ford Magna would be, as anyone who knew her would readily agree, a gross understatement. Rather it was the Rector who by his parishioners and neighbours for many miles around was spoken of, if at all, as Mrs Large's husband. Apart from the public appearances which church ceremonies made obligatory, he was little seen and less regarded by his flock. Mrs Large, on the other hand, could never be disregarded, and as for seeing her, the one object of any villager with a guilty con-science was to avoid being seen by her. Indomitable, inquisi-tive, and untiring, she had the eye of a hawk for any back-sliding from her own standards of conduct, the nose of a bloodhound for any hint of scandal, and a tongue that was all her own with which she spoke her mind without restraint or regard for the feelings of her audience. Nobody could have described her character as an amiable one, but it was remark-able that in any crisis where practical help was needed in the village, it was to her that the sufferer instinctively turned. Mrs Large was well aware that she was not loved, and indeed seemed to take a malicious pleasure in the fact. That others should find themselves dependent on her for help she took for granted as part of the incurable weakness of humanity, herself excepted. One weakness, indeed, she had, and that in full measure – an overpowering desire, amounting to a passion, to know exactly what was going on within her little kingdom down to the last detail and to display to those concerned the fact that she did so know. All in all, an individual less calcu-lated to harmonize with Jimmy's state of mind at that moment it would have been difficult to find.

The path that he was following must bring him right past her, and at all costs he wished to avoid speaking to her.

Cautiously he began to retreat, hoping that she would soon be gone, but as he did so, Mrs Large turned round, caught sight of him, and waved. He had no option but to wave in acknowledgement. Then he thought he saw salvation in a tiny fish splashing in the shadows on the far side of the stream. Surely if she saw him fishing she would soon lose patience! With immense care he began to cast over it. In vain. Her high-pitched voice floated clearly down to him.

'It's no use trying there, you know. They're only tiddlers!'

With a groan, Jimmy acknowledged himself beaten, reeled up his line and walked up to the bridge. From her vantage point Mrs Large looked down on him with quizzical eyes that seemed to Jimmy to hold more than a hint of malice.

'How de do, Jimmy?' she began, as soon as he was in ear-shot. 'How's Father?'

Jimmy was, as always, irritated by her gambit. The fact that she had known a fellow ever since he was a kid didn't entitle her to go on talking to him as though he was still in the nursery. Why couldn't she say: 'How is your father?' as from one grown-up to another? He mumbled that his father was pretty well, 'considering'.

'Rheumatism no better, I suppose?' said Mrs Large brightly. 'Ah, well, I don't suppose it ever will be. Once that gets into your bones, it doesn't get out, you can tell him that from me! Not that I've ever had it, of course,' she added, apparently accepting her invulnerability and her omniscience as matters equally axiomatic.

Jimmy made incoherent noises and tried to get away. But Mrs Large was far from being so easily disposed of. She waved a bunch of what looked to Jimmy like rather bedraggled weeds in his direction.

'What d'you think of these?' she demanded. 'Nice, aren't they? *Veronica beccabunga* and *Butomus umbellatus*. I found them in the water-meadows just now, on my way back from Runt's Farm. The girls there have been missing Sunday school lately, and I've been finding out the reason why.'

Jimmy's knowledge of wild flowers was about as profound

as his interest in Sunday schools, and he could think of nothing better to say than: 'Oh?' But Mrs Large's next remark recalled his wandering attention with a jerk.

'Seen anything of your friend up at the Manor lately?' she shot out.

His face burned. She would bring that up! He had known all along she would.

He managed to get out: 'No, not much.'

'I don't know what *she* thinks of these goings on in the village.'

Jimmy had made up his mind not to be drawn into any discussion with her, but this took him by surprise.

'What goings on?' he asked.

'Susan Bavin's baby, of course. Haven't you heard? Born last night, and I saw the doctor's car going down the lane when I came up it this morning. Very fast he was driving too – nearly knocked me down. It's disgraceful! Poor little thing – Marian, I mean!'

'But what's it got to do with M – with Lady Packer?' asked Jimmy.

'Bless my soul, boy, but don't you know anything? Sir Peter and that Bavin girl have been an open scandal in the village for months! I wonder Marian hasn't spoken to you about it. The little wretch – Susan Bavin, I mean. She's been walking out with that nice young Carter boy in White's Cottages – going to be married at Michaelmas, and all the time – '

But Jimmy wasn't listening. The pulses in his ears were drumming too furiously to let him hear anything else. So it was true, then! This Packer creature, not content with neglecting and ill-treating her – she had never said it in so many words, but he knew it well enough – had actually – and with a common village trollop! That she should have any contact with anything so sordid! But Mrs Large was still talking.

'– and not only one either, I'll be bound!' she was saying. 'If I had my way with a man like that, I – '

'I must go,' said Jimmy abruptly. 'Good-bye, Mrs Large.'

She took his sudden departure with good humour.

'I must go too,' she said. 'The Rector will be wanting his tea, and if he doesn't get it, there'll be no sermon tomorrow. Good-bye, Jimmy. You won't catch any fish before seven o'clock today. There won't be any fly on the water till then. But there's no harm trying.'

How did Mrs Large know such things? But it was useless to inquire. Mrs Large knew everything.

Jimmy went his way, feeling for once in his life utterly indifferent to fishing. The peace of the river, in which a few moments before he had been delighting, was destroyed for him. The brilliant summer day seemed to mock the misery. To his disgust, he found his eyes filling with tears. But they were tears, he told himself, of manly sympathy and manly rage. Thank God, Marian had one real friend in the world! And as for her husband, if ever he could lay hands on that man, by George he'd – he'd –

He clutched the inoffensive fishing-rod as though it were a weapon.

CHAPTER FIVE

Encounter at the Road Corner

O F all the pools in the Polworthy water, it is probable that the syndicate talked and thought most often of the one known by them as the road corner pool. In the first place, it was from the purely fishing point of view outstanding. Year in and year out, more and heavier fish were taken from it than any other, with the possible exception of the willow-tree pool, two or three hundred yards above, the lowest and favourite spot on beat three. Nor was the water between the two pools to be despised. During the mayfly season, or when the evening rise was propitious, the whole reach was sometimes alive with feeding trout. A visitor from the lordly Walton Club at Didford Parva had been heard to say that it almost put him in mind of some of the Club water – than which there could be no higher praise.

The pool was also noteworthy in that it was the only place above the lowest beat where the water could be conveniently reached by road. Here the great bulk of Didbury Hill, crowned with its beech-grown prehistoric camp, shoulders into the valley, and squeezes the road close between its flank and the river that skirts it. It had therefore become the custom for anglers making for the upper beats to drive to that point, leave their cars in an opening just off the road and walk thence up the stream. Inasmuch as to follow the bank all the way would involve a lengthy detour, besides the awful risk of disturbing another man's water, they naturally used instead a path which led direct from the road corner to the bend just below the willow-tree pool. This path, locally known as 'the causeway', was in fact a narrow strip of made ground across a marshy tract of land which had once no doubt been a part of the river-bed. At this season of the year, it was less a path than a green tunnel cut through bulrushes and osiers higher than a man's head, murmurous with warblers and other birds whose identity it was Matheson's perennial delight to establish.

The last and most regrettable reason for the road corner's celebrity had been canvassed at length at the 'Polworthy Arms' overnight, and on many previous nights. The sawmill which Sir Peter had set up and which was now fast devouring the shapeliest trees of his estate was, to put it mildly, an abominable nuisance. By some trick of acoustics, the noise was barely audible from a distance; on a near approach it became atrocious. The hills, which shut off the sound from the other parts of the valley, intensified it to anyone within their circle. It was a circumscribed inferno of noise in the very heart of the quietude of the valley.

Jimmy Rendel heard it as he approached the point where the river curved to make the famous pool. First the heavy 'thud, thud' of the water-driven engine, then a piercing scream as the circular saw met the tree trunk, descending by slow degrees to a deep-throated but still overpowering snarl as it bit deeper and deeper into the wood, rising once more to another high-pitched shriek, then the crash of the severed timber falling asunder, followed by an interval of comparative peace, while the monotonous 'thud, thud' continued, until a fresh victim was brought forward to be riven with the same agonized and agonizing sound. It was difficult, while the noise continued, even to think of anything else, and for a moment Jimmy was conscious of a certain relief as the overpowering din drowned the clamour of his previous thoughts. But an instant later he remembered that this hideous onslaught on the peace of the river he loved was but another manifestation of Packer's iniquities. Damn him! Could he leave nothing unspoiled?

Jimmy fought down the sense of nausea that assailed him. Here at least he would not be beaten. He had come to fish, and fish he would even though his head was splitting. Shutting his ears to the noise, which gained in volume with every step he took, he advanced slowly up the bank, looking anxiously for any sign of a feeding trout. He had not gone far before he realized that Mrs Large was right. The wind had dropped, and the river seemed asleep. Under the hot sun it flowed smoothly, its surface unbroken but for an occasional fragment of floating weed. No fish was stirring, and look as he might, he could see no fly on the water to tempt them to the surface. He reached the head of the pool and began to explore the reach above, where the bank on which he stood curved gently to his left. Under the alders opposite, he knew, there was sometimes a chance of a trout, even on the least promising days. He moved slowly, his eyes fixed on the farther bank, as it opened up foot by foot while he advanced round the curve. Then he glanced at his own side of the river and something that he saw there made him stop suddenly in his tracks.

What he saw was no more than a pair of rather bright, yellow-brown brogue shoes, and two chequered knitted stockings attached to them, protruding on to the path less than ten yards away. The rest of the wearer was hidden from sight by a thick growth of reeds. Another two or three paces would have brought him into full view, but Jimmy did not need to go any farther to know to whom the shoes and stockings belonged. He had seen them too often to be mistaken.

Jimmy stood stock-still looking at the motionless limbs for what seemed to him a very long time – long enough, in fact, for the sawmill to repeat its shattering performance twice over. His thoughts raced. Sir Peter Packer, he realized, must be sitting on a little patch of hard, dry ground, familiarly known to the syndicate as 'the tump'. It was a favourite spot for anglers on beat two to choose for lunch as it gave a good view of the water in both directions. It was quite unheard of for him to appear on the river bank at all, and Jimmy's first reaction was simply one of surprise, reinforced by the reflection that of all spots on the river it was the least agreeable to choose for a quiet siesta. Then the full horror of the situation dawned on him. To follow his course up the bank, he would have to go right past Packer, to meet him face to face, to speak to him – that could hardly be avoided – to hear once more those odiously patronizing tones. (He blushed as he recalled how, at the beginning of his acquaintance with the Packers, he had been pleased and flattered at the condescension of the man of the world.) For some time past it had been an ordeal to be adequately civil to the man, but today, after his talk to Mrs Large, how could he so much as look at him?

Then it was as if a very quiet distinct voice were speaking, close to his ear. 'Well,' it said, 'and who said anything about being civil to the beast? That wasn't your attitude just now, was it? Didn't you swear that if ever you could lay hands on the man, you'd – what? It would be easy enough to lay hands on him now, wouldn't it? He couldn't hear you if you walked up quietly enough – if you chose your time when the sawmill was at its loudest. It would be as easy as anything, don't you think?

'Of course,' the voice went on after a pause, 'if you are afraid – '

Jimmy walked slowly down the bank the way he had come. His hands trembled violently. He felt at once relieved and deeply ashamed. For suddenly he had been brought up against the truth that lay behind all his heroics. He hated the man and he had not the courage so much as to set eyes on him.

He walked back towards the road corner with the intention of going up the causeway to the top of his beat. There seemed little prospect of successful fishing anywhere for some time yet, and further up he would at least be able to rest in the shade. At the moment, rest and solitude were what he needed most. His feet dragged wearily in his heavy fishing boots and his empty bag weighed on his shoulder in the heat as though it were filled with lead. But exhausted though he was with the emotional stress through which he had just passed, never had his senses seemed so acute. He was alive as never before to the green bravery of trees and grass, to the unsullied blue of the sky and the swallows that described evanescent black arabesques against its background. His ear, too, seemed no longer dulled by the intermittent din of the sawmill. Between the moments of intensely loud noise he was able to distinguish clearly the normal sounds of the waterside, and while he was still some distance away, he could hear quite distinctly, above the noise of the engine, the sound of a car being reversed from the road into the opening at the corner.

He wondered absently whose the car might be. The place was scarcely used at all except by the syndicate, and neither of the men who were on the upper beats that day would be likely to be on the move at that time in the afternoon. To reach the end of the causeway it was necessary for him to pass close to the gate which led into the road, and as he did so, he satisfied his curiosity with a glance over his shoulder. Two cars stood there side by side, and he recognized them both. One, new and glossy, belonged to Wrigley-Bell, the other was the scarred veteran of Dr Latymer. Obviously, Wrigley-Bell had left his car there on his way up to beat three, and the doctor was the newcomer. Jimmy had no desire to meet him, or indeed anyone else, at that moment, and he walked on hastily towards the causeway. His hopes were disappointed. He had not taken more than a few steps before he heard his name called from behind.

'Hey!' said Dr Latymer.

Jimmy's fatal good nature was too much for him. He halted

and turned round. The doctor was just getting over the gate, his usual cheerful smile sending his high-coloured face into a thousand wrinkles. Jimmy noticed that he carried his bag in his hand.

'Good afternoon,' said Jimmy.

Latymer opened his mouth, and it was to be presumed that words came from it, but a renewed access of noise from the sawmill made it impossible to hear them.

'What did you say?' Jimmy asked when the conversation became possible again.

'Are you going up the causeway?'

'Yes.'

'We'll go together, then. I'm – ' The rest of the sentence was drowned by a renewed onslaught from the saw, but Jimmy thought he could distinguish the word, 'cottage'.

'Going up to the cottage?' he shouted.

The doctor nodded, and jerked his fingers towards the mill.

'Chap working there yesterday ... top of his finger off,' Jimmy heard.

They walked on a few paces until the next interval of silence.

'D'you generally come up this way?' asked Latymer.

'Yes. We all do. It's the quickest way up to the top, you know.'

Latymer grinned knowingly.

'Better not let Packer see you at it, then.'

'What do you mean?'

'Last time I saw him he said you had no right –'

Again the outcry of protesting timber filled the air. The doctor waited till he could be heard again, and then went on:

'He says the fishing only includes the right to walk on the bank, and that you've no business on his land. Very sore about it, is our Peter. If he sees you here, he'll make trouble.'

'He won't see me here this morning,' said Jimmy confidently enough. 'I happen to know he's *there*.'

He pointed towards the 'tump' as the saw began to scream once more. Latymer stopped abruptly, and Jimmy, stopping too, looked at him with astonishment. He saw in his face an intense expression of concentration and interest that reminded him of something. He puzzled to think what it was for a moment and then remembered. He had seen the same look in the face of another doctor – the very young man who had been called in one summer holiday to treat him for a bad stomach-ache, at the moment when he had diagnosed – incorrectly as it turned out – acute appendicitis. There was the same professional awareness, the same controlled excitement. But why on earth should Latymer –? He strained his ears to catch what he was saying.

'Over there?' he was shouting. 'What was he doing? standing up?'

Jimmy shook his head, and tried to indicate by pantomime that Sir Peter was on the ground.

'Lying down?'

'Lying or sitting; I couldn't see. I didn't go near enough to – '

Talking was easier now again, but Latymer did not wait to listen.

'Had he his hat on, do you know?'

'I didn't see, I tell you. What does it matter? He was there. That's all I know.'

The doctor was looking around him. They were about halfway along the causeway.

'Which is the nearest way to him, do you think?' he asked. 'On to the end, or back to the corner?'

'Back, I should think,' said Jimmy, quite mystified. 'But why shouldn't he sit there if he wants to?'

The doctor was already walking away.

'When a man who's had a bad go of sunstroke sits in the open on a day like this, it's time something was done about it,' he shouted as he went.

Jimmy stared after him for a moment, then walked on. It was not for some time that it crossed his mind that perhaps he should have offered to go with Latymer. He excused himself with the reflection that he would probably have been of no use. What did one do for a man with sunstroke, anyhow – if Sir Peter had sunstroke? Then he remembered the feet and legs as he had seen them, unnaturally still, projecting outwards into his line of sight as stiffly as though there had been two sticks inside those hideous stockings. He ought to have guessed – how was it that he had not guessed? – that there was something wrong about it. What did a man look like with sunstroke? he wondered. Pale and unconscious, or red-faced, stertorously beathing? He tried to imagine Packer's coarse, self-assured countenance first with one symptom, then with the other. He shuddered. He knew quite well now why he had not gone back with the doctor. Then a final thought struck him, and the sky went black for an instant as his heart missed a beat. Did one die of sunstroke? And if so –

He came out of the causeway on to the bank without looking where he was going. A woman who was standing almost in the entrance jumped aside as he blundered past her. Her exclamation of surprise recalled him to himself. He stopped, his face not two feet away from hers, tongue-tied and embarrassed, looking, and worse, knowing that he looked, utterly boorish. It was Marian Packer.

'Jimmy!' she cried. 'You – you startled me.'

Jimmy opened his mouth to speak, but no words came. He stood there, goggling at her, as mute as any trout in the Didder. She was a slightly built, small-boned woman, of a fragility that never failed to make him feel intolerably clumsy; and his first reflection was that if he had cannoned into her, as he well might have done, he must infallibly have sent her flying into the river. He cursed himself for his stupidity. Was he always to appear at a disadvantage with her?

'I'm frightfully sorry,' he mumbled.

They were both silent for a moment. Everything seemed strangely quiet. The sawmill, for the time being, must have ceased work. But Jimmy did not seek any explanation of the phenomenon. She was there, and all was peace. It seemed in the nature of things. Marian Packer was not by ordinary standards a beauty, though her candid, wide-spaced grey eyes and her silvery voice, fresh as a rill of spring water, might remain in the memory long after more striking faces had been forgotten. Her charm lay above all in a cool serenity of manner and speech that in Jimmy's eyes set her above all the petty troubles of the world. He gazed at her hungrily, and as he looked he saw, what anyone less infatuated would have noticed at once, that all was not well with her. Something had shattered her tranquillity. She was unnaturally pale, her breath came fast, and one hand clutched at her breast, as though to stifle the uncontrollable beating of her heart.

'What are you doing here?' she asked at last – almost angrily, he thought.

'Fishing,' he stammered. 'I mean, I was going up to the willow pool and – '

'You haven't been *that* way?' she pointed down the bank.

He shook his head. Then the unreality of the conversation got on his nerves. It was absurd to talk like this when there was so much to be said.

'Look here, Marian,' he said in as commanding a tone as he could assume, though his voice wobbled dangerously: 'I know all about it.'

'About what?' She spoke barely above a whisper.

'About – about your husband and Susan Bavin.' He blushed furiously as he said it.

'Oh, that!' she said, in a tone almost of relief. She began to walk along the bank, upstream, and Jimmy followed.

'I've only just heard,' he said. 'Mrs Large told me, and – '

'Oh, Mrs Large! Naturally! And it's all over the village now, of course. That poor girl! We shall have to do something for her, I suppose.'

She spoke kindly enough, but without any emotion, as though her mind was not going with her words. She might have been discussing a purely abstract problem. Then she stopped, and turning to Jimmy, said in an altogether different tone of voice:

'Jimmy, were you speaking the truth just now?'

'What do you mean?' he asked.

'You haven't been up the bank?'

'No, of course not. I came along the causeway. You saw me.'

'Then you haven't seen him today?'

'Him? Who?'

'Peter.'

Jimmy was taken aback by the question. For the time being, he had actually forgotten all about his encounter with Dr Latymer or the events that had preceded it. It occurred to him, too late, that the least he could have done was to tell her that her husband was all this time within a stone's throw of them, probably in need of help. But as he opened his mouth to reply the sawmill woke from its slumbers with renewed clamour. While its echoes still filled the air, a bird flew past them low over the water, and settled with a splash in the stream twenty yards above them.

'What was that?' she cried. Her hand tightened nervously on his arm.

'It's all right, darling, nothing to be frightened about. Only a wild duck.'

The endearment slipped out unawares. It went unheeded.

'No, no, not that. I heard something.'

'Heard something? How could you with all that – '

But this time there was no mistaking. Above the loud beat of the engine came a voice from the reeds farther down the bank.

'Jimmy!' it cried. 'Jimmy Rendel!'

Marian fairly thrust him from her. 'What are you waiting for?' she cried. 'Go at once! Something must have happened.'

Thoroughly alarmed by now, Jimmy began to walk back along the way they had just travelled together. As he reached the mouth of the causeway, the doctor appeared round the bend of the river bank. His usually cheerful face was a mask of anxiety. He was about to speak when he caught sight of Marian, standing where Jimmy had left her, a few paces behind. Her appearance evidently startled him, for he stopped, and instead of speaking, silently beckoned Jimmy to approach. They were within speaking distance when the sawmill once again made speech impossible. Until it had gone through its gamut of searing sound, all three remained motionless, Jimmy and Latymer face to face, Marian ten yards away, two of them intently watching the third, waiting for the word that should resolve their perplexities. At last came the crash of falling logs, and then the words came, spoken very low, so that Marian could not hear.

'Jimmy,' said the doctor. 'A dreadful thing has happened. Sir Peter is dead.'

CHAPTER SIX

Murder

'DEAD?' Jimmy repeated, staring at him stupidly.

'Yes.'

Latymer was looking at him very hard, his full lips compressed to a straight line. It flashed across Jimmy's mind that for a doctor, to whom death must be a familiar presence, he seemed strangely disturbed. Then he heard him go on, in the same low, urgent tone.

'Do you know anything about this, Jimmy?'

'I? Of course not! What do you mean?'

'You didn't hear anything – see anything beyond what you told me?'

'No.' Jimmy, in spite of himself, was beginning to feel frightened. 'Why should I?'

'He didn't die of sunstroke, Jimmy.'

'He didn't – ?' Jimmy began, and then shut his mouth, for in competition with the saw, which elected to recommence work at that moment, he would only have wasted his breath. Helplessly, he turned towards where Marian was standing, but the doctor shook his head and put out a restraining hand. Jimmy obeyed, and stood in sickening anxiety until the noise had died down. Then he said:

'Are you sure?'

'Quite sure,' Latymer replied. 'Unless,' he added grimly, 'having the back of your head blown off is a symptom of sunstroke. Come and see for yourself.'

Jimmy did not move or speak. He could only shake his head dumbly. Not for anything in the world could he have gone to look at the horror that lay behind the tall reeds. For a moment he thought he was going to disgrace himself by fainting. Then he caught the eye of the doctor, who nodded understandingly.

'You needn't, of course,' he said.

Jimmy pulled himself together.

'What can I do to help?' he asked.

'We shall have to get the police, and the sooner the better,' said Latymer. 'Before anyone else comes here, if possible. Can you do that?'

'Yes, of course I will.'

'Good lad! You had better take my car, and drive down to the village. There's a telephone at the inn, isn't there? I shall stay here till they come.'

He shouted the last words above the renewed outcry of the sawmill, and Jimmy turned to go. He looked towards where Marian had been, and noticed to his surprise that she had disappeared. Had she heard anything of his colloquy with the doctor? he wondered. He knew from experience that her hearing was very acute. But he gave himself no time for speculation. He plunged down the green corridor of the causeway as fast as he could, intent on nothing but getting away from the ill-omened place as quickly as possible. As he went, he remembered with irony that only a short while before he had been rejoicing in the river as a place of rest and peace. Then his mind went back to Sir Peter's feet and legs as he had seen them. Another few steps and it would have been for him and not the doctor to make the discovery. Fervently he thanked the luck that had at least saved him a sight that he knew would have haunted him for the rest of his life. 'The back of his head blown off' – horrible! The *back* of his head? Then it couldn't have been suicide. It must have been some horrible accident or – murder!

46

Murder! He framed the ugly word with his lips. Murder was a thing one read about in the evening papers, made a parlour game of it – it didn't happen to people one knew. But here it was, in plain, everyday reality, murder done on the body of someone he knew, murder – he steeled himself to face the thought – perhaps committed by someone he knew.

Just before he reached the gate, he was surprised to find the doctor close behind him. He must have walked very fast to catch him up, Jimmy thought.

'Just wait a moment,' he said. 'I forgot something.'

Jimmy paused expectantly. The doctor went on in an unnaturally loud voice.

'I want you to drive my car first to the inn. You can telephone from there to the police station at Parva. Then ring up my surgery and tell them I shall not be back for some hours. After that you had better see if you can find the constable and bring him back with you.'

'Yes, certainly I will,' said Jimmy.

'That's all, I think,' Latymer concluded, and turned away. Jimmy opened the gate and went through. His nerves felt thoroughly unstrung, and he wondered whether he would be capable of driving safely even for such a short distance. But clearly he was not the only one so affected. The fact that Latymer had come after him all the way merely to give him directions for the most part unnecessary and for the rest trivial, and the strident tones in which he had spoken, so unlike his usual quiet, confident manner, was evidence that he too was suffering from reaction. Jimmy, who always felt acutely conscious of his own rawness in the presence of those more experienced than himself, felt comforted at the realization that in a crisis they were as much a prey to their nerves as he was.

It was not until he opened the door of the doctor's car that he remembered how encumbered he was for the business of driving. He was still carrying his rod, which from force of habit he had never abandoned, though it had become as useless to him as one of the spears that the Wagnerian deities trail about with them on the Covent Garden stage; and his legs were heavy with long waterproof boots, slimy with the mud of the riverside. The rod was too long to lie inside the car, and he did not wish to waste time in dismantling it. He solved the problem by laying it on the running-board. The spare wheel, which was carried in the old-fashioned manner at the side, and the front wing, served to keep it in place. The boots he slipped off altogether, put them in the back with his net and bag, and drove in his stockinged feet.

The car started easily, and he swung out into the road. Just as he did so, he was aware of a woman a few yards ahead, walking away from him. She was in the middle of the road, and he was almost upon her before he knew it. He tried to brake, but his foot slipped on the pedal, and if she had not leaped to one side while he swerved to the other he must have run her down.

He threw an anxious glance over his shoulder to make sure that no harm was done. The woman was standing by the roadside, staring after him. At the very moment that he looked she put her head down, as though not wishing to be recognized. But he had had time to see who it was. It was Mrs Matheson, and her appearance just at that place and at that moment seemed to add yet another complication to a day of mystery and misery. If he had knocked her over, it would have capped everything! And what possible excuse could he have had, coming out into the road in that criminally careless way? At the same time, he was puzzled that he had not been able to stop the car. He had driven in stockings before, and his experience was that they gave a very secure, if painful, contact with the controls. But he was quite clear in his mind that something had made his foot slip. He must look into the matter.

Jimmy had none of the instincts of a detective, and no liking for the business of detection. He wished to have as little as possible to do with the hideous affair in which he found himself involved. Nonetheless, he could not help his mind turning on the succession of unexpected events that seemed to be accumulating. What was Mrs Matheson doing there, and why had she been so anxious to avoid notice? There might be a dozen reasonable explanations, but it was odd, to say the least of it, that she should have appeared so close to the place where murder had been committed. He supposed that anybody who was about the neighbourhood would come under suspicion.... Resolutely he shut his mind against the thought that there was another woman, even closer to the scene of the crime, who might reasonably be suspect. But the thought remained, nonetheless.

He pulled up outside the 'Polworthy Arms'. He must keep quite calm, he kept telling himself. Nothing seemed quite real – neither the familiar aspect of the plain, red-brick inn, nor the feel of the leather seat of the car, warm with the sun. It was all a nightmare, and he would wake up quite soon. Meanwhile, he must concentrate very hard, take things slowly and do one thing at a time. He opened the door of the car and put out a leg. The ground felt very hard beneath his feet. What was the matter? Ah, yes, of course, he had no boots on. And his boots were – where? With an effort he remembered that they were in the back of the car. He took them out and drew them on with exaggerated care. Now to telephone. He took a step towards the house and then stopped with a puzzled frown. There was something else he had to do if he could only recollect it. The clue was only just over the edge of his mind – it had been in his head just now.... He remembered suddenly. Stockings! Not – his mind shied away from the picture like a frightened horse – not those horrible chequered things of Sir Peter's, but the honest grey pair on his own legs. Why had his foot slipped so badly on the brake? For some reason that question had assumed immense importance in his mind. Before he did anything else he must find out. Very carefully he bent down and inspected the foot brake. Something green caught his eye. He touched it. It was wet and slimy. He pulled up a fragment of waterweed, coated in viscous mud. So that explained it! He regarded the thing stupidly for a moment or two, and then walked into the inn.

He lifted the telephone receiver and after the usual leisurely delay, old Mrs Jenkinson the postmistress inquired: 'Number please?'

'I want the police station.'

'What number did you say, my dear?'

'The police station, I said.'

'Oh, dear!' came Mrs Jenkinson's ready sympathy. There was a pause during which Jimmy knew she was silently inviting him to tell her the news, and then grudgingly she went on: 'Just a minute, my dear, and I'll put you through.'

Followed a long and animated conversation between Mrs Jenkinson and the Didford Parva exchange, at the conclusion of which there came a number of clicks and burrs, and at last a bored official voice, saying: 'Hullo? *Hullo*?'

'Is that the police station?' asked Jimmy.

'It is. What's your trouble?'

'Murder.'

It was not in the least the way he had intended to put it, but the temptation of startling the unseen policeman out of his calm was too much for him. He certainly succeeded.

'Eh? What's that?' snapped the voice. 'Who's speaking?'

Jimmy wished, too late, that he had begun his story properly. His head was aching violently, but he collected his thoughts as best he could, cleared his throat and began:

'Look here – Sir Peter Packer – '

'Oh, Sir Peter Packer!' he was deferentially interrupted. 'I beg your pardon, Sir Peter. I – '

'No, no!' protested Jimmy. 'Will you listen, please? Sir Peter Packer has been murdered.'

This time there was no doubt he had caused a sensation.

'Hold on, please!' gasped the voice.

Jimmy heard a murmur of subdued tongues, and a succession of those metallic clangs that on the telephone mean footsteps, doors shutting, the movement of furniture or almost anything else. Then a fresh voice broke in, quiet, kindly and forceful, with a hint of rustic richness beneath the clipped, official tones.

'Superintendent White speaking,' it said. 'Now what have you got to tell me?'

Everything seemed to have become suddenly much easier, at the sound of that unruffled voice.

'Sir Peter Packer's body has been found,' Jimmy heard himself saying smoothly, 'on the river bank, near the saw-mill.'

'I know the place. We'll be along there directly. Did you say he was murdered?'

'The back of his head is blown off.' Was it possible that he, Jimmy, could be saying all this so calmly?

'Yes....Who are you, and where are you speaking from?'

'My name is Rendel. I'm speaking from the "Polworthy Arms".'

'You're one of the fishing gentlemen, I suppose?'

'Yes. I – '

'Did you leave anyone with him?'

'Dr Latymer is there. He sent me to telephone.'

'Dr Latymer? Good. That will save us a lot of trouble. Thank you, Mr Rendel. Will you meet us at the road corner in a quarter of an hour?'

He rang off. Jimmy put up the receiver with an immense feeling of relief that the matter was now off his shoulders and in the hands of competent authority. Then he rang up Latymer's surgery and left his message. As he turned away from the telephone, Dora, her face flushed and anxious, appeared in the hall.

'Please, sir,' she breathed, 'I couldn't help hearing – '

Jimmy cut her short with an unwonted air of authority.

'Will you go down to the policeman's cottage,' he said, 'see if he's there and ask him to come up at once? I can run him up in the doctor's car.'

It was only a matter of a hundred yards or so to the cottage, but Jimmy was overcome by a feeling of sudden weariness, and he felt that any further effort would be utterly beyond him.

The girl fluttered away, and he walked outside. The afternoon was melting into the glow of a serene summer's evening. He thought, inconsequently, that the prospects for the evening rise looked good. That put him in mind of his rod, still reposing on the running-board of the car. To occupy himself he picked it up and began to dismember it. He noticed as he did so the bit of weed, now dried, still clenched in his right palm. While he busied himself with the joints of the rod, his mind played with the problem that it presented. Why should the brake pedal be coated in river-weed? The doctor had arrived in the car only a few minutes before the murder was discovered. Nobody, surely, could have driven it between then and the time that he, Jimmy, took it away. Then Latymer's foot must have left that mud. Why? It was river-weed undoubtedly, there was no mistaking the stuff. He tried to remember what his shoes had looked like when he first appeared at the gate, but in vain. Later, of course, they would be muddy with walking along the bank, but before? If they were muddy then, it could only mean one thing – that the moment when the doctor drove his car up to the gate was not the first time he had been on the riverside that day.

Jimmy had just reached the conclusion when heavy and hurried footsteps behind him proclaimed the arrival of the stout and genial Police Constable Bowyer, still fumbling at the last button of his tight-fitting tunic. His red face shone with sweat, and his eyes danced with happy excitement as he climbed into the car.

'This is bad doings, Master Rendel,' he said in a voice of pure joy.

He said no more as the car rattled back along the winding road, and Jimmy was glad of his silence. But just before they reached their destination, the constable leaned confidentially towards him and remarked:

'They do say down the village that Peter Packer picked a peck of peppercorns when he started after Susie Bavin!'

Jimmy swung the car round and backed into the entry off the road. As he opened the door to alight, an open car roared up, and came to a standstill with a squealing of brakes. Three uniformed men got out.

The police were in charge.

CHAPTER SEVEN

Superintendent White and Major Strode

'MR RENDEL?' said Superintendent White.

He was a grey man – grey-eyed, grey-faced, and his close-cut moustache and the hair that showed beneath his uniform cap were of the same non-committal colour. Years of official life seemed to have drained the blood from his cheeks and the personality from his expression. Only the loose-limbed body and the occasional touch of Doric in his speech proclaimed the countryman.

Jimmy came forward.

'I got here just before you,' he said. 'Shall I show you the way?'

'If you please,' answered the superintendent. Then, looking round him, he asked: 'Whose car is this?'

'The doctor's. I drove down in it to telephone.'

'The other one, I mean.'

'That is Mr Wrigley-Bell's. He's fishing farther up the river.'

'Was it here when you first arrived?'

'Yes. I noticed it when I passed the gate.'

The sawmill here interjected another blast of sound. White beckoned to Bowyer.

'Go round and tell those fellows to knock off work,' he shouted. 'Don't let any of them leave the place until I've seen them, though.'

Bowyer departed, and Jimmy led the superintendent and the other two officers through the gate.

'The Chief Constable will be up here-along, pretty soon,' said White. 'Meanwhile we'll just have to see what is to be seen. It was you that found him, I suppose?'

'Not exactly,' Jimmy attempted to explain. 'Dr Latymer found him, but I told him where he was.'

'That sounds rather complicated,' remarked White. 'But we won't bother about that now. Time for statements and all that later. You know where he is?'

Under Jimmy's direction they walked to the river bank and turned upstream.

'This the way you came before?' the superintendent asked. 'Yes.'

He examined the ground. The bank was soft and in many places waterlogged. Every footprint as it was made almost immediately filled with water.

'Not much use looking after footprints here,' he observed.

Just round the bend in front of them a wisp of blue smoke appeared above the reeds. A pace or two farther, and they came in sight of Dr Latymer. He was standing looking across the river, smoking a cigarette. At their approach he turned to greet them.

'Good afternoon, Superintendent,' he said. 'You haven't wasted much time.'

'We reckon to be pretty quick on a job of this kind,' answered White. 'The Chief Constable's not far behind, and I've ordered an ambulance up from headquarters. I allowed you'd want to do your post mortem down along at the mortuary at Parva.'

'Quite right,' answered Latymer. 'Not that a post mortem will show very much more than I know already, in this case. But there's always my fee as police surgeon to be considered, isn't there?' He grinned cheerfully. Whatever his reactions to the discovery had been at first, he was now evidently entirely at his ease. 'Well,' he went on abruptly, stepping aside to let the others pass, 'here you are.'

The body lay upon the little raised platform of dry ground, just where Jimmy had foreseen that it would be. The legs were thrust forward stiffly towards the stream, and looking at them now, he wondered that he could ever have supposed that they belonged to a living man. Sir Peter was on his back, his head almost touching the dense bank of reeds that bordered the 'tump' on three sides. He wore plus-fours and a sleeveless pullover. In life he had been a florid, paunchy man, and Jimmy sickened at the sight of those full cheeks and thick lips now unnaturally pallid, and at the fat belly thrust indecently upwards by the angle of the ground. In the now quiet air of the waterside there was an ever-present hum of flies. The grass and reeds around the head were spattered with dark stains.

Latymer went on one knee beside the body, and putting one arm under its shoulder, pulled the head forward.

'You can see what happened,' he said, as unconcernedly as though he were lecturing a class of medical students. He casually brushed away a swarm of flies. 'The bullet penetrated the right eye very nearly. It came out *here*' – he indicated a hideous wound in the back of the head – 'and took most of his brains with it. It probably broke into fragments against the *dura mater*, which would account for most of the mess. We shall find that out when we come to open him up.'

He released his arm and let the head sink back into its former place.

'What sort of a bullet would that be?' asked White.

'Pretty small, to judge from the entrance wound. An automatic, say – or a rook rifle might have done it.'

'Range?'

'Fairly close. Within a foot or two, I should fancy. You'll observe that there are no signs of burning round the wound.'

'Just a bit far for suicide, I reckon,' said the superintendent thoughtfully.

'And did you ever find a man who shot himself in the eye?' said the doctor. 'Added to which, where's the weapon? I can't see it anywhere. No, I'm afraid it's not suicide. I'm afraid not,' he repeated regretfully.

'Only one more question, I think,' said White. 'How long would you say he has been dead?'

The doctor shook his head. 'It's confoundedly difficult to tell,' he answered. 'Let's see, it's nearly six now. I didn't take the time when I found him. Did you, Jimmy?'

'It must have been five or thereabouts,' said Jimmy, 'but I can't be sure.'

'Say five o'clock. Well, at that time the body was still warm. He might have been killed at any moment up to the time I saw him.' Was it only Jimmy's fancy, or did Latymer's eye seek his as he said this? 'Or', he went on, 'he might have been lying here some time. The body has been fully exposed to a hot sun, and that of course would keep it warm. For the matter of that, it's warm still. Conversely, if he had just been killed when I found him, I should have expected to find the blood-stains still wet. But there again, a sun like this would dry them up in no time. I'm sorry, Superintendent, but the conditions are about as bad as they could be for making an accurate estimate.'

'Yes,' said White patiently. 'But you can give us some sort of a limit each way, I reckon, doctor?'

Latymer pursed his lips.

'The limits are so wide that they won't be of much use to you,' he said. 'Doctors aren't magicians, you know. He had been dead not more than seven hours when I found him. That's about the best I can say.'

'And the other limit?' pursued White.

'A matter of minutes.'

'Thank you, sir, and now – Oh! Good afternoon, sir!'

The superintendent's last remark was addressed to a short, thick-set man of military bearing who now appeared beside them. The other officers drew themselves up and saluted. The whole atmosphere of the group became sensibly more formal. Major Strode was a chief constable well liked by his sub-ordinates, but he saw to it that discipline came before all things in his force.

He returned the salutes punctiliously, nodded a greeting to Latymer, and then looked with expressionless eyes at the body. After a brief survey he turned to White.

'Suicide?' he asked.

'The doctor thinks not, sir.'

'H'm. Then somebody must have shot him down as he stood, eh?'

'You'll notice, sir,' said the superintendent smoothly, 'that deceased is in his shirtsleeves. His coat, I think, is underneath him.'

'Meaning that he was sitting on it when he was killed?'

'It would look that way, sir.'

Major Strode frowned.

'Potted him sitting, by Jove!' he murmured. Evidently in his eyes the murderer's lack of sportsmanship aggravated the offence. He remained silent for a moment, and then went on: 'Well, and who was the first to find him? You, I suppose?' he barked at Jimmy.

'Well, I –' began Jimmy confusedly.

'What's your name?'

'Rendel, sir.'

'Any relation to Gervase Rendel, who used to shoot with me at Charbury?'

'He's my father, sir.'

'Good!' The chief constable became decidedly more friendly now that he had Jimmy securely placed. 'Well, what's your story, eh?'

'I was coming up the bank, when I saw Sir Peter lying here. That is, I didn't see him altogether, only his legs. I thought he was sitting by the waterside. I – I didn't want to disturb him,' he went on hastily, 'so I went back to the corner to come up the other way. At the gate I met the doctor, and in the course of conversation I mentioned what I had seen. He went round and – '

'Why did you go round, Latymer?' Strode shot out.

'He was a patient of mine,' said the doctor, 'and I knew he ought not to be sitting in the sun.'

'Good Lord! Why on earth not?'

'He had a bad go of sunstroke last year, and nothing would ever induce him to wear a hat. When I heard what he was doing, I thought it my duty to warn him.'

'And you found – that?' said Strode, jerking his thumb disrespectfully at the body.

'Precisely.'

'H'm. Bad business, doctor, bad business.'

He remained silent for a moment or two, while his subordinates awaited the slow process of his thoughts. Then he said: 'Well! Body will have to be moved, I suppose. Have you made any arrangements, White?'

'I have ordered an ambulance, sir,' said the superintendent. 'It should be here by now. Dr Latymer thought he had better do the post mortem down at Parva.'

'Quite right. Taken any statements yet?'

'Not yet, sir. If you approve, I propose to see the men at the sawmill first, and see if they have anything to say about it. Then I thought I would take statements from this gentleman' – he indicated Jimmy – 'and the other fishing gentlemen at the "Polworthy", later. Then there's her ladyship, sir – '

'Who? Oh, the widow! Yes, poor girl, someone's got to break it to her. I think perhaps that would come best from me. She – er – I think we should understand each other, you follow me?' Having in this delicate manner indicated the social gulf that lay between chief constables and baronets' ladies on the one side and superintendents of police on the other, he cleared his throat, went rather red, and continued: 'That's settled, then! White, you'll let me have copies of all statements tomorrow morning at my house. I'm dining out this evening, but if I can get away I may join you at the "Polworthy Arms" later.'

'Very good, sir. The ambulance is here now, sir.'

'Then carry on! Doctor, I suppose you'll go down with it?'

'No,' said Latymer. 'I have a patient to see at the cottage just above here, and I must deal with that first. I shall follow later. The P.M. won't take me long, I expect.'

'We want your report as soon as possible, y'know.'

'Perhaps,' suggested the superintendent, 'the doctor could come up along to Magna when he's finished, and I could have his statement along with the rest?'

'That'll do, that'll do. Let's get on with it!' said Strode impatiently. 'Now what's my best way up to the Manor?'

'You can walk up through the grounds,' said Latymer. 'It's on my way. I'll show you.'

'I should like to come too, if I may,' said Jimmy, surprised at his own boldness.

'Eh? You? Why?' Strode shot out.

'She's – she's rather a friend of mine,' Jimmy faltered, 'and I thought perhaps – I mean, I'd like to – ' His voice trailed away in silence.

'Very decent of you,' observed the chief constable. 'Shows a very decent feeling and all that. If she's a friend of yours, may help to soften the blow and so forth. Any objection, White?'

'Not a bit, sir, if the young gentleman will be back at the "Polworthy" for his statement.'

'I'll drive him down myself. Have my car sent round to the Manor, will you? Now, come on!'

Jimmy, the doctor, and Strode walked on together. A few paces took them round the bend and out of sight of the 'tump'. A mellow sun flooded the river bank with gold. A light breeze set the tips of the reeds and the leaves of the alders whispering together. In mid-stream a trout rose with a quiet 'plop'. Jimmy's heart felt ready to burst at the beauty of it all, at the cruel contrast between their business and its setting.

'Jolly evening, what?' said Major Strode.

CHAPTER EIGHT

The Widow

MAJOR STRODE and Jimmy left the waterside just above the end of the causeway and took a path parallel to the fence that bordered the Manor grounds. They crossed the little leet which provided the power for the sawmill, and here the doctor left them, turning into the cottage near by. They went on past the beech wood, now a devastated area of stumps and trampled brushwood, and came out into the miniature park surrounding the house. The Manor stood well above river level, looking down the valley, so that they were walking steadily uphill. The chief constable was silent, breathing heavily through his nose. Jimmy had the impression that he was setting a rather quicker pace than was really comfortable for him, and that he kept his mouth shut to conceal the fact.

A few minutes' walk brought them to the gate which divided the park from the garden, and, passing through, they turned parallel to the side of the house in order to reach the drive. The path ran through a little grove of flowering shrubs, and then skirted a broad expanse of lawn. In the middle of the lawn stood a great copper beech, beneath which was a garden seat. On the seat, quite motionless, sat Marian Packer. Her hands were idle in her lap, and she was gazing vacantly before her. The sound of their feet on the gravel evidently roused her, for she turned her head in their direction, but otherwise she did not move. The pair left the path and came towards her across the silent surface of the grass, while she watched their approach. Her eyes, Jimmy noticed, were not on him but upon his companion.

They came to a halt in front of her. The chief constable saluted. Jimmy was in terror that he would say something brutally tactless, but he need not have been alarmed.

'Lady Packer,' he began in a voice of unexpected gentleness, 'I think you know me. I am Major Strode.'

She nodded, without taking her eyes off his.

'I am sorry to say that we have some very serious news for you,' he went on.

'My husband?' she asked. The words came clearly and without visible effort. Her face displayed no emotion whatever. It was as if a statue had spoken.

'Yes,' answered Strode.

'You have come to tell me that he is dead?'

'Yes.'

There was a frozen silence for a moment before he went on. 'He is dead, Lady Packer, and further, it is my duty to tell you that all the evidence points to his having been murdered.'

'Murdered!' She was on her feet in an instant. 'Is that true, Jimmy?'

Jimmy was utterly at a loss, finding himself appealed to in this manner, over the head of the chief constable.

'I'm afraid so,' he murmured uncomfortably.

'Murdered!' she repeated quietly to herself. For a moment she stood quite rigid, then passed her hand across her eyes, and said quite calmly: 'I think we had better go indoors, hadn't we?'

Turning, she led the way to the house, which she entered through an open french window. After the sunbaked garden, the long drawing-room in which they now found themselves was cool and dim. She settled herself in the corner of a sofa with its back to the window, and the two men sat down awkwardly in chairs confronting her.

'Now, Major Strode,' she said.

'Afraid this is a terrible shock to you,' said the chief constable. 'Can I get you a glass of water or anything?'

She shook her head.

'There will have to be an inquest, of course,' he went on, 'and inquiries and questions and all that sort of thing. Naturally, I don't want to worry you now, but I thought you ought to be prepared. '

'Please ask me anything you wish to know,' she answered. 'I quite understand that there will have to be full inquiries of all kinds, but in the meantime I am at your service now.'

'That's very sporting of you,' said Strode. 'If you're sure you feel up to it, you can help us a lot. Now in the first place – '

'In the first place', she interrupted him, 'you must tell me what has happened. My husband has been murdered, you say. How and where?'

'He was shot through the head on the river bank. At least, that is where he was found. Close to – what is the name of the place, Rendel?'

'Just above the river corner,' Jimmy explained. 'About half-way between that and the end of the causeway, where – '

'I know the place,' she put in.

'Have you any idea what he would be doing there?' asked Strode.

'He often went down that way,' she answered. 'To see how the sawmill was going, especially.'

'And this morning in particular – what can you tell me about his movements?'

'Let me see. After breakfast he and Mr Cawston went off to talk business.'

'Mr Cawston? Who is he?'

'He is a business acquaintance of my husband's, I understand. I had never met him before.'

'Staying in the house?'

'Yes, he arrived here late last night, and left after lunch today. I don't know, of course, what the business was.'

'They were talking business all the morning, then?'

'No. A little before eleven, they came back to this room, where I was, and my husband asked me to look after Mr Cawston, as he had to go out for a little. We waited for him till lunch, and then when he had not returned, sat down without him. Mr Cawston was rather annoyed, I remember, because he had to leave without seeing him again.'

'Weren't you surprised at his not turning up?' asked the major.

Marian smiled wanly.

'I certainly thought it rather inconsiderate of him,' she admitted. 'But my husband is – was – inclined not to consider other people's convenience, I'm afraid. I understood that he had finished all the business matters and thought that he simply didn't want to be bothered with Mr Cawston any more. That was rather like him in some ways. So when he didn't come in, I took it for granted that he had taken his lunch with him. He often did. It was only after Mr Cawston had left, when he did not come in for tea, that I began to feel at all anxious. Then I made inquiries, and found that he had made no arrangements to be out. That surprised me.'

'What did you do?'

'I walked down to the river by the way I thought he had probably taken.'

'Yes?'

Marian Packer went on slowly and deliberately.

'I went down to the river. When I got there, I saw Mr Rendel and Dr Latymer talking together. The sawmill was making too much noise for me to hear very much. Presently in a pause I heard the doctor say: "Sir Peter is dead." I turned round and came straight home.'

'God bless my soul!' ejaculated the chief constable.

'That seems strange to you, Major Strode, no doubt?' she went on, as calmly as ever. 'I suppose it must. But the plain fact is, I couldn't face it. I was a coward, I suppose, but at the moment I simply felt that I had to be alone – to think over things and face the position. Can you understand?'

'Er – yes, I think so,' said the major, though it was apparent that he did not.

'Ever since then I have been sitting on the lawn outside, waiting for someone to bring me news. Though of course,' she added, 'I did not expect to see you.'

'Of course not,' said the chief constable vaguely.

If her story had seemed strange to him, to Jimmy it was completely bewildering. He did not trust himself to look at her, but he was certain that every word of her story – so plausible, so utterly misleading in its omissions – was directed at him. He realized with a sickening dread that in a short space of time he would have to tell his story and make his choice between prevaricating and proving hers to be untrue. Why was she afraid to say what they both knew to be the fact? Why was she, in effect, appealing to him to support her version? He stared miserably at the carpet, conscious that his face was going red and white by turns, in mortal fear that at any moment Strode might notice his discomfiture. But Strode was too absorbed in his questioning to spare any attention for his companion.

'Had you any particular reason,' he was asking, 'to anticipate your husband's death?'

'His health was not very good,' she replied, 'and he wouldn't take any care of himself. He had already had one attack of sunstroke.'

'Just what the doctor feller thought it was in this case, until he came to look at him,' commented Strode. 'You hadn't any reason to suppose that anyone wanted to do him harm, I suppose?'

'There were a good many people who had disagreements with him,' she answered evenly, 'but I can't say that any of them had ever threatened his life.'

'Just so,' murmured Strode. He stared vaguely at the ceiling for a moment and then added: 'Well, that's what our business is – to find out who had a motive for doing the job – for this dreadful crime, I should say. And when we have, we shan't be long fixing it on him, I can promise you.' He rose to his feet and said: 'I'm not going to bother you with any more questions, Lady Packer. You'll have the superintendent up here tomorrow to put your statement shipshape, but he's a nice fellow, and you needn't let that worry you. Now I'm only going to ask you to do one thing more before I clear off. Would you please show me where your husband kept his private papers and so forth?'

She took him to Sir Peter's study, an aggressively masculine room, hung with coloured prints representing sports the owner had never practised, and with all the antlers of deer he had never shot. Jimmy knew the room well. He hated it, because to him it seemed the quintessence of the man he detested. On this occasion he was doubly glad to take the opportunity to remain behind in the drawing-room.

The chief constable found himself faced with a large roll-top desk, its pigeon-holes stuffed with papers of every description, all neatly folded and filed away.

'These are all business papers,' Marian explained. 'His personal papers, so far as I know, he kept in these two drawers.'

She indicated them. They were both locked.

'Where are the keys?' asked Strode.

'In his pocket, I expect,' she told him. 'He was hardly ever parted from them.'

'In that case, the superintendent will bring them up with

him tomorrow, go through the drawers and take away anything he thinks may prove material. It may be rather unpleasant for you, but in a case like this – '

'Please don't bother to apologize, Major Strode. I had not the least objection, in any case.'

'Good. And in the meantime, you won't mind my locking the door of the room and taking away the key?'

'Of course not.'

'Housemaids dusting and so forth might destroy a valuable clue without knowing it, y'never can tell,' the major explained jerkily. 'Well, I think that's all now. One moment, though, I quite forgot to ask – had your husband a revolver, or anything of that sort?'

'Yes. I know that he had a small automatic.'

'Where did he keep it?'

'In this desk. It was always in this drawer. It is locked, of course.'

Strode tried the handle of the small drawer to which she pointed. It slid open. It was empty.

'Hullo, hullo!' said Major Strode.

'I cannot understand that at all,' said Marian quietly.

'Anywhere else that it can be, d'you think?'

'No. I cannot. I shall have a search made, of course.'

'The only other alternative is that he took it with him when he went out today. Was there any particular reason why he should?'

'None that I can think of.'

'He hadn't had any threatening letters or anything of that sort?'

Marian reflected a moment.

'He had one letter this morning that seemed to cause him some annoyance,' she said. 'I remember that he tore it up and threw it into the fire.'

'He didn't say what was in it, I suppose?'

'No. I took no particular notice. It was not so very uncommon for him to treat letters he disliked in that way.'

'And you haven't a notion who it was from, of course?'

'No. I fancy that the envelope was written in a rather un-educated hand. And now, if you'll excuse me, Major Strode, but I have had rather a·trying day – '

'Of course, of course, my dear lady,' said the major. 'I won't trouble you any more. And if you'll allow me to say so, you've been dashed plucky about the whole business. Really, I wouldn't have believed it possible. I'll go at once. My car's at the door, I expect. Perhaps you'd ask young Rendel to come along?'

He made his way to the hall. The butler, a tall, bleak-looking man, was at the open door in earnest conversation with the policeman chauffeur. He drew himself up as the chief constable approached.

'I suppose you've heard, my man,'·said Strode to him as he passed out, 'that your master is dead?'

'I have, sir.'

'Just tell me – what terms would you say he was on with her ladyship?'

The man looked blankly a foot above the major's head.

'It was not a subject her ladyship ever discussed with me, sir,' he replied.

Before the other could make any rejoinder, Jimmy had appeared on the steps, and the two climbed into the car together.

'Marvellous little woman that,' remarked Strode, as they drove away. 'She took it pretty calmly, don't you think?'

'Yes.'

'Seeing that she's a friend of yours and so on, I thought she might like the chance of a word with you alone.'

'Thank you.'

'Did she say anything to you?'

'No. She only said good-bye, and thanked me for coming up with you.'

Jimmy spoke the truth, and the fact that it was the truth only added to his perplexities. Her actual words had been: 'Good-bye, Jimmy. It was good of you to come up and hear what I had to say.' But he could not tell the chief constable what those words had conveyed to him, or describe the searching look that had accompanied them. She had squeezed his hand as he left, he could feel the pressure on his still. He felt that against his will he had been bound in some kind of compact with her against the world. Would he have the strength to keep it?

Strode's voice broke in upon his reverie.

'By the way,' he asked, 'so far as you remember, is her story correct about your chat with the doctor?'

'Oh, quite correct,' answered Jimmy.

'I've done it now,' he said to himself.

CHAPTER NINE

Questions and Answers

SUPERINTENDENT WHITE did not reach the 'Polworthy Arms' until after eight o'clock. The bar was full, and the intake of beer and the output of excited conversation proved that the village was in possession of the news. White had with him an officer to assist him in taking statements. This man he sent into the bar with a request that the landlady should see him immediately. Standing in the hall outside, he could hear the noise of talk stop abruptly on the appearance of the constable, and rise again to hurricane force as he left the room with the flustered woman.

'I shall be wanting to take some statements here,' he told her. 'Is there a room that you can let me have?'

'I don't know, I'm sure,' said the woman perplexedly, wiping her hands on her beer-stained apron. 'There's only the parlour, and Mr Rendel is in there, eating a bit of supper. The other gentlemen will be in some time, I expect.'

'They all use the parlour?'

'That's right.'

'It wouldn't hardly be suitable for me, asking them all questions, would it?'

'Well, perhaps you wouldn't mind using my sitting-room at the back?' suggested the landlady. 'Dear knows, I shan't be in there this evening, with all there is to do in the bar, and the gentlemen to wait on, and that Dora in such a state she might just as well not be here at all – '

'That's very kind of you,' said White gravely. He knew the capacity of the 'Polworthy Arms' perfectly well, and had intended from the beginning to borrow this room for his purpose. He knew also that if he had asked for it straight out he would have met with a blank refusal.

'You're welcome, I'm sure.'

'Is Mr Rendel the only person in?'

'Yes, sir, all except Mrs Matheson. She came in about six o'clock. Terrible put out she was when she heard the news. Went straight up to her room and hasn't been down since.'

'I see. Now will you show us the room, please?'

In a small back room, encumbered with ferns and stuffed birds, the two men sat down. The landlady found them some bread and cheese and beer, and promised to send Jimmy to them as soon as he had finished his meal.

'Not that he's making much of a supper, poor young man,' she commented. 'So put out he is – nearly as much as the lady upstairs. Well, you can't wonder, I say.'

White drank his beer and crumbled his bread in silence. While he did so he was glancing through the notes he had already made, and adding a comment here and there in pencil. The constable watched him with respect, while demolishing his share of the cheese at an astonishing rate. Presently the quiet was interrupted by an uproar from the direction of the bar.

'Go and see what that is,' said the superintendent. 'I expect it's only a drunk, but have him got out quietly.'

The officer went out and returned in a few moments.

'It was a drunk all right,' he said. 'Some friends of his were getting him out and the row began when he wouldn't go.'

'That's not like the "Polworthy",' the superintendent observed. 'They usually know when to stop serving a man with liquor here.'

'He wasn't served here at all, they tell me,' the constable explained. 'He was fair drunk when he came in.'

'That explains it, then.'

'Kicking up a fearful row, he was,' the officer went on with relish, 'and saying such things about Sir Peter you wouldn't believe.'

'Indeed? What was his name, by the way?'

'Carter, sir, Philip Carter. A steady-going young man in the ordinary way by all accounts. Seems funny, him breaking out like that all of a sudden.'

'I dare say he'll be able to tell us what the reason is to-morrow. No good asking a drunk man questions, you know. It's when he's got a splitting head next morning that he'll talk.'

The constable had scarcely had time to savour this piece of wisdom before Jimmy Rendel came in. The superintendent glanced sympathetically at his pale tired face, and hastened to find him the least uncomfortable of the room's inhospitable chairs.

'I shan't be keeping you long, sir,' he said. 'I think we know most of your story already, but we want it all shipshape, if you don't mind.'

'I don't mind at all, of course.'

'Good. Then we'll begin at the beginning. Your full name and address, please?'

Jimmy's narrative, reduced into writing by the attendant officer, was succinct enough, though when he came to sign it he had some difficulty in recognizing his own words in the stiff police phraseology. It ran as follows:

'I arrived at Didford Parva this afternoon by the train due at 2.15 p.m., proceeding to the "Polworthy Arms", Didford Magna, by hired car. The train being late, it was nearly 3.0 p.m. when I reached the hotel. I did not look at my watch again until after the events in question. It is not customary to take much account of the time when fishing. I changed my clothes and proceeded to the river, with the intention of fishing the bottom stretch of the water. When I had gone a short distance up the river I met Mr Matheson. He told me that he was fishing my beat and that I was to go to the next beat above. That is beat two. There are four beats altogether, numbered from the bottom upwards. Mr Wrigley-Bell and Mr Smithers were on beats three and four respectively. To reach those beats one must go past the road corner, but not necessarily by the river bank. Mr Matheson had caught two fish, and caught another while I was with him. I proceeded up the bank of the main stream, keeping the river on my right. Mr Matheson came with me a short way, and then I left him. At the road bridge I met Mrs Large. We had a short conversation. I then proceeded to the road corner. I arrived there approximately half an hour after leaving Mr Matheson. I proceeded up the bank. I saw Sir Peter Packer on the bank. I did not see him, I saw his legs. I recognized his stockings. I went back to the corner. While I was there Dr Latymer arrived by car. We walked up the causeway together. In consequence of what I said to him he went back while I proceeded to the junction of the causeway and the bank. Shortly after I had arrived there Dr Latymer called to me. I went back and spoke to him. In consequence of what he said to me I proceeded to the road corner, and drove in his car to Didford Magna, where I summoned the police. I last saw Sir Peter Packer a week ago.'

'Thank you,' said White, as Jimmy signed the document. 'Now is there anything else?'

'Anything else?' Jimmy looked at him with a misgiving which he tried hard to keep from his face. 'I don't understand.'

'There are lots of things which don't get into police reports,' the superintendent explained, 'which nonetheless they get to hear about, and which sometimes are uncommon helpful. Just little bits of information, you follow me, sir, which a bright young man might notice and not even know they were important. Now in a case like this, I needn't tell you, we are bound to consider everybody as more or less under suspicion – '

'Including me, I suppose,' Jimmy put in.

White inclined his head gravely.

'Including you, sir,' he said. 'So you'll understand that it's all to the good if you can give me any scrap of knowledge concerning any person or thing you may have noticed which isn't here in your statement.'

Jimmy thought for a moment. He had not expected this development. The taking of his statement had proceeded so smoothly that he had hardly realized himself that in an all-important particular it was virtually untrue. Now the superintendent's appeal and the hint of a threat that accompanied it threw him for the moment off his balance. But his mind was made up. He had gone too far to recede. On one point at least he must remain silent. Then, as he looked at White's expectant face, he remembered with a feeling half of relief and half of guilt that he could after all satisfy his curiosity without trespassing on the forbidden ground.

'Yes,' he said. 'There is one thing – or rather two things which you may as well hear.'

'And they are?'

'Well, it may have been just a coincidence, but when I was driving the doctor's car on to the road to fetch the police I saw Mrs Matheson – nearly ran over her, in fact.'

'Where was she at the time? On the main road?'

'Yes.'

'That doesn't seem to come to very much, then, does it, sir?'

'No. Only it struck me at the time that she seemed anxious not to be seen.'

'Ah!' The superintendent fingered his pencil absently for a moment and then asked: 'This Mrs Matheson, now – she's not a fisher herself, I suppose?'

'No.'

'How does she spend her time down here? Walking about the countryside and that sort of thing?'

'Yes.'

'She might have been up to Didbury Camp for a stroll, like, and come down that way?'

'I suppose she might. The path from the Camp comes into the road quite close there.'

'I thought so. Well, it'll do no harm asking the lady, at all events. And what was the other thing?'

'Simply this. I was puzzled because my foot slipped on the brake. That was why I nearly ran down Mrs Matheson. When I got back here, I looked and found that the pedal was slimy with mud.'

'Off your own boots, like as not.'

'No. I was driving in my stockings. They were quite dry.'

'And what did you think about that?'

'I thought it odd that the doctor should have been on the river bank before that afternoon.'

'You're jumping a bit, aren't you, sir?' said the superintendent sceptically. 'There's lots of places you can pick up mud in, besides the river, I reckon.'

'But this was river mud, I'll swear,' said Jimmy. 'Besides, there was a bit of water-weed as well. There was no mistaking it.'

'Did you keep the bit of weed?'

'No, I'm afraid not.'

'A pity that. That would have been a real bit of evidence. What the story-writers call a clue. Now let's see. The mud was quite fresh when you found it?'

'Yes, quite fresh enough to make my foot slip, anyway.'

'Do you think there was time for anyone to have used the car between when you saw Dr Latymer arrive in it and when you came to drive away?'

'I suppose there was – time to drive quite a short distance and back, but it certainly seemed to be exactly where the doctor had left it, when I came back.'

'H'm. We don't know anything of the doctor's movements before that, of course?'

'I only know what Mrs Large told me, that he drove down the road towards the village some time before she met me.'

'She told you that, did she, sir? A useful lady, Mrs Large, to have about the village, I reckon,' commented the superintendent, something very like a grin illuminating his grey features for an instant. 'Well, Mr Rendel, I'm very much obliged to you for your help. I'm afraid you'll be wanted to give evidence at the inquest, but you needn't let that trouble you very much.'

'When will that be?' Jimmy asked.

'That depends on Mr Severn. He's the coroner in these parts. But I reckon it can hardly be before Tuesday. Unless we find out a lot between now and then, it will be little more than a formality. Till then, sir, you won't take it amiss my warning you, best not talk about this to anyone, and don't you let any of they newspaper chaps get hold of you! Good night!'

When he had gone, White turned to the constable.

'It's mortal hot in here,' he remarked. 'Just see if that window will open a little wider.'

The officer went to the window.

'It's come all over cloudy outside,' he said.

'There was a nasty little wind beating up when we came in,' the superintendent said. 'Did you notice it? Dry and gusty like. It'll turn to thunder tonight, you mark me. Well, that's all to the good. It'll bring the fisher folk in early, and that'll save us trouble.'

One of the fisher folk, as a matter of fact, had already returned. As he left the landlady's room, Jimmy Rendel met Matheson in the hall. He stamped in, obviously very tired but contented, swinging a heavy fishing-bag in triumph.

'Two brace, my boy!' he exclaimed as he met him. 'I thought I was going to make it the half-dozen, but the rise stopped dead in the most extraordinary way. Change in the weather coming, I suppose. Never mind! I've done enough to put a spoke in Wrigley-Bell's wheel, I fancy. Is he in yet?'

'No.'

'Have you seen my wife anywhere about?'

'No, but I believe she is upstairs. She – she's had a bit of a shock, sir – in fact we all have.'

'What the devil are you talking about?'

'Sir Peter Packer is dead. The police think it is murder.'

73

'God bless my soul!'

'He was found on the bank this afternoon, just above the road corner. The police are here now, inquiring into it. As a matter of fact, I think they want to see you.'

'Me? But that's ridiculous! What should I know about it? I was on the bottom part of the water the whole day. You're my witness for that.'

'Yes, of course, sir,' Jimmy assured him. 'I expect it's just a matter of form.'

Grumbling, Matheson agreed to humour the police. First, however, he sought out Dora and handed over to her his fish, with instructions that they should be laid upon a lordly dish to await Wrigley-Bell's return. Then he mixed himself a strong whisky-and-soda, and having drunk it off, declared himself ready for the interview. He did not, Jimmy remarked, go upstairs to see his wife, or allude to her again.

'I'm told you want to see me,' he began somewhat defiantly to the Superintendent.

'I thought it would be as well to get statements from all the fishing gentlemen,' White explained quietly, 'seeing that this affair happened on their river, in a manner of speaking.'

'Well I can tell you in advance that I don't know the first thing about this "affair", as you call it. I only heard two minutes ago what it was all about.'

'Quite so, sir,' said White non-committally. 'Now may I have your name and address, please?'

Matheson gave him the particulars with an ill grace.

'You were fishing on what you call beat one today, I'm told?'

'Yes.'

'All day?'

'Yes. From about a quarter past eleven in the morning till less than an hour ago.'

'Sir Peter was found a little way above the road corner. Did you go there at all?'

'Certainly not. It's not on my beat.'

'Have you a map,' the superintendent asked, 'which will show me just where these beats begin and end?'

'Certainly,' said Matheson.

From a poacher's pocket in his coat he produced a large-scale ordnance survey map, well worn and grimy with much usage. This he spread out upon the table. It was neatly marked to show the boundaries of the different beats, and in addition it was copiously covered with small crosses in red ink, to each of which a date and initials were appended.

'What are all these?' White asked.

'Birds and birds'-nests,' Matheson explained.

'You collect eggs, then?'

'Good heavens, no!' exclaimed Matheson, deeply wounded. 'I should think not! But I happen to be a bird lover and – '

'Of course, of course, I understand you, sir. I'm very fond of birds too, if it comes to that.' He examined the map with interest, and then, pointing to one mark, asked: 'What's this, sir, just up by the road corner? "B-T, 5.5.37", it reads.'

'I told you just now – a bird.'

'Yes, but what bird? Let me see now – "B-T", up by the road corner among all them reeds.... It can't be – you don't really mean you found a bearded tit, sir?'

'I certainly do.'

'Last year?'

'Yes.'

'Wonderful, sir, wonderful! I thought they were extinct in these parts, altogether.'

'Well, you can take my word for it that they are not,' said Matheson, with a smile of triumph.

'Well, I can only say that I congratulate you, sir. It must be years since I set eyes on one. Why, the last time must have been near thirty years ago, when I was a young constable down at Whittingfield. I don't know if you've ever been in the marsh there, sir – '

To the astonishment of the young constable the pair continued to talk birds with animation and interest for a full five minutes, until, when the topic was reluctantly abandoned, every trace of Matheson's former antagonism had disappeared.

'I wonder if I might borrow this map, sir,' said White at last, 'to mark my own copy with the various beats?'

'Of course, of course. No objection at all.'

Friendly relations having been by now firmly established, Matheson's examination proceeded smoothly enough.

'Where were the other gentlemen fishing today?' White next asked.

'Mr Wrigley-Bell was on beat three, Mr Smithers on beat four.'

'To reach either of these, according to this map, you have to pass by the road corner?'

'That is so.'

'I shall have to ask them themselves, but perhaps you can tell me, sir, when did they leave the hotel?'

'Mr Smithers went first. I'm not sure when, but it was before half past ten. He walked up. I should imagine he took the short cut through the copse. Wrigley-Bell didn't start till about eleven. He went by car.'

'So that beat two, where the road corner is, was unoccupied?'

'Until Rendel came along, yes.'

'Mr Rendel tells me, sir, that it was his day for the first beat, and that he was surprised to find you there.'

Matheson reddened slightly.

'Yes,' he said. 'I – er – had occasion to change my beat last night.'

'How was that, sir?'

Somewhat shamefacedly, Matheson recounted the story of the bet which had resulted in his choosing the bottom beat for the second time in succession.

'I may not be so young as I was,' he concluded, 'but hang it all, I had to show the fellow that I could still catch fish. You can understand that, Superintendent?'

White smiled sympathetically.

'I reckon I can understand how it all came up, sir,' he said. 'I expect you gentlemen often have little bets among yourselves, in fun like.'

'Nothing of the sort,' Matheson answered with some heat. 'I've never known such a thing before, all the time I've fished here. I don't approve of betting on field sports. I shouldn't have done it last night if I hadn't been fairly goaded into it.'

'Indeed, sir. Was there anything special that made Mr Wrigley-Bell goad you, as you say?'

'Nothing at all. He just suddenly turned nasty, that's all. And I was feeling tired and cross, or I shouldn't have let it affect me. It was a silly business altogether.'

'It certainly had an unlucky result, sir,' said the superintendent gravely. 'It left beat two free for somebody to do what was done there with none to see.'

'I quite appreciate that,' Matheson replied. 'I can only say that I did in fact fish beat one, and the fish are there to testify that I was well occupied. Also' – he tapped the map, and spanned the distance from the road corner to the boundary post with his fingers – 'I am an old man, officer, and you will have observed that I walk slowly.'

White nodded. 'Only one more thing, sir,' he said. 'You can, if necessary, of course produce evidence as to when you left the hotel this morning?'

'Certainly. For one thing, there's Wrigley-Bell himself. He was writing letters in the parlour this morning while I was going through some notes I was contributing to *British Birds*. He left a little before me. Then there's my wife. She left about the same time as he did.'

'Ah yes – Mrs Matheson,' murmured White. 'I wonder if I could ask her a question or two.'

'My wife? You want to question my wife?'

'If you please, sir.'

Matheson stared at him a moment, and then grumbled, 'Very well, if you say so.'

He listened without comment while his statement, rendered in the same police jargon as its predecessor, was read over, scrawled his signature at the foot of the page, and left the room.

CHAPTER TEN

Questions and Answers (continued)

WHEN Matheson entered the bedroom which he shared with his wife, he was surprised to find the blinds drawn and the room in semi-darkness. Euphemia was lying on the bed, a handkerchief steeped in eau-de-cologne pressed to her forehead. She started up as her husband switched on the electric light. Her face was very pale, except for her nose, which was unbecomingly and unusually pink and shiny.

'Robert, darling!' she exclaimed. 'I didn't know you were back. Do turn out the light. I've got such a horrible headache. There's going to be a thunderstorm in a minute, I know.' Then, as he did not reply: 'Did – did you have some good fishing?'

Matheson did not turn out the light, nor did he reply to her question. Instead he sat down wearily in a chair and asked curtly:

'Have you heard what has happened?'

She nodded and blew her nose vigorously.

'You mean about Sir Peter? Robert, isn't it too *dreadful*? I feel so upset about it.... Darling, would you mind if I don't come downstairs again this evening? I am so wretched.'

'The police are here,' Matheson went on heavily. 'I've just been talking to them. They want a word with you.'

'With me? But why?'

'I don't know. I suppose they'll tell you when that you see them.'

'But Robert, I can't see them! I'm not feeling at all well, and there's nothing I can say that will be of any sort of use to them. They can't think that I –' She got off the bed, and crossing the room, put her arms round his neck. 'You don't imagine that I know anything about it, do you, Robert?' she murmured.

He detached her arms from him, not ungently, but did not look her in the face.

'All the same, I think you had better go down and see them, Phemy,' he said.

She stood up, and going to the dressing-table began to powder her nose.

'I think you are horribly unsympathetic,' she answered. 'But if you insist, I shall go.' There was silence between them, while she made good the disorder of the last few hours to her hair, dress, and complexion. 'I'm ready now,' she answered at length. 'Are you coming with me?'

'I'll come downstairs with you,' Matheson replied. 'But I think it would be best if you gave them your statement alone.'

'You want me to see those horrors of police alone?'

'You can always insist on having a lawyer to advise you if you like.'

'I suppose you want me to have that hateful sneering Smithers? No, thank you. Besides, it isn't a lawyer I want. Simply I feel so tired and unwell.'

'Would you like me to send for Latymer, then?'

There was something in his tone that made her turn and look at him.

'Latymer?' she repeated. 'Why do you mention him?'

'He is a doctor, isn't he? He wrote a very pretty prescription for me last night, did he not?'

She stared at him in surprise.

'What on earth are you talking about, Robert?' she said.

'Well, that is right, isn't it?' he persisted.

'He gave a prescription for you last night – yes,' she said. 'I took it to the chemist's today to have it made up. But what –'

'Ah, so you took it to the chemist's! You are always solicitous of my welfare, Phemy! And what did you think of it?'

'Robert, I shall begin to think you have gone crazy in a moment! How on earth should I know what was in the prescription? You're not mad enough to suggest that there was something wrong with it, are you?'

Matheson looked his wife in the eyes.

79

'Do you really mean that you never read the prescription that Latymer gave you last night?' he said slowly.

'Of course I didn't read it. That's the chemist's business, not mine. I shouldn't have understood it if I had. Robert, do be sensible!'

Her husband stared at her for a long minute, and then suddenly threw back his head.

'By God!' he exclaimed, 'I believe you're telling the truth! And in that case –' He burst into a sudden roar of laughter.

Then, to her complete surprise, he went up to her and kissed her gently on the forehead.

'The police will be waiting,' he said.

Without a word she turned and ran from the room.

The Mrs Matheson who confronted Superintendent White a few minutes later was a very different-looking woman from the Mrs Matheson who had spent the evening distraught upon her bed. In the short distance that she had had to cover between the two rooms, she had contrived to shed every trace of agitation. Her forehead was unruffled by any sign of care, a hint of a smile played round the corners of her full lips, and if her manner was subdued, even melancholy, that was after all no more than fitting in the circumstances.

She apologized prettily for keeping the police waiting.

'I have had such a terrible headache,' she explained. 'I think it must be the thunder in the air.'

A distant mutter of thunder gave point to her words.

'I can quite understand it,' said White. 'Besides, this news must have been a great shock to you.'

'Yes, indeed it has.'

'Was Sir Peter a great friend of yours?' the superintendent asked.

'Not a great friend exactly. My husband and I had been to the Manor once or twice, you know, and I had seen something of them in London. It's mostly his wife I was thinking of. She seemed such a nice little thing.'

Nobody could ever have described Euphemia as a nice little

thing, and she paid this tribute to Lady Packer with a touch of condescension that made it quite clear that she was agreeably conscious of the fact.

'Now, Mrs Matheson,' White went on, 'we are naturally anxious to eliminate as far as possible everybody who could have been in the neighbourhood of the scene of the crime at the material time. Your husband has already given us an account of his movements. Perhaps you can help us in that direction.'

'I shall be glad to, of course.'

In reply to White's questions, she described her husband's movements up to the time when he had left the hotel. Her account tallied exactly with his. Her description of the scene of the night before when the bet was made added nothing to what the police already knew. although her manner of telling it was a good deal more vivid, and so far as Wrigley-Bell was concerned, decidedly more adjectival. The threatened storm had by now broken, and her story was punctuated, not inappropriately, by flashes of forked lightning and bursts of thunder.

'The nasty little beast,' she concluded. 'I slapped his face for him, and that's some consolation.'

'Did you, indeed, ma'am?' said White gravely. 'I don't recollect Mr Matheson mentioning that.'

'He didn't know anything about it,' Euphemia explained. 'He had gone up to bed.'

'And you remained behind to – er – have it out with the other gentleman?'

'Oh, no. I went upstairs with my husband. Then I found that I had left my bag in the parlour and came back for it. Meeting Mr Wrigley-Bell again was just an accident. Not that I'm sorry for what I did. I'm rather pleased about it. In fact, I wouldn't have missed it for worlds,' she concluded with a touch of defiance.

'I see,' said the superintendent. He coughed to cover his evident embarrassment and then went on: 'And now as to your own movements today, Mrs Matheson?'

'Mine? Oh, they were simple enough. Immediately after breakfast I drove down to Didford Parva and left a prescription to be made up at the chemist's. That was one that Dr Latymer had given me for my husband last night. When I got back I had a packet of sandwiches made up and went out for a walk. That would be shortly after eleven, I suppose. I remember that my husband was just preparing to go out fishing, and Mr Wrigley-Bell's car left the inn while I was waiting for my sandwiches. I didn't return here till quite late.'

'Where did you go?'

She waved her hand vaguely towards the west.

'Up on the downs,' she said. 'I found my way to the Camp eventually, and spent the afternoon there lazing in the shade.'

'Which way did you come back?'

'The same way – more or less.'

'By the downs?'

'Yes.'

'If anyone says he saw you on the road between here and the Camp, that wouldn't be right, then?'

She looked him straight in the eyes and said in a low clear voice:

'Oh, no, superintendent. That would be absolutely wrong.'

And upon this note the interview terminated.

As White had foreseen, the thunder had brought the anglers home early. While he was reading over Euphemia's statement to her, with the patter of the first big raindrops on the window-panes as accompaniment, Wrigley-Bell and Smithers arrived together in the former's car. They found Matheson at a solitary supper and learned from him of the tragedy at the road corner. It was, therefore, no surprise to them when, just as they were sitting down to their own meal, Dora approached them with the intimation that the superintendent wished to speak to them.

Smithers looked up from his plate in disgust.

'There is no reason, in law or common-sense, why the police should interrupt my meal-times,' he observed. 'Give the bobbies my compliments, Dora, and tell them to wait.'

Wrigley-Bell got up from the table.

'I'll go,' he said. 'I really don't feel like eating anything this evening after this – this shocking news.'

'Just as you please,' said Smithers. 'Personally, I don't intend to let Packer's disappearance affect my appetite. But then you always were a sensitive plant, Bell.'

The other made no attempt to answer the sarcasm, but made his way directly to the back room.

'It is good of you to assist us, sir,' said White, when the preliminaries of name and address had been completed.

'Oh, but of course – of course, I am most anxious to assist the police in every way possible,' Wrigley-Bell insisted with a grimace. 'But naturally, I don't know anything about this matter at all – on my word I don't.'

The superintendent disregarded the protestation and began his questions without further preamble.

'You were on beat three today, sir?'

'That is right.'

'To reach it you have to pass the road corner, I think?'

'Yes. I generally leave my car there when I am going to the upper water.'

'You did so on this occasion?'

'Yes.'

'About what time would that be?'

'About ten minutes past eleven, as near as I can say.'

'And from there you walked up to your water, I suppose?'

'Yes.'

'By the bank, or by the short cut?'

Wrigley-Bell hesitated.

'By the cut, I think,' he said. 'Mind you, I can't be sure, but I think so.'

'Did you see Sir Peter on the way?'

'I most certainly did not.'

A heavy frown added emphasis to his words.

'Or anybody else?'

'Nobody else.'

'Was there any other car at the road corner when you left yours there?'

'No. Mr Smithers had walked up in front of me. He hasn't his car with him. Nobody else uses that place for leaving cars that I know of.'

'At all events there was none today?'

'No.'

'When did you last see Sir Peter?' was White's next question.

'I couldn't say, I'm sure. Indeed, superintendent, you mustn't press me about that. I really couldn't be sure. It must have been – let me see, now – oh! some weeks ago, at least.'

'Where would that be, sir? Hereabouts?'

'Oh no! in London – in the City, in fact. I should explain that Sir Peter was – not exactly a friend of mine – rather the reverse in fact – but our paths crossed in business to some extent. You see, I happen to be Managing Director of Brandish & Brandish, Ltd, and Sir Peter of course was Chairman of Packers – both in the same line of trade – wholesale clothiers and textile merchants, you know. In fact we were business rivals – that is, our firms were – are, I should say. And that's how it was.'

Wrigley-Bell ended his somewhat breathless explanation with a grin that bared all his gums.

'I follow you, sir,' said White. 'Then you have not seen Sir Peter for some weeks?'

'No.'

'Or communicated with him in any way?'

'No. As to that, though,' he added hastily, 'it may be that you will find among Sir Peter's papers letters from my firm signed by me – business letters, you will understand. I can't answer for that, of course.'

'Thank you,' said White. He remained silent for a moment and then added: 'By the way, was the sawmill working when you passed that way this morning?'

'Really I don't know. I didn't pay any attention to it at the time.'

The superintendent put no more questions, and Wrigley-Bell retired, to be succeeded after a short interval by Smithers.

'I understand that you wanted to see me,' said Smithers.

'That is so, sir.'

'Then please observe that I do not admit your right to question me. Any statement that I may make is made purely as a matter of grace, and I reserve the right to refuse to reply to any questions which I may find it inconvenient to answer.'

Having delivered this tirade with a seraphic smile, Smithers sat down at the table.

'Well, sir –' began the superintendent.

Smithers took not the smallest notice of him.

'My name is Stephen Fortescue Smithers,' he began, precisely as if he were dictating a letter in his office. 'I am the senior partner in the firm of Smithers, Cartwright & Smithers, solicitors, of 46 New Square, Lincoln's Inn. I am fifty-nine years of age, and was admitted a solicitor of the Supreme Court of Judicature in the year nineteen hundred and five.'

He paused and turned to the frantically scribbling constable.

'What is the matter?' he asked icily.

'You're going a bit too fast for me, sir,' the man complained.

Smithers shrugged his shoulders.

'Really,' he said, 'this is somewhat ridiculous. The least I should expect would be to have a properly trained shorthand writer. If I am to oblige you by making a statement at all, I should be allowed to do it in my own way. However, I will endeavour to moderate my pace. Are you ready now?'

'Yes, sir.'

'Very good. If you do not catch anything I say, or want assistance with the spelling, stop me and I will put it right.

'I have been in the habit of fishing on the Polworthy water for the past seven or eight years. Members of the syndicate fish a different beat each day during the season, in strict rotation. Today it was my turn to fish the fourth or upper beat of the water. I had arranged to go by car with Mr Wrigley-Bell as far as the road corner, but as he was occupied with some correspondence he had to attend to, I gave up waiting for him and left the inn on foot at about ten-fifteen. I walked up the road as far as the first gate, and thence by the footpath through the copse to the road corner, which I reached at approximately eleven. My intention was to walk along the causeway, as is customary for members of the syndicate who wish to reach the upper part of the water. Before I could do so, however, I was met and stopped by Sir Peter Packer. Is anything the matter?'

Smithers' last question was prompted by the young constable, who at the mention of the name had laid down his pen, and was staring at the speaker with large, round eyes.

'Not the least bit wrong, sir,' the superintendent reassured him with a smile. 'You go on. This is very interesting.'

'I imagined that it would be. It has the additional merit of being strictly accurate. To continue:

'I should explain perhaps at this point that relations between Sir Peter and the syndicate in general have at no time been cordial. Mr Matheson, who has odd ideas of his own on what he describes as "neighbourly" conduct, has remained on calling terms with him, and young Mr Rendel, as a friend of Lady Packer, has been to the house more than once; but I have no reason to suppose that Sir Peter welcomed any social contacts with our body. For myself, I had reason to believe that he harboured a particular dislike, because he suspected – quite correctly, as it happened – that it was only due to my acumen that he was prevented from extruding the syndicate from their water altogether.'

Smithers stopped and looked at the constable.

'You are not taking this down,' he said sternly.

'On my instructions, sir,' White put in. 'You see, we only want evidence in police reports. What you've been telling us is very interesting, but it isn't quite matter of fact, is it, sir?'

'Very well. You must take your own course. I shall continue to give my statement in my own way.'

'I should much prefer that, sir.'

'Your preferences have no bearing on the matter. As I was saying:

'I was somewhat surprised to see him there, as he was not in the habit of frequenting the waterside, at all events during the fishing season. As the freeholder of the land, he was no doubt entitled to do so, though not to do anything which might interfere with the enjoyment of the fishing rights. I will do him the credit of saying that he had made no attempt at such interference, except to annoy us considerably by setting up his objectionably noisy sawmill near by. The sawmill, I may add, was not working at the moment I am speaking of.'

'You are quite certain of that?' the superintendent interposed.

'Of course. It is not a matter on which one could be in any possible doubt. Perhaps you have heard it yourself? Very well, then:

'Sir Peter, as soon as he saw me, remarked aggressively: "Oh, it's you, is it?"

'As the statement seemed too obvious to call for any confirmation from me, I said nothing and walked on. He immediately pushed past me, stood in front of me in the causeway with his arms extended like a scarecrow, and shouted:

'"Damn you, this is my land! You can't come this way!"

'He appeared to be in a high state of excitement, and I may add that I was not in the best of tempers myself. It was a warm morning, and I had walked a considerable distance carrying the usual fisherman's impedimenta. I was not minded to put up with impertinence from him or anybody else, and I told him so in quite clear tones, adding, to the best of my recollection, that he could go to hell and that I should walk where I pleased.

'Sir Peter, however, persisted in his attitude and, I think, made use of the conventional expression that I should not pass save over his dead body – an example of dramatic irony which I have only this moment fully appreciated. I did not accept his invitation, and indeed, Superintendent, from what I have been told about the subsequent disposition of the corpse, it never became possible. Be that as it may, the dispute continued for some time, becoming about as violent as it is possible to be without resorting to physical force. My difficulty was' – Smithers allowed himself a charming smile at this point – 'that so far as I could see, Sir Peter was perfectly in the right. It *was* his land, and although I had made all possible inquiries I had been quite unable to find any evidence of a public right of way over the causeway. The mere fishing rights carried with them the right to pass along the bank only – there is a decision of the House of Lords directly in point. But it would never have done to let our Peter know that.'

He chuckled serenely at the thought.

'And then?' White prompted him.

'Then? Oh, the whole ridiculous business came to an end quite tamely. For some reason or another, he suddenly stopped arguing, drew to one side, and said: "All right, then. Go on, and get out of my sight, damn you!" So I went.'

'And what did Sir Peter do?'

'I have no idea. I did not look back.'

'You can't say what made him abandon his point?'

'No. He seemed suddenly bored with the whole affair – rather as if he had remembered something more important.'

There was a pause, and then Smithers said abruptly: 'That's all.'

The constable finished his writing and handed the last sheet over to Smithers to sign. Smithers took the whole bundle, read it through carefully, initialling each page at the foot, and finally put his signature at the end.

'A disgusting travesty of my language,' he observed, 'but it seems to convey the gist of it accurately enough.' He stood up. 'And now, Superintendent, I will wish you a good night.'

'Good night, sir.'

'There are no further questions you wish to ask me?'

The superintendent smiled faintly.

'Quite a number, sir,' he said. 'But I don't know as I dare hardly ask you, after what you were saying just now.'

'Don't be an idiot,' replied the solicitor. 'Any proper question which you choose to ask, if I consider it reasonable and relevant to this inquiry, I shall be prepared to answer. But I am for this purpose the sole judge of what is reasonable and relevant.'

'Very good, sir. Now can you tell me anything about the dispute between Mr Bell and Mr Matheson last night?'

Smithers pursed his lips.

'I am not sure that this is relevant,' he remarked.

'Perhaps not, sir,' White admitted. 'But what I was thinking was this: It was a very fortunate thing for whoever killed Sir Peter that number two beat was vacant until Mr Rendel came along in the afternoon. The beat would not have been vacant if it had not been for the bet which sent Mr Matheson off fishing down on number one. Therefore – '

'Therefore,' interrupted Smithers, 'one of the parties to the bet must have been guilty of the murder. A very pretty piece of police logic!'

'I wouldn't go as far as that, sir,' said the superintendent seriously. 'But I should just like to know how the bet came to be made. You see, Mr Bell didn't strike me as the kind of man to force a quarrel in the ordinary way, and I thought – '

'I see your point,' said Smithers. 'I was surprised myself. It was certainly somewhat out of character, but I can't explain it any better now than I could at the time. We were all of us feeling fairly sympathetic to old Matheson, who is decidedly not the man he was, until Wrigley-Bell, when he came back into the room – '

'Back into the room?' It was White's turn to interrupt. 'He had been out, then?'

'Yes. He had been called to the telephone.'

'I see, sir. You don't know who he had been speaking to, I suppose?'

'You can ascertain that from the telephone people in any case – so I suppose there is no harm in my telling you. The call was from the Manor.'

'Indeed!'

'That is to say, Dora asserted that it was from the Manor. She is unreliable on the telephone as members of the uneducated classes usually are, so I give the information with all due reserve.'

'Thank you, sir.'

'Is there anything else?'

'No, thank you, sir.'

'Good night, then.'

'Good night, sir.'

CHAPTER ELEVEN

'Call in the Yard!'

AFTER Smithers had gone, the superintendent remained for some time in silence. He gathered up the sheets of paper on which the various statements were transcribed, pinned them together, arranged them in an orderly pile and contemplated them gloomily. He scratched his head in perplexity and then carefully rearranged his grey hairs again with the flat of his hand.

'It's a fair do!' he said at last.

'Yes, sir,' said the constable meekly.

'And what do you think of it?' the superintendent asked.

'Me, sir? Well, sir, I – I reckon much about the same as you do, sir.'

White laughed.

'Now just you take my advice, young man –' he began, but before he could tender any counsel he was interrupted by the entrance of the landlady.

'Is there anything further you'll be wanting?' she inquired. 'Thank goodness, I've got the last of them out of my bar. Such a rumpus there's been, you wouldn't believe.'

'I heard a bit of it,' remarked White.

'Ah, you mean Phil Carter, I expect. Now don't you go believing any nonsense about him. He's a nice straightforward young feller, as anyone in the village will tell you, and if he did forget himself this evening it isn't hardly surprising, with him so upset about Susie Bavin and all.'

The superintendent changed the subject abruptly.

'You saw nothing of the fishing gentlemen all day, I suppose?' he said.

'No, to be sure. They none of 'em came in to lunch – not even Mr Matheson, and he hadn't any sandwiches.'

'Indeed?'

'No. I had his lunch all hot and waiting for him, as he was only just up the river. I looked out of my bedroom window for him about a quarter to one to see if he was coming, and there he was, by the water, fishing. I gave him a quarter of an hour, and he was still there, looking through his glasses at the birds. Quarter past – half past – still the same thing. Then I had me own dinner, and when I looked again he was still at it. He's a fair caution, that old man! When he was still there at half past two, I gave him up as a bad job. I ask you, a whole day without a square meal, and all for a few fish! It's nonsense! These gentry don't know when they are well off, if you ask me, and they never stop to think of the trouble they give, any more than you policemen do. And now will you be wanting anything more tonight?' she concluded with a touch of asperity.

'I'm sorry to keep you up,' said White gently, 'But we're still waiting for the doctor. He promised to report to me here, and I wonder he hasn't come yet. That's him, I expect,' he added, as the front door bell sounded.

It was not the doctor, however, but Major Strode who came into the room.

'Glad to find you still here, White,' he exclaimed. 'Have you got all the statements?'

'Yes, sir. I am only waiting for Dr Latymer's report now.'

'Confound the feller! Hasn't he turned up yet? It can't take him all this time to do his job. What the devil does he mean, keeping me waiting like this?'

'He doesn't know, sir,' the superintendent pointed out, 'as it's you he's keeping waiting. I didn't expect to see you myself tonight.'

'You wouldn't have, if it hadn't been such a damn' dull dinner,' observed the chief constable. 'And when they expected me to sit down at sixpenny bridge with a couple of dowagers, I thought I should be better employed here. Now, what have you got to show me?'

'Quite a lot, sir,' White began, picking up the pile of statements.

'Can't read all that lot through at this time of night,' said Strode abruptly, eyeing the bundle with disgust. 'Just give me the gist of it, can't you?'

'Very good, sir. To begin with, I interviewed the men at the sawmill, while you were seeing her ladyship.'

'Yes, yes. That reminds me, I've got something to tell you about that. Never mind, it'll keep till later. You didn't get much out of them, I suppose?'

'No, sir. That is, they hadn't seen or heard anything unusual. But I learnt one rather curious fact from the foreman.'

'Ah! What was that?'

'In the ordinary way their hours for work on a Saturday would have been from eight till twelve. Sir Peter, who was anxious to get the work finished, had for the last three Saturdays been paying them overtime to work all day.'

'Well? What about it?'

'This morning,' the superintendent went on impressively, 'about an hour after they had started work, a message came down from the Manor telling them to knock off work, and not start again till twelve-thirty.'

'Any reason given?'

'No, sir. They were told that the time would count on their wage-sheets as working-time, so they were perfectly satisfied, though naturally rather puzzled. But then Sir Peter was given to unexpected actions, I gather.'

'He wasn't given to paying people for nothing, was he?'
'I understand not, sir.'
'How did the men pass the time until twelve-thirty?'
'Playing cards, the foreman told me. None of them left the mill, at all events. There wasn't time to get down here after the bar had opened and back again to start work, so there was nothing else for them to do, in a manner of speaking.'

The chief constable grunted.

'Well, that's that. What else do we know?'

'The last person who admits to seeing the deceased alive is Mr Smithers,' White went on. 'That would be about eleven, so near as I can reckon. He left here at a quarter past ten, and it's about three-quarters of an hour's walking up to the corner, going slow as I expect he would.' He briefly outlined Smithers' statement and continued: 'Now Mr Wrigley-Bell, who was on the spot about ten minutes later, says that he did not see him.'

Something in his tone caused Strode to interject: 'Any reason to disbelieve him?'

'Well, sir, it may be just forgetfulness, but Mr Wrigley-Bell's statement isn't altogether satisfactory. You see, he doesn't remember whether he went up through the causeway or along the bank. He can't say whether the mill was working when he reached the corner or not, though as Mr Smithers says, it's not a thing you could be in any doubt of. And,' he added clinchingly, 'he denies most positively having had any communication with the deceased for some weeks – yet he certainly spoke on the telephone to someone at the Manor only last night.'

'He sounds an unsatisfactory blighter altogether,' commented Strode. 'Now, what about the others?'

In a few words the superintendent repeated the salient points of the narratives of the Mathesons and of Rendel. When he had done, the chief constable sat silent for a moment or two, chewing the ends of his moustache in an effort of thought which seemed to be positively painful.

'One thing strikes me, White,' he said suddenly. 'Perhaps it wouldn't occur to you.'

'Indeed, sir?'

'No. I'm a bit of a fisherman myself, and what strikes me is this. All these fellers were uncommonly late on the water.'

'You think so, sir?'

'Think so? It sticks out a yard. Weather like we've been having, your best chance of getting fish is early in the day. After that it's likely to be pretty dull till the evening rise comes along. But here are all these fellers spending the best of the morning hanging about – dammit! they seem positively to have been waiting on one another!'

'I don't quite follow you, sir.'

'Well, look here. We can leave Rendel out of it. He didn't get down till the afternoon. But Smithers, now – he was on the top beat of all, and he didn't even leave here till a quarter past ten.'

'He was hoping that Mr Wrigley-Bell would take him up in his car.'

'Exactly. And Bell keeps him hanging about till he goes off on foot. Even then, *he* doesn't start till the other chap has been gone the deuce of a time.'

'Until, in fact, sir,' put in White, 'Mr Smithers has had time to get past beat two altogether.'

'By Jove, you're right! And what should he be writing letters for on a Saturday morning? If he wrote 'em tomorrow they'd get to London, or wherever it is, at just the same time. Then take Matheson – that's an odder case still. Here's a man with a bet on his hands. He's got to catch fish or lose a fiver. And what does he do? Messes about with his writing until Bell is off the premises. Why, it simply doesn't make sense. I tell you, White, it looks confoundedly fishy to me – no, that's exactly what it isn't – too *un*fishy, if you take me – all these men supposed to be keen on catching trout, but refusing to make a start till they see the coast is clear.'

'It does seem strange, certainly,' the superintendent admitted. 'But it's not enough to justify us in suspecting any of them.'

'If I found a fisherman who sat at home when he might have been on the water, I'd suspect him of anything,' said Strode emphatically. 'But I quite agree – we shan't have a jury of anglers to put this case before, worse luck. We've got to find lawyer's evidence, and where are we? Motive, for instance?'

'There's one man who seems to have had motive enough,' said White, and he told the chief constable what he had heard of Philip Carter. 'But if he did this, what puzzles me is where

94

he got the weapon from. Revolvers are scarce in these parts.'

'Ha! That reminds me,' put in Strode. 'Where is Packer's revolver?' In a few words he acquainted the superintendent with the result of his interview with Marian Packer. 'What d'you think of that?' he asked.

White shook his head mournfully.

'It's getting beyond me, sir,' he admitted. 'If you'll permit it, I think this is a case for calling in the Yard.'

Major Strode grunted.

'Can't stand those fellers,' he said. 'I like to run my own show myself. Calling in a man from outside is like borrowing a huntsman to hunt your own pack. It only unsettles 'em.'

White said nothing. He had made the same suggestion in other cases and met with the same objection. But he had gained his point in the end and he did not lose hope of doing so now. Meanwhile Strode was still elaborating metaphors drawn from the hunting field when Dr Latymer made his tardy appearance.

'So here you are at last!' the chief constable exclaimed.

'Good evening!' said Latymer, quite unruffled at the other's peevish tone. 'I didn't know I was going to see you again tonight.'

'Perhaps if you had, you wouldn't have kept us waiting such a confoundedly long time.'

'I doubt if it would have made any difference. I have had a good deal to do this evening.'

'Ha! Autopsy more of a job than you expected, eh?'

'On the contrary, it was, as I anticipated, simplicity itself. But I had other things to do.'

'Other things?'

'Certainly. I have been brought up to regard a patient as taking precedence in the scheme of things over a corpse, however produced. Policemen, I know, have a different scale of values. However, we need not discuss that. For the purposes of this evening, I am the servant of the police. Here is the report, drawn up in the best official jargon at my command.'

He threw a closely written document on the table.

Strode glanced at it, frowned and handed it to the super-intendent.

'What does it all amount to?' he asked.

'Precisely what I told you this afternoon. He was killed by a bullet of small calibre fired at close range which penetrated the right eye and emerged through the back of the head. Death instantaneous. Body well-nourished, as you might expect – a good deal too well-nourished as far as liquids go, I should suspect – if I did not know it already from my knowledge of the man. His liver was in a thoroughly amusing condition. But I don't expect you want to hear about that?'

'No.'

'Very well. Then I suppose I may be going now?'

'I think so – don't you, Superintendent?' said Strode, turning to White.

'If I might suggest it, sir,' White put in, 'it would perhaps be as well if we could have a statement from the doctor, to put alongside the others. It would be more regular, like, and he is by way of being a witness of fact, besides an expert.'

'Very well, if you think so, Superintendent. Just tell us your story, doctor. But make it short. We're late enough as it is.'

'Story? God bless you! I have none to tell, sir.'

'Eh? What's that?'

'A quotation only. I apologize – it's a bad habit of mine. I never have been able to see why it should be regarded as a sign of intelligence to be able to say things in other people's words rather than in your own. But one does it.'

'Dr Latymer!' growled Strode impatiently.

'Once more, I apologize. Here goes, then: I was at the road corner about five o'clock this afternoon, on my way to see the man at the mill who had been injured.'

'Yes, yes,' said Strode. 'We know all about that. You drove up to the corner just as young Rendel was passing.'

'Oh, you know that, do you?'

'It's all in his statement. That's right, isn't it?'

'Perfectly right, of course. I had been on my rounds and had just parked my car when young Reginald came past. We had a short chat, in the course of which he mentioned, quite casually, that Sir Peter was sitting, or lying, on the bank a little farther up. I was rather uneasy to hear this. Sir Peter had been my patient for some time. He had suffered from a very nasty attack of sunstroke last year and I had warned him seriously of the danger of exposing himself in hot weather. He was just the type, physically, to collapse again – his blood pressure for his age was – '

'Never mind the medical stuff,' the chief constable interrupted. 'You went round to look at him, anyway.'

'I did. I found him where Rendel had indicated, in the state which you'll find set out in the report I have given you. As soon as I had satisfied myself that he was dead – which was not a very long matter – I called for Rendel. He was round the corner, out of my sight. I moved on and found him and Lady Packer there. I told him as quietly as I could – '

'Stop!' cried Strode. 'What was that you said? You found Rendel and Lady Packer together?'

'Certainly.'

'This is important. What were they doing? Talking, or what?'

Dr Latymer paused a moment.

'I am sorry,' he said. 'I had no idea that this might prove important. I must think.... No, they were not talking. They were not, strictly speaking, together. They were ten or fifteen yards apart. Rendel, who had evidently heard me calling him, was coming towards me. She was standing behind.'

'What did she do?'

'While I was talking to Rendel she walked away. I didn't try to stop her. I thought it as well not to.'

'So Mr Rendel had his back to her all the time you were speaking to him?' put in White.

'Yes.'

'Do you think he could have been unaware of her being there at all?'

'I am quite certain that he knew she was there. He would have turned round to speak to her if I had not stopped him.'

The superintendent and the chief constable looked at each other in silence.

'Have I said anything improper?' asked the doctor, quizzically.

'You've said something that may be important,' said Strode. 'How important you'll understand when I tell you that Rendel denies having seen Lady Packer at all.'

'Not denies, sir,' said White gently. 'He just doesn't mention it in his statement at all.'

'It comes to the same thing. And Lady Packer admits seeing him but didn't say a word about his seeing her, when I spoke to her just now. In fact she said just the opposite, or practically said it. You'll interview her tomorrow, White, and pin her down to it.'

'This all sounds very interesting,' said Latymer drily, 'but hardly in my line. May I go to bed now?'

After the doctor had gone, Strode flung himself back in his chair.

'Dammit, if that fellow is right, those two must be in it together! Who'd have thought it? That little woman!'

'And Mr Wrigley-Bell, sir?'

'He's not out of it, certainly.'

'And Phil Carter?'

'We don't know anything about him yet.'

'And Mrs Matheson, sir?'

'Yes, confound it, and her husband too, for the matter of that!'

'And the doctor himself, sir?'

'Eh? What do you mean? What's the doctor got to do with it?'

'If Mr Rendel is to be relied on, the doctor had been on the river bank before he admits in his statement,' White explained.

'But how can we rely on what Rendel says, when we know he's been lying to us?'

'We don't know it, sir. We only know that his story doesn't agree with the doctor's. And if the doctor hasn't been telling the truth – '

'Why shouldn't he?'

White pursed his lips and remained silent. Presently the chief constable burst out: 'Damn it all, I can't make head or tail of this case! Can you?'

'No, sir.'

'Then for God's sake let's get hold of someone who can!'

'You mean the Yard, sir?'

'Yes, and the sooner the better!'

CHAPTER TWELVE

Mallett goes over the Ground

A VERY tall, very broad man, with a mild red face set off with an unexpectedly ferocious-looking waxed moustache, deposited his suitcase at the 'Polworthy Arms' early on Monday afternoon. His arrival did not pass unnoticed, for Didford Magna, to its mingled embarrassment and delight, had found itself over the week-end a focus of curiosity for the whole of England. Inspector Mallett had been seen off at Waterloo by representatives of three leading news agencies, he had been photographed in the act of stepping out of the train at Didford Parva, and there were two reporters awaiting him at the door of the inn. He made no statement to any of the pressmen. Indeed, warned by past experience, none of them even ventured to ask him a question. They were there merely to establish the all-important fact, and to publish it to a world which might be sceptically disinclined to accept the chief constable's official statement, that Scotland Yard had been called in.

Mallett was accompanied by the superintendent and the chief constable. P.C. Bowyer, in a glory of excitement and hero-worship, importantly moved on the group of children that had gathered in the village street. The inspector had declined the offer of police hospitality at Didford Parva. He preferred, he said, to be on the spot. He preferred also, though he did not say so, to be in a position to work alone as much as possible, while able to call in assistance when he needed it.

Having arranged for the inspector's comfort at the 'Polworthy Arms' – and having alarmed the landlady a good deal more than was necessary in the process – Major Strode proposed to drive him to the road corner. Mallett, however, announced his intention of walking to the scene of the crime by way of the river bank.

'I'm in strange country,' he explained modestly, 'and I'd like to get the lie of the land.'

In fact, he had already had an opportunity of studying a large-scale map of the district, and it was not long before he made it clear that he had done so to good purpose.

The little party walked down the lane towards the ford and climbed the fence in the same place that Jimmy Rendel had done the day before. If Mallett's reactions to the view were the same as Jimmy's, he did not express them in words. He merely gazed reflectively at the stream and remarked: 'So this is the Didder!'

'It's pretty small here, of course,' said Strode apologetically. 'Lower down, at Parva, it's nearly twice the size. The fishing there is really worth having. Here, there are only a few pools that are really first class. That's why the beats are so long You may have to walk a long way before you find a rising fish.'

'And when you do, you sit down and put your bait over him?'

'Bait? This is fly-fishing water – dry fly-fishing.'

'I'm a Londoner,' said Mallett humbly. 'Is there much difference?'

'All the difference in the world. In this kind of fishing you – oh, hang it! It's difficult to explain, you ought to see it done – but roughly, you've got to find a fish that's feeding on flies floating downstream, and then you've got to float your fly over him so that he thinks it's a natural. That's the idea.'

'What sort of fly does one use?'

'That depends on what's on the water. See that fish rise up

there? He took an olive. If you wanted to catch him you'd put on an olive, too. But you never can tell with trout. Lots of fish about here are caught on different kinds of fancy flies – things that don't imitate any particular fly in nature, but seem to attract the trout just the same. Personally, I don't think it's quite playing the game,' added Strode virtuously, and to Mallett quite incomprehensibly, 'but they all do it, so I suppose it's all right.'

Mallett's curiosity on this point satisfied, the little party proceeded up the bank.

'Is there a path on the other side?' he asked.

'A path of sorts,' Strode explained. 'I've been given a day or two on this water, and I find that nearly everyone fishes from this bank, unless the wind makes it quite impossible. You can only get to the other side by the Runt's Farm bridge above us there, and by another one, right at the top of the water.'

'You could wade across at some places, I expect,' Mallett observed.

'Wading! God bless my soul! That's never allowed here,' said the chief constable, genuinely shocked, leaving Mallett to marvel once more at the intricate etiquette that governed the killing of trout on the Upper Didder.

The little party walked on in silence until they had passed the post at the top of beat one.

'That will be Didbury Hill, no doubt,' remarked the inspector. The beech-crowned summit had just come into full view.

'That's right. The highest point for twenty miles.'

'You must get a fine view from the top.'

'Oh, tremendous! You can see Salisbury spire, I believe.'

'I meant, a fine view of the place where Sir Peter was found.'

'I'm not so sure of that. What do you say, Superintendent? I've never been up there myself.'

'I was there last year, sir,' said White. 'From the top you couldn't see anything of the river for about a hundred yards either side of the corner, for the trees. It may be different now that so many have been cut. You can see the road at the corner, though.'

'How do you get there?'

'You can walk up from the village to the top of Didbury Down and then along the crest,' the superintendent explained. 'That's the way Mrs Matheson went on Saturday – so she says. If you go up from the road corner there's a steep little path just round the shoulder of the hill. You can't see it till you get to it.'

'It occurs to me,' said the inspector, 'that the road corner pool is a remarkably secluded part of the river. You'd think this valley a fairly open one, yet that particular place can hardly be overlooked from any direction.'

'This is about the best view-point you can get,' remarked the chief constable.

They had reached the bridge which carried the track to Runt's farm. Together they climbed on to its high arch and looked up and down the stream.

'You can see the whole of the corner pool from here,' Strode explained, 'but not quite as far as the place where Sir Peter was found. That is just round the bend higher up.'

Mallett looked long and thoughtfully, but said nothing. They then resumed their journey upstream. It was a slow progress, for the inspector was strangely, and irritatingly, dilatory. He seemed to be interested in every track and path that crossed their way, and muddied his trousers badly in an attempt to follow one of them. When they had almost reached the road corner he noticed the short cut through the copse and insisted on following this back almost to its junction with the highway before he was satisfied. Finally, he allowed himself to be led up the bank to the fatal spot. The rain of Saturday night had obliterated almost all traces of the tragedy, save a few dark stains which still remained on the undersides of the reeds. Mallett listened in silence to the explanations which the others had to give him. Then he asked White to lie down as nearly as possible in the attitude of the corpse, while he himself approached the spot from below. At the point where the superintendent's feet and legs came into his view he stopped, and drove a stick into the ground to mark the place. This done, he walked up the bank round the bend and repeated the performance from the other direction. Then he surveyed the tangled mass of vegetation which divided the bank from the causeway with a look of despair on his good-humoured countenance.

'You've looked for the weapon, I suppose?' he asked White.

White shrugged his shoulders.

'My men have made the best search they could,' he said. 'But you see the sort of place it is. All this is marsh-land. If you try to walk on it you go in above your knees. I've tried experiments with stones, and anything heavy sinks at once. There are a score of places here where you could hide a pistol where it wouldn't be found this side of Doomsday.'

'Alternatively, you could drop it in the river,' Mallett suggested.

'I might drag this stretch, perhaps,' said the superintendent doubtfully.

'Drag the Didder!' exclaimed Strode. 'But damn it all – what about the fishing?'

'I don't think that will be necessary,' the inspector consoled him.

He retraced his steps to the gate and walked slowly up the causeway. Once or twice he attempted to leave the path, and on each occasion found that, as White had said, the treacherous ground would not bear a man's weight.

'It doesn't look as if the murderer could have approached from this side,' he remarked. 'Wait a minute, though – what's this?'

They were about half-way up the causeway, and the inspector was pointing to a slender sapling which showed itself among the bulrushes a yard or so from the right-hand side of the path.

'I'm no countryman,' he observed, 'but isn't that an oak?'

'You're right,' said the superintendent. 'A funny thing, that. You don't often see them growing in places as wet as this. It must have been just a stray acorn that blew here some time.'

Mallett was peering through the rushes, holding them apart with his hands. Presently he said: 'I think I can manage it.' He stepped back to the other side of the causeway, ran forward and took a flying leap into the air in the direction of the oak sapling. As he came down, he grasped its trunk with both hands, almost breaking it with his weight. The watchers from the path heard him grunt with the effort, heard also the thud of his feet as he hit the ground. A moment later they heard him say:

'I'm on sound ground here. And – someone's been here before me!'

His flushed face appeared on a level with the tops of the reeds.

'Eh? What's that?' cried Strode. 'Let me have a look!'

'Better, not,' Mallett warned him. 'There's only just room for one to stand here and – '

A splash and the sudden disappearance of his head below the level of the vegetation announced that he had stepped off the island of firm soil. There followed an interval of plungings and heavings which shook the whole surface of the marsh and brought clouds of protesting song birds into the air. Finally, with the assistance of the young oak, which must have been nearly torn up by the roots by this time, the inspector re-established himself.

'Silly thing to do, that,' he said philosophically. 'But you can see for yourself, sir, that there's no room for two.'

'I'll take your word for it, at all events,' said Strode. 'Are you coming out now?'

'Just a moment,' Mallett replied. 'There's a blackberry bush just beyond me here. That ought to mean another bit of solid ground. I want to see if I can get through this way to the bank.'

A long stride brought the inspector, by now dripping with sweat above and with liquid black mud below, to the patch of coarse grass that surrounded the roots of the bramble bush.

Here his further progress was checked by its thick thorn-laden branches, but dropping gingerly to his hands and knees he was able to see that beneath it there was room to crawl, and that beyond it stretched a narrow strip of comparatively dry land. He was quite unable to tell where he was in the green forest that surrounded him, but he knew that the strip must lead roughly in the direction of the river. He therefore called to the superintendent to go round to the bank, and set himself to follow it.

Whoever had first made the track – for that it had been made by someone he was convinced – must have been of slimmer build than Mallett. The thorns tore at his coat as he wedged his broad shoulders beneath the arching shoots of the bramble, and when he emerged on the other side his body continued to make a wider passage through the herbage than his predecessor's had done. There was now room to stand once more, but Mallett, who had by now reached the stage of wetness and muddiness when further mud and water can make no difference, continued to advance on hands and knees until he heard a hail from the superintendent. It sounded quite close, and within a few yards of him.

'Where are you?' Mallett asked.

'A yard or two below the "tump",' answered White.

'What is the "tump"?'

'That's what they call the place where we found him,' White explained. 'You're not far from it now.'

'I can't go any farther this way,' said the inspector. 'At least, nobody has been farther this way. The track ends in a little ring of beaten-down grass. Can you see me?'

'No.'

Mallett stood up.

'Can you see me now?'

'Just the top of your head.'

'And we're both pretty tall men,' commented Mallett. 'Now go to the "tump".'

White did so, and presently Mallett saw his head and shoulders appear above the reeds about three yards away.

'Try sitting down,' he suggested.

The superintendent sat down, and Mallett peered in his direction, first standing, then sitting, and finally prone on his stomach.

'I can just make out that there's somebody there, and that's all,' he announced. 'Now let's see if I can reach you.'

He blundered forward among the reeds, wading knee-deep in the waterlogged ground. Stumbling and splashing, he made slow headway, and it seemed more than once that the effort would be too much for him. At last, however, the thick growth of reeds behind the superintendent parted, and Mallett drew himself, triumphant and exhausted, on to the 'tump'. A broad swathe of trampled vegetation marked his passage.

'One thing's pretty certain,' remarked White, while the inspector recovered his breath, 'nobody's been through that way lately.'

'Looks as if we'd discovered a mare's nest,' said Strode, who had watched the whole performance with growing impatience.

'I dare say so, sir,' said Mallett apologetically. 'But I think it was worth investigating, all the same. And someone has been in there lately, though he didn't come the whole way through.'

He displayed two small objects.

'This', he went on, exhibiting a brown bone button, 'was just underneath the blackberry bush. It looks as if it had been torn off when whoever it was crawled through. Then when I got to the end of the solid ground I found this.'

The second exhibit proved to be a small piece of paper. Mallett unfolded it carefully. Though sodden with water, it was quite recognizable as the wrapping of a popular brand of chewing gum.

'Ha! That has an American look about it!' remarked Major Strode.

'There's quite a lot of it used hereabouts,' said White. 'The farm hands, who can't very well smoke at their work, have picked up the habit, they tell me. Some of the men in our force chew quite a bit on duty, too.'

'Well, don't let me catch them at it, that's all! Filthy

Yankee habit!' the chief constable fumed. 'Anyhow, that doesn't tell us much. It may have been here any length of time.'

'It tells us something, though, doesn't it, sir?' Mallett put in. 'For one thing, chewing gum is not such a very common habit. And for another, it rather limits the class of person who might have left this behind. I mean, sir,' he went on, 'a constable might very well chew gum on his beat, but one wouldn't expect to find a gentleman in your position doing it.'

'I should hope not!'

'Then as to the length of time it has been here,' the inspector continued hastily, 'that one can't tell, of course. But if it was left by the same man who lost this button, it hasn't been here very long. Just look at these threads, sir. They've been quite recently broken, if I'm not mistaken, and in spite of the wet, they don't seem to have rotted at all.'

'You may be right,' said the chief constable grudgingly. 'But if you are, where are we? The feller in there couldn't even see a man out here, let alone shoot him.'

'It would seem so, sir. But he might be a very valuable witness all the same, if we could find him.'

'If – if — That reminds me, superintendent, you haven't laid your hands on the Carter boy yet?'

'No, sir. But I don't think it will be very long before we do. He's a local lad and he won't get far without he's noticed.'

The party returned to the road corner, Mallett's shoes squelching loudly with every step. Before they left the water Mallett asked a question which proved that his mind was still running on fishing.

'How long does it take to catch a trout, sir?'

'Eh? What d'you mean?'

'I mean, sir, if a man – a good fisherman, say – set out to catch a trout on this water, how long would it take him?'

'God bless my soul! I can't answer that one! It all depends. Nobody knows how long it's going to take him to catch a fish – or whether he's going to catch any, for the matter of that. He can't tell whether the fish will be rising, for one thing.'

'But assuming there is a fish rising?' Mallett persisted.

'Well, if a fish is rising, in a place where you can get a line over him, a good fisherman ought to catch him – in theory, anyway. But there's so much to be done. First you've got to find what's the right fly, then you've got to put it over him, hook him, play him, and land him. It all takes time. On the other hand, it may be quite a quick business. I remember Matheson telling me that once on the Kennet, when the may-fly was up, he caught two brace while he was smoking one cigarette, and lost the fifth just as his moustache began to singe. But that wasn't on this water – and I'd take that story with a grain of salt anyhow,' he added.

Mallett's thirst for knowledge was not yet satisfied.

'Then if there is more than one trout rising and you catch the first, it may be quite a quick business to get the next?' he asked.

'That depends, again. In playing the first fish you are very likely to disturb the second, if he is at all close, unless you are very lucky. That varies with the state of the water, of course. On a quiet still stretch like that carrier you saw at the bottom, it's next door to impossible to catch one fish without scaring everything else for a long way.'

'Thank you, sir,' said the inspector. 'I think you've told me all I really want to know.'

Strode shrugged his shoulders, whether in contempt for the Londoner's ignorance or in bewilderment at the trend of his questions, it was impossible to say. On the road, his car awaited them. Before getting into it, Mallett carefully reconnoitred the junction of the path with the road and the road itself for some little distance in either direction.

'Is there much traffic along here?' he asked.

'Very little,' White told him. 'It doesn't lead to anywhere special, you see. Just up to the Manor, and then round the hill to join the new main road that goes the other side of it. We call it the new road,' he added, 'but it's been there nigh on two hundred years.'

Mallett climbed into the car – the state of his shoes earning him a scowl from the policeman-chauffeur – and the chief constable was just following him when a sharp feminine voice accosted him.

'How de do, Major?' it said. 'Looking for fingerprints in the river?'

The Major reddened, saluted stiffly and told the chauffeur to drive on.

'Who was that?' asked the inspector.

'Mrs Large – parson's wife – damnedest old gossip in the whole county. Pokes her nose into everything and then screams about it like a jay in a pheasant covert.'

Mallett had never heard a jay in a pheasant covert, but he made up his mind to have a chat with Mrs Large at the earliest opportunity.

CHAPTER THIRTEEN

Philip Carter

MALLETT finished his third cup of tea and leaned back luxuriously in the best arm-chair that the 'Polworthy Arms' could produce. Major Strode had gone, and with him had gone the inevitable sense of constraint that the presence of a commanding officer entails. The two detectives looked at each other over the teacups. It was a look of instinctive liking and mutual understanding. On White's side, perhaps, the understanding did not go very deep. Essentially a simple-minded man, who had risen to his position by hard work and unswerving fidelity to his duty, he found in the other's mentality a quality of elusiveness and subtlety that baffled him. Mallett was not unaware of this feeling, but he had already seen enough of his collaborator to be assured that it would in no way affect the loyalty of his support.

'And now –' said the inspector, and without further preliminary the two men set themselves to work. The pile of statements was produced once more, and for a full hour they worked upon them, sifting, analysing, and questioning every assertion contained in them. At last Mallett felt that he had extracted from them the last atom of enlightenment. He lit a pipe and puffed at it slowly while the fragments of the multiple story slowly took shape in his mind.

'Except for one point,' he said at last, 'the mechanics of this crime are easy – too easy. Sir Peter, for some reason or another, elects to place himself on this particular part of the river bank – handy to his home, to the road, and handiest of all to the anglers who come and go that way – but remarkably secluded from observation at the same time. And any one of these people could have had access to the place and got away unobserved. Yes – it's too easy.'

'Except for one thing, you said,' the superintendent reminded him.

'Exactly, and that one thing, of course, is the weapon that killed him. I think we can assume that it was a revolver, and not a rifle, though Latymer seems to think that a possibility. Sir Peter had a revolver, and it's missing. That's a long way from saying, still less proving, that that was the weapon that killed him, but it is at any rate a probability. What does that suggest?'

'That his wife killed him,' said White promptly.

'You're skipping a bit, aren't you? Let us say that someone who knew where the weapon was, and who had access to it, killed him.'

'And who should that be if it wasn't his wife?'

'If it was, Super, you'll admit that she behaved very strangely. Why did she tell Major Strode that he had a revolver at all, and in addition lead him straight to the place where it ought to have been, and wasn't? I should have expected her to deny that she knew anything of his possessing such a weapon, or alternatively, after using it, to clean it carefully and put it back in its usual place, so that it should seem to have no connexion with the crime at all.'

White was silent, and the inspector went on after a pause:

'Of course, there is another possibility.'

'What is that?'

'Why, that Sir Peter had the pistol in his pocket that day –'

'And was killed with it?'

'Yes.'

'Why, then,' said the superintendent slowly, 'in that case –'

'It opens up an interesting lot of possibilities, doesn't it? How did the murderer get it from Sir Peter? By force? There are no signs of a struggle.'

'It may not have been much of a struggle,' White pointed out. 'Suppose Sir Peter was threatening the other man, and began to fish his pistol out of his pocket. The other fellow, if he was strong enough, could twist it out of his hand before he knew what had happened. It can be done, I think.'

'It can be done,' Mallett agreed. 'I did it myself, once, down Limehouse way, when I was a good many years younger than I am now, or I shouldn't be speaking to you now.'

'Well, there you are.'

'But there's one objection to that theory. Sir Peter was sitting down, to all appearances, when he was killed. You don't generally quarrel with people sitting down, do you? And if you're threatening someone, isn't your first instinct to get up?'

'You've an objection to everything,' said White with a laugh. 'Then what is your theory?'

'I'm not committed to a theory yet. I'm only considering possibilities. One possibility I have in mind is of the murderer sitting down beside Sir Peter, in a perfectly friendly way, and taking the pistol out of his pocket without his knowledge.'

'How did he know it was there?' It was the superintendent's turn to object.

'Alternatively,' Mallet went on, 'the pistol was not the one that killed him at all, but was taken from him after death.'

'This all sounds a bit fine-spun to me, if I may say so,' said White. 'What seems to me the common-sensical view of it is that the wife took the pistol and shot him with it, threw it in the river when she'd done it, and then lost her head when the Chief came along.'

'That depends on whether she's the kind of woman to lose her head or not – and I haven't been able to judge of that yet,' returned Mallett. He was silent for a moment and then went on: 'So much for the mechanics of this crime, anyway. The other side is, of course, the personal one. Who had a motive to kill Sir Peter?'

'The wife,' reiterated White.

Mallett could not repress a smile.

'You're on sound ground there,' he admitted. 'But leaving her aside for a moment, who else is there who we know at present to have had a motive?'

'Why, next to her, I suppose it would be young Carter.'

'Carter? I should hardly think he would want to kill Sir Peter just at that time.'

'What!' said White in astonishment.

'Just consider,' said Mallett slowly. 'You think that Carter had a motive for murdering Sir Peter because his girl had had a baby and Sir Peter was the father. But babies aren't born all at once, without some preliminary warning – at least not in London, and I expect the same rule applies to this part of the world. And do you mean to tell me that Carter, who had been walking out with this girl, didn't know all about it months before?'

'It's odds he did,' the superintendent admitted.

'Very good, then. If he had murder in his heart, the time you'd expect him to do it was when he found out that Sir Peter had been monkeying with his Susie, or the time when she told him that a baby was on the way. Why should he wait to find out if it was a boy or a girl before he takes his revenge?'

'And why does he drink himself silly and run away if he has nothing to do with it?' White retorted.

'There may be several good reasons for that. Don't misunderstand me, Super. I'm not saying that it's impossible for Carter to have committed this crime. I'm only arguing that the motive which you suggest is really no motive at all. In fact, I should say that Sir Peter's death at this moment was just about the last thing he wanted.'

'Well –' said the superintendent in a dissatisfied tone.

Before he could say more there was a loud knock at the door. 'What is it?' he cried.

The shining red face of Police Constable Bowyer appeared round the half-open door.

'Mr White, sir!' he whispered hoarsely, 'I've got 'im, sir!'

'Got him? Who?'

'Phil Carter, sir!' Bowyer answered, in the same conspiratorial tone which he seemed to think appropriate for detective work.

'Then bring him in, for goodness' sake!' said White impatiently. 'Where is he?'

'Here, sir!' breathed Bowyer between clenched teeth. Opening the door to its full extent with his left hand, he kept his right hand behind him for an instant, and then triumphantly brought it forward, firmly attached to the collar of a limp and wretched-looking youth whom he propelled before him into the room. The effect of the performance was somewhat marred by the too audible aside in which he said to his victim: 'Cheer up, Phil, lad. They can't eat yer!'

The superintendent contrived to keep a perfectly straight face. He merely asked:

'Where did you find him, Bowyer?'

'Knowing the 'abits of the suspect, sir,' replied Bowyer with relish, 'I kept observation on the Bavins's cottage. As I 'ad anticipated, sir, 'e – well, 'e come along, and there you are,' he concluded, his supply of official verbiage failing him at the last moment.

'I see. Thank you, Bowyer.'

The constable saluted and withdrew. Meanwhile Mallett had been studying the newcomer with close attention. He was a thin, undersized lad, whose age might have been anything between eighteen and twenty-five. He looked pale, hungry, and more than a little frightened, but his sharp features bore an expression of wary self-confidence that surprised the inspector, who had thought that he was going to see a raw country bumpkin. It was odd, he reflected as he gazed, that none of the country people whom he had so far met conformed to the country bumpkin type. Perhaps it did not exist at all – was a mere invention put about for the confusion of Londoners.

'Well, young man,' White was saying, 'you're in a pretty pickle, aren't you?'

Carter looked down at his stained and shabby clothes, rubbed his unshaven cheek and chin and mumbled sheepishly, 'Yes, sir.'

'Been sleeping out, haven't you?'

'Yes, sir.'

'Why?'

Carter said nothing.

'Why?' repeated the superintendent.

''Ad a drop too much Saturday,' he managed to get out at last.

'Where did you get it?'

'Started at the "Wayfarer" and then come on 'ere.'

'The "Wayfarer"? Ah!' said White with satisfaction.

The 'Wayfarers' Arms', mid-way between Magna and Parva, was a house with a bad reputation, which the police would have been glad to see closed. White was not sorry to have another black mark to put against it. He went on:

'What made you do it, Carter? You're a steady sort of chap in the ordinary way.'

Carter's small eyes peered for a moment at the other's face, then dropped to the floor.

'I dunno,' he muttered.

'Oh yes you do,' the superintendent insisted. 'What was it, now? And why did you stay out all Sunday?'

'I was upset, like.'

'That's more like it,' said White encouragingly. 'And what had happened to upset you?'

Carter said nothing.

'Was it Sir Peter Packer's death that upset you?'

Carter gulped and nodded.

'Was it? Speak up, my lad!'

'Yes, sir.'

'Oh, it was! And why should you care about Sir Peter! Was he a friend of yours?'

Carter shook his head.

'I thought not! Ever spoken to him in your life?'

Another shake of the head.

'Then why should you worry about whether he was dead or alive?'

Still Carter was silent.

'Was it because you knew something about his death?'

'*No, sir!*' screamed Carter in an accent of terror.

In the silence that followed, all the more oppressive by reason of the sudden outburst, White turned and looked at Mallett. The look was probably intended to convey satisfaction, for the superintendent seemed well pleased at having reduced his witness to a state of abject fear. Mallett, however, preferred to interpret it as a call for help. He stood up, walked across the room and brought another chair forward.

'Sit down, Carter,' he said quietly. 'Do you smoke?'

'No, sir,' answered Carter in a voice barely above a whisper.

'Chew perhaps?'

Mallett rummaged in his pockets and produced a packet of chewing gum. Carter accepted a piece eagerly. Nothing was said between them for a moment or two, while the young man's jaw moved in steady rhythm.

'When were you and Susie Bavin going to be married?' asked Mallett after a while.

'Michaelmas, sir.'

'That's all off now, I suppose?'

'That's right, sir.'

'Pity,' said Mallett reflectively. Then he asked, as an afterthought: 'Since when has it been all off?'

'Since Saturday, sir.' Carter looked him straight in the face, and the inspector was conscious once more of the cunning intelligence in those little eyes. 'She – she don't know it yet, sir.'

'Ah!' Mallett permitted himself a wink. 'You'd promised to stick by her in her trouble, eh?'

'That's right,' said Carter with a knowing grin as from one man of the world to another.

'But things have changed a bit since Saturday?'

'Well – I'll allow they 'ave, sir.'

'I see ... Sir Peter hadn't done anything for Susie, is that it?'

'No, sir, but 'e'd got to, 'adn't 'e? Pound a week the lawyer up to Parva told me. That's the law, ain't it? Pound a week till the kid's sixteen. That's summat, ain't it?'

'And now it's all gone,' said Mallett sympathetically.

'All gone!' muttered Carter in dejection. 'Susie wouldn't do nothing about it – kept on putting it off – said there'd be time when the kid was born – and now – '

'Now you're in a bit of a hole, eh? I take it that she'll still be looking to you to marry her?'

'What should I want to marry 'er for now?' Carter said in a tone that made Mallett feel that Miss Bavin was well out of her engagement.

'Well, that's your business and not mine. But tell me, Carter, if Susie wouldn't make Sir Peter do the right thing, did you ever try yourself?'

Carter's face went completely blank.

'No,' he said.

'Sure?'

'Sure.'

'When did you last see Sir Peter yourself?'

'I dunno, sir.'

'You saw him on Saturday,' said Mallett in a calm, matter-of-fact tone. 'Just above the corner pool.'

'No, sir.'

'You were hiding in the reeds just off the causeway. You lost a button getting there.' He indicated the broken piece of thread on Carter's coat. 'Here it is.'

Carter stared at the button as if mesmerized.

'Did you speak to Sir Peter, Carter?'

'No, sir.'

'Why not?'

'There were too many people about, sir.'

'What?' exclaimed White violently, but Carter took no notice. His eyes were held by the inspector's, his ears attuned only to the soft, bland voice.

'Too many people about, eh? Well, that's just what I thought it was. Suppose you tell us all about it. Very likely they're the people we want to get hold of.'

Carter remained silent for a moment or two, fumbled for the missing button on his coat, chewed once or twice, swallowed convulsively and at last began to speak.

'I was goin' up to the Manor to see if Sir Peter would do right by Susie,' he began, 'when I seed 'im coming down the causeway. So I slipped into the reeds. I knowed the place – been there bird-nesting afore.'

'Why did you do that, if you wanted to talk to him?' interjected the superintendent.

Carter turned on him a look of animal cunning.

'Thought I'd take 'im by surprise, like,' he said.

'Go on,' said the inspector quietly.

''E come past me without 'e see me, and presently I put my 'ead out and sees 'im at the bottom of the causeway talking to a man with a fishing-rod. So I put my 'ead back again. Presently t'other man come along past where I is. I don't see 'im, but I sees 'is rod above the reeds, like. I stays there a bit, thinking on what I'm going to say to Sir Peter and 'as a chew while I'm thinking, and all of a sudden I 'ears 'im and another man talking the yonder side of me, next the water. I didn't 'ear what they was saying, but Sir Peter sounds main angry. I crawls up closer to see if I can catch what they're saying – '

He stopped abruptly.

'Yes?' Mallett encouraged him:

'An' then I come away again, quick as I can.'

'And what made you do that?'

'It was along of what I 'ears Sir Peter saying.'

'And what was that?'

'"'Taint no good your threatening me," Sir Peter 'e says, "I've a pistol in my pocket," 'e says, "an' I don't give a damn for your threats," 'e says.'

'And what did the other man say to that?' asked the inspector.

'"I don't believe a word you're sayin'," 'e says, "What for would the likes of you be walking about the place with a pistol?" 'e says. But Sir Peter just laughs at 'im and says: "I didn't bring it for you, you poor rabbit" – that's what 'e call 'im, sir, a poor rabbit – "I brought it along of a letter I got this morning, which is a threatening letter," 'e says. "And if you don't shut your mouth I'll soon show you I'm speaking the truth, for I don't care a damn for you, and that's a fact," 'e says. And that's why I come away, sir.'

'But he wasn't speaking to you!' White exclaimed.

'But he was speaking about you, wasn't he?' said Mallett. Carter nodded.

'You had threatened Sir Peter in a letter he received that morning?'

'Yes, sir.'

'Silly sort of thing to do, wasn't it?'

'Yes, sir, I allow it was. But then you see, sir, I didn't reckon for fire-arms when I wrote like that. I ain't going to threaten anybody with a pistol in 'is pocket!'

'I see. Now tell me, what sort of a man do you think it was, you heard talking to Sir Peter?'

''E sounded rather like a gen'leman,' said Carter doubtfully.

'But you never saw his face?'

'No, sir.'

'Do you think it was the same man you had seen talking to Sir Peter before, or another one?'

'I dunno, sir.'

'Thank you, Carter. I think that's all. One moment, though,' he added, as the young man prepared to go. 'How was Sir Peter dressed when you saw him?'

'Coat an' breeches, sir, same as anybody else might be.'

'Anything else you'd like to tell us?'

'No, sir.'

And Carter left the presence of the detectives, to arrange his tangled affairs with Miss Bavin as best he could.

CHAPTER FOURTEEN

Private Papers

MALLETT spent the evening alone. His only companions were the documents which White had left behind him. These included not only the witnesses' statements, from which he felt that there was nothing new to be gleaned, but also the papers removed by the superintendent from Sir Peter's study on the previous day. The chief constable had left strict instructions that these should be kept under lock and key at the police headquarters at Didford Parva, but the two detectives had elected to disregard them.

'You'd better keep them yourself for the present,' White had said. 'I haven't had the time to go through them all myself, but from the look of them, they won't help us much. Maybe you'll find something worth while, though.'

It was to these papers that Mallett turned after he had demolished his supper with an appetite all the keener for his violent exercise of the afternoon. He began his labours without very much hope and with the expectation that a cursory inspection would enable him to endorse the superintendent's valuation, but when he at length rose from his reading and made his way to bed the church clock was chiming three and the night air was already chill with the wind that heralds the dawn.

Mallett wondered, in the brief interval that elapsed between putting his head on the pillow and the onset of sleep, how much of what he had read was really germane to the case. Possibly, when he came to analyse it, very little. But he did not regret the time that he had spent. It had all been very interesting, and he had acquired a variety of knowledge which would certainly prove useful at some time or another.

The papers which had first attracted the inspector's attention, consisted of a large file of typewritten matter, almost every sheet of which was marked: 'Confidential', 'Private and Confidential', or 'Secret'. The file did not appear to be complete, and on the other hand there were added to it letters and documents which did not seem to belong to the rest, but taken as a whole it presented a fairly clear picture which Mallett, as its features became plainer to him, found increasingly odd. It depicted a fragment of the inner history of two limited liability companies. One of them, naturally enough, was Packer's – the concern which Sir Peter the first had founded and of which his son was chairman up to the time of his death. The other was Brandish & Brandish, an old-established firm in the same line of business.

It took Mallett some time to gather what the purport of all these documents could be. First in series came a number of lists of figures – balance sheets, profit and loss accounts, extracts from ledgers, garnished with a variety of trade terms that meant little or nothing to him. Interspersed among these were cryptic references to interviews between individuals – identified only by their initials – of which no written record had been kept. Then followed a number of letters, exchanged between the same individuals, and matters became a little clearer. Negotiations of a sort were going on between the two companies – or rather between 'P.P.' on one side and 'Q.V.' on the other. The former was obviously Packer himself; the latter could be identified from one of Brandish & Brandish's letter-headings as Quentin Valance. Mallet knew Valance by repute as a man of great wealth and wide financial interests. From the fact that he had a seat on the board of Brandish & Brandish he could assume that he was probably in a position to control the company. The negotiations were evidently prolonged. The fat file on the inspector's knees covered a period of over two years. But little by little, with all the caution and almost all the mutual distrust of two dictators engaged in forming a new 'axis' in European affairs, the two parties drew together. At last they began to come out into the open, so that it was possible for a stranger, reading their carefully guarded correspondence, to see what they were driving at. Their object was, nothing so crude or obvious as an amalgamation, but an 'understanding' between two companies which had been, and still were, while the negotiations proceeded, at deadly rivalry with each other. The competition between them was to be eliminated by parcelling out the territories which they now disputed, they were to agree between themselves the prices at which their respective products were sold, and a concerted effort was to be made to absorb or drive out of business certain troublesome small competitors, to the mutual benefit of the two giants.

At this point matters began to grow really complicated. The principle having been decided, it seemed for a long time as though the deal would break down on questions of detail. Each side, in the best tradition of diplomacy, began to make reservations. Certain lines of goods, certain areas especially valuable to one of the parties, were to be excepted from the scope of the agreement. Elaborate financial provisions were suggested by way of compensation for the surrender of different monopolies, and in arriving at an agreement a price had to be put upon each branch of the business of the two companies. Mallett was not long in discovering that each was extremely reluctant to give the other any information which might be of service in the event of the negotiations breaking down, and he observed with amusement that on more than one occasion the late chairman of Packer's had gone to the trouble of preparing two sets of figures – one for his own information, and the other for submission to his rival.

So far, Mallett had been reading merely with the interest that even a file of business documents will evoke, where it involves the clash of human interests and wills that is the stuff of drama. But now his mind was violently recalled to the case in hand by a scribbled pencil memorandum at the foot of one of 'Q.V.'s' letters to 'P.P.'. 'W.-B. 1st May, 3.30,' it ran. That was all, but it was enough to cause the inspector to plunge anew into his reading with keener attention. He had been struck by the fact that the papers so far contained no allusion to Wrigley-Bell, the managing director of Brandish &

Brandish, behind whose back the negotiations seemed to have been carried on, and he scanned the papers eagerly for the next appearance of the tell-tale initials. Before long he came upon a scrap of paper which had evidently been jotted down by Packer after the interview of the 1st May. It consisted mainly of figures which without any context were unintelligible, but at the foot were these words: 'W.-B. Agreement – £5,000, seven years. Query, renewal?' Evidently this referred to Wrigley-Bell's agreement with the firm that employed him – a contract for seven years at a salary of £5,000 per annum. It seemed also that the renewal of this very handsome engagement at the end of the seven years was a matter of some doubt. Mallett recollected that one of the advantages of the proposed arrangement, much stressed by Quentin Valance, was the reduction in overhead and administrative expenses.

The inspector grinned sardonically. What was Wrigley-Bell's position to be under the new arrangement, he wondered, and what was he doing, conferring thus with the head of Packer's? The correspondence between 'Q.V.' and 'P.P.' made it quite clear that hitherto Valance, at any rate, had disclosed his plans to none of his associates. He consulted an almanac, and saw that the 1st May in that year had fallen on a Sunday. Packer and Wrigley-Bell had taken care to meet out of office hours, most probably in the country, where they would be safe from observation. The inference was clear. The managing director of Brandish & Brandish was going behind the back of his employers to convey information to the other party in these negotiations – no doubt in return for some substantial recompense.

The very next document in the file made this conjecture a certainty. It was a letter from Wrigley-Bell to Packer, addressed to the Manor, which ran as follows:

Private and Confidential

My dear Sir Peter,

I return herewith the copy of Valance's letter with which you supplied me at our interview, with the figures amended to display the true position. This will, I think, enable you to make an offer more in accordance with the real value of the connexions surrendered by Brandish & Brandish than the sum hitherto demanded. I am happy to think that I have been able to be of some genuine service to you in this matter. As you know, my position is in the circumstances a somewhat delicate one, and I am glad to have your assurance that it will, in your own expressive phrase, be 'taken care of'. I need not say that I should not have taken the course that I have done, had I not been convinced that it was, in the widest sense, in the best interests of my company.

> With kind regards,
> Yours very sincerely,
> THEODORE WRIGLEY-BELL.

'I wonder what exactly he meant by "in the widest sense"?' was Mallett's comment. He turned the page and read on.

Sir Peter had wasted no time on receipt of the letter. Two days later in date was a note addressed to him by Valance:

Dear Packer,
Thank you for your note. I am glad to hear that you are now in a position to put a concrete offer before me. I shall be delighted to lunch with you at the place and time you suggest.

At the lunch, the two business potentates had evidently come to terms, and it needed only the exchange of a few more or less formal letters to arrive at an agreement in principle, which would have become an agreement in fact but for the sudden death of Sir Peter. The reader was left to imagine how far this happy result had been contributed to by the fact that one of the two poker players was now able to see the other's hand. But there still remained something of interest in the file – another letter from the managing director of Brandish & Brandish, written in a somewhat different style from the first.

Dear Sir Peter,
As you will no doubt have heard, the board today decided to accept in principle the scheme of arrangement which has been under discussion between you and Valance. I think it right to tell you, however, that the board at the same time came to another decision, namely, to terminate my appointment, under the terms of my contract, on the 1st January next. I was officially informed that the reason for this step was that the new scheme will enable the

Company to effect economies in administration which will render my post redundant; but the Company's secretary, Mr Cawston, in conversation let fall something which led me to believe that this was not the real motive behind the board's decision. I find it difficult to credit the imputation which he conveyed, but his words gave me quite unmistakably to understand that the decision to which I have alluded was in fact made at your request, and as part of the consideration insisted upon by you with Mr Valance for entering into the agreement. It is possible, of course – and I would gladly believe – that Mr Cawston is mistaken. He has not, I am sure, been wholly in Mr Valance's confidence during the negotiations of the last few months. He has not, I need hardly say, shared my confidence during the same period. Circumstances may arise, however, which will make it advisable for me to mention certain matters to Mr Cawston, and this would be scarcely calculated to facilitate the conversations on various points of detail which he tells me you are to have with him over the week-end.

I should be reluctant to take such a step. I am reluctant even to hint at it. I prefer to assume – I am indeed entitled to assume – that you have in mind some other arrangement for my benefit. I shall be interested to know what it is, and I shall take the earliest opportunity of hearing from you exactly what your intentions are. As I shall also be in your neighbourhood next week-end, perhaps you will make an appointment. *In your own interests, it would be as well not to refuse this request.*

Yours truly,
T. W.-B.

Mallett turned the last page and put down the bulky file.

'And that,' he murmured to himself, 'is that! It certainly suggests a reason why – But all the same, I don't see how – Confound that fellow Carter!' he added inconsequently. 'He certainly seemed to be telling the truth!'

With a sigh, he turned to the other papers. They were a mixed collection. There are two types of men who cause particular trouble to their executors when the moment comes for their affairs to be finally wound up. There is the type who keeps no record whatever of his transactions, who loses receipts and insurance policies, whose share certificates may be discovered lurking in the backs of bookcases, whose will, if it is found at all, turns up in a housemaid's cupboard, long after all hope of finding it is abandoned. At the opposite extreme is the man who sedulously preserves every scrap of paper which has ever had any conceivable value or interest, leaving to his hapless survivors the work of sorting them out. Sir Peter clearly had belonged to the latter class. Fortunately, if he was a hoarder, he was a methodical one, and this lightened the inspector's task considerably.

The papers with which he was now dealing represented, of course, merely a fraction of the mass which Sir Peter had accumulated. They were the contents only of the drawers which Marian Packer had indicated to the superintendent as holding his personal papers, and which had been opened subsequently with one of the keys found on the body. They had therefore this in common with one another, that they were all records of matters which for one reason or another Sir Peter had seen fit to keep under lock and key. There were some of the personal documents which men ordinarily keep in a place of safety, such as a passport and an enviably fat little note-book of investments. There were also two or three neatly folded bundles of receipts. These the inspector examined with interest. Most of them, he was not surprised to find, were from dressmakers, jewellers, and florists. It did not need much perspicacity to guess why these should find their way to his private papers apart from his more orthodox accounts. A receipted bill for 'sundry books' puzzled Mallett for a moment, until he looked at the name of the bookseller and then he understood Sir Peter's motive, as well as that of the tradesman in not particularizing his wares more exactly. There remained one other account, the presence of which in this company did not so readily explain itself. It was from a firm of builders and decorators in Crabhampton, the county town about twenty miles away, and was dated in July of the previous year.

'To work done in accordance with our estimate No. 46802 ... £152 10s. od.'

That was all, and Mallett, with sleep weighing heavy upon his eyelids, stared at it stupidly. What was it doing here? Sir Peter, he had no doubt, had somewhere a file of his estate accounts, where an item such as this would normally be placed. Had it been placed carelessly in the wrong bundle? Somehow Sir Peter did not leave the impression of having been the kind of man who would make such mistakes. If not, it must be something of a private nature, to justify its place among the others, and the inspector had read enough that evening to assure himself that with Sir Peter, 'private' entailed something more or less disreputable. At all events, it represented something that must be investigated, whether it would eventually prove to have any bearing on the present inquiry or not.

Yawning heavily, Mallett copied the builders' names and the number of the estimate into his notebook.

There remained only a few letters, apparently unrelated to one another or to the other documents which he had examined. The inspector glanced through them rapidly, and as rapidly threw them aside one by one as hopelessly irrelevant to the matters at issue. He was by now almost reading in his sleep, and only the conscientiousness born of long training kept him to his task. It was not until he reached the last letter of all that a familiar name at the bottom of a long typewritten document jerked him fully awake once more. The document was signed: 'Hilary Sneyd', and Mallet was immediately conscious of having met the name before. He cudgelled his sleep-ridden brains for a minute or two, and then his mind went back to a dull, undistinguished case of fraudulent company promoting on which he had been engaged a year or two before. Hilary Sneyd, he recollected, was one of the innumerable persons whom he had interviewed in the course of that outstandingly tedious investigation; a person, moreover – it was becoming clearer now – who, if he had not so obviously been a mere tool in the hands of abler, wickeder men, would probably have been a defendant. An unimportant young man – an unimportant case, except to the unfortunates who had lost their money in the company promotion, but it was satisfactory to be able to remember all about it, and to know that if it should become necessary to investigate the affairs of Mr Sneyd at any time, his complete history up to quite a recent date was already on record in the files at Scotland Yard.

Mallett turned back to the body of the document. In form it was a letter, addressed to Sir Peter, but the envelope in which it was contained bore no sign of having passed through the post. Its matter was interesting enough. It was a confession, signed and witnessed, of a number of frauds evidently committed by the author of the letter upon Sir Peter's company. The precise method was in every case indicated, and the evidence by which the confession could be substantiated was carefully identified. So exact and detailed was this part of the document that it might almost have been a brief for the prosecution in a court of law. It was apparent that if anybody, armed with this information, chose to take proceedings against Sneyd for his delinquencies, he would have no difficulty in proving his case. The inspector smiled appreciatively. The man who had inspired this record had known his business. A confession extorted by promises or threats would be inadmissible in law. But here was matter which would enable the prosecutor to prove guilt without recourse to the confession at all.

That some pressure had been used to secure the admission could be readily gathered from the rest of the letter, which was in marked contrast to what had gone before. It was an apology, grovelling and undignified, to Sir Peter for the wrongs which the writer had done him, coupled with expressions of gratitude for his leniency, couched in terms of such servility as made the reader's gorge rise. Throughout there were references to Sneyd's family, and in particular to 'one dear to us both', the meaning of which did not immediately appear. It was altogether a degrading spectacle of self-abasement, and Mallett was not sorry when he came to the end of it and of his night's labours together.

Somewhat nauseated, decidedly interested, and excessively tired, the inspector finally gathered all the papers together and went to bed.

CHAPTER FIFTEEN

Mrs Large Enlarges

ON Tuesday morning ten good and lawful men of the county
duly appeared on summons at Didford Parva, and there took
a solemn oath that they would diligently inquire and a true
presentment make of all such matters and things as were
there given them in charge on behalf of their Sovereign Lord
the King, touching the death of Peter Packer, baronet, then
lying dead, and would without fear or favour, affection or ill
will, a true verdict give according to the evidence and to the
best of their skill and knowledge. An hour later they separated,
having, under the guidance of a wily coroner, who was himself under the guidance of the police, inquired with more
speed than diligence and brought to the matter very little skill
and no knowledge whatever. As to the evidence, this had been
scanty enough. The widow had given formal evidence of iden-
tification, the doctor had spoken of the cause of death and the
only other witness had been Jimmy Rendel. Verdict, true or
false, there was none, and the proceedings ended in an
adjournment.

Jimmy left the town hall, where the inquest had been held,
with his mother, who to his annoyance had insisted on accom-
panying him. The business of giving evidence had not been
nearly so bad as he had feared – far less of an ordeal than his
interview with the superintendent. His worst moment had
been, not when he was in the witness-box himself, but when
Marian was called. He had felt a ridiculous impulse to cry out
and warn her to be careful what she said, and his relief had
been enormous when she stepped down again after answering
the few simple questions put to her by the coroner.

'Poor woman,' said Mrs Rendel, as they stood on the steps
of the town hall, amid a crowd of curious onlookers, 'I must
go over and speak to her.'

'Don't, mother,' said Jimmy wretchedly. 'She's got some-body with her – a solicitor or someone. We would only be in the way.'

'But Jimmy, I thought you were such friends! Of course, I've hardly seen her since her marriage, but she used to come to the house quite often – don't you remember?'

Did Jimmy remember!

'I dare say she did,' he answered. 'But I don't see why we should worry her now, all the same.'

Mrs Rendel allowed him to gain his point, and then sug-gested going to the nearest hotel for lunch. Jimmy shook his head.

'Let's have a late lunch at Crabhampton on the way back,' he said. 'This place will be simply stiff with reporters and policemen. I want to get out of it as soon as I can.'

'As you can drive the car and I can't, I suppose I shall have to lunch where you please,' said his mother philosophically. 'But I must say, Jimmy, that you are rather a spoil-sport. This is the first time in my life I have ever had anything to do with a murder mystery, and now you want to take me away.'

'If you'd seen as much of it as I have, you'd want to get away too.'

'Isn't that the Scotland Yard person over there? I wonder if he'll discover anything.'

'I wonder.'

'You are infuriating, Jimmy! Don't you want to know who did it?'

Jimmy found some difficulty in answering. Finally he said:

'I don't see how lunching here will help us to find out, anyway.'

But they were not to get away so easily as Jimmy had hoped. As they were getting into the car in the market-square, Mrs Large hailed them.

'How de do, Mrs Rendel,' she said, shaking hands vigor-ously. 'Nice to see you again! You came down to hear Jimmy give his evidence, I suppose? He did it very well, I thought, very well indeed. You must have felt quite proud of him.

Only, Jimmy, you want to hold your chin up a bit more when you speak. Otherwise your voice doesn't carry to the back of the hall. That's what I always tell my G.F.S. girls. Keep your head up and speak to the back row.'

Jimmy glowered at her. A moment ago he had been contradicting his mother with complete assurance, but before Mrs Large he was dumb.

'The funeral's to be at Magna tomorrow,' Mrs Large was saying. 'I've told the Rector he must keep the churchyard gates locked – except for the family and the better class people, of course. He talks a lot of nonsense about parish rights and so on, but I'm not going to have a lot of Nosey Parkers swarming all over the place. You can look right into the Rectory gardens from the churchyard, you know. I remember what happened the year before last, when old Harman was buried, and he was only a suicide. I told the Rector at the time that he had no right to be buried in consecrated ground at all, and what was the result? There wasn't an apple left on that side of my orchard!'

'I don't think anybody would want to steal your apples in June,' Mrs Rendel observed gently.

'That makes no difference. It's the principle of the thing. Nasty lot of people! Why can't they keep where they belong?'

'I suppose it's only human nature,' said Mrs Rendel.

Mrs Large paid no attention. Her sharp eyes were darting in every direction round the square.

'That's Mrs Jenks's car, isn't it?' she said. 'And there go the Fosters! They must have come in by the bus. Everyone in Parva seems to be here. It's quite a gathering, isn't it? I'm surprised none of your fishing friends came, Jimmy.'

'Perhaps they had something better to do,' said Jimmy.

If Mrs Large appreciated his sarcasm at all, she showed no signs of it.

'I thought the Mathesons would have come, anyway,' she went on. 'They tell me that Euphemia Matheson was very upset at Sir Peter's death – quite unnaturally upset. Have you any idea why?'

130

'No,' said Jimmy.

'Well, I dare say there is nothing in it, but of course her husband is a very old man, and Sir Peter – '

'Really, Mrs Large,' Mrs Rendel protested. 'You mustn't say such things! I am sure Sir Peter – '

'Well, we know what Sir Peter was, don't we, Jimmy? I expect he told you all about it, Mrs Rendel – one of our village girls – a baby born the very day he was killed. D'you remember, Jimmy? I was telling you all about it just before you – found him.'

Mrs Large's eyes looked into Jimmy's face with a sudden gleam of purposeful intelligence. Do what he could, he could not prevent the flush which he felt spreading over his cheeks. Damn the woman, oh damn the woman!

'Mother,' he said, in as calm a voice as he could manage, 'if we are going to get any lunch at Crabhampton, we had better be starting now.'

'Good-bye, Mrs Rendel,' said Mrs Large amiably. 'Give my love to your husband. He's as bad as ever, I suppose? You ought to take him to Droitwich – not that I expect anything will do him any good at his time of life. Good-bye, Jimmy. And don't forget what I told you about keeping your chin up.'

'Extraordinary woman,' Mrs Rendel observed as they drove away. 'And did you notice, Jimmy, that she never so much as mentioned that poor, bereaved Marian Packer?'

Jimmy felt that that was one thing at least for which he could feel grateful to Mrs Large.

'I don't suppose anybody takes what she says seriously,' he said.

The remark was an expression of hope as much as of opinion. For, as they rounded the corner, he had looked back and seen Mrs Large talking to the man whom his mother had identified as 'the Scotland Yard person'.

'I wonder whether you could give me a little of your time,' said Mallett.

Mrs Large looked him up and down, and then ejaculated: 'Ah! Busy!'

'I beg your pardon?'

'Busy, I said. Isn't that what you people call yourselves? My husband reads a lot of those nonsensical crime novels, and he tells me that's the proper word.'

'I have been called that – and worse things, before now,' the inspector admitted. 'Though never by a lady.'

'It's what you are, though, isn't it?' Mrs Large persisted. 'Nothing to be ashamed of,' she added kindly.

'I certainly am busy just now, and busy about this case. That is why I am anxious for your help, if you can give it me. I dare say the present time is not very convenient to you – '

Mrs Large was looking at the clock on the town·hall tower.

'Quarter to twelve,' she observed. 'I have to meet the Rector at a quarter past, and he's certain to be late. Not that he has anything to make him late, he just always is late. So we've plenty of time. Where shall we go?'

'Perhaps it would be a good plan – '

'Because I was going to suggest the Baghdad tearooms, and then if the Rector is punctual, by any chance, he'll find me there. Come along!'

And Mallett found himself meekly following the redoubtable old lady into a panelled, angled room readily recognizable as Mesopotamian in character by reason of its bead curtains, bamboo tables, and lampshades hung round with strips of jangling glass. It was crowded with townspeople, who looked curiously at the pair as they entered, and the inspector wondered whether a less suitable place for a confidential chat could possibly have been found. But Mrs Large was equal to the occasion. In a moment she had seized upon a waitress, addressed her in tones that suggested that she was speaking to one mentally deficient – which was probably the fact – and whisked Mallett upstairs into a small empty room on the first floor.

'I have ordered some coffee,' she told him. 'That will suit you, I suppose?'

'It's very kind of you,' said Mallett. 'But really, I couldn't let you – '

Mrs Large waved aside his protestations.

'The Rector will pay when he comes,' she said. 'He will have been at the bank this morning, so *that's* all right.'

The coffee was brought, in cups that had overflowed generously into their saucers. The inspector sampled it and found that by dosing it liberally with milk he was just able to swallow it without nausea. He eyed the plate of little cakes that made up the repast and then told his hostess that he preferred not to spoil his appetite for lunch.

'Fiddlesticks!' said Mrs Large, munching heartily. 'That's what the Rector always says.' Apparently the fact that the Rector agreed with it was enough to condemn any proposition. 'Well, Mr Busy,' she continued. 'What do you want to know?'

'In the first place – ' Mallett began.

'I can tell you this much, to begin with,' she interrupted him. 'Young Jimmy Rendel is sweet on Marian Packer. Always has been. He's been up there making sheep's eyes at her whenever he's had the chance. Not that *he* minded much – her husband, I mean. Nasty fellow! He and that Bavin girl – but you know about that, I expect?'

Mallett nodded.

'I'm sorry for young Carter. Now there's a nice young man for you!'

'I have seen him,' Mallett ventured.

'A straightforward, honest boy. Though the Rector always had a down on him when he was in the choir – I can't for the life of me imagine why. I don't believe he had anything to do with that business about the cat at the Harvest Festival – not for a moment. I can always tell when a lad's to be depended on,' she added sagely.

Mallett thought it wise to make no comment.

'I told Jimmy all about it – about the Bavin business, I mean – on Saturday afternoon,' she went on. 'Just before – you know. I dare say that isn't news to you either?'

'Well, I thought I heard something to that effect.'

'Ah! You were eavesdropping when I was talking to Jimmy's mother just now. Just what I might have expected.

Oh, don't apologize, Mr Busy! It's all in the way of your trade, I know. I don't bear any malice.'

She laughed, and took a large bite from a cake topped with sugar of a livid green.

'Suppose,' said Mallett, 'you were to begin at the beginning.'

'Just so, the beginning! And where does anything begin, may I ask? Susan Bavin's baby began in'— she counted rapidly on her fingers — 'September last year, I suppose. And Peter Packer's neglecting his wife began on their honeymoon, by all accounts. At any rate, I know she had a very woebegone look when she first came to the Manor as a bride, poor child! It's not so easy to find the beginnings of things in this world, I can tell you!'

'I know that,' said the inspector humbly. 'I really meant something much simpler. All I want, in the first place, is for you to tell me what you can about the events of Saturday last. Your own movements, to start with.'

'Ha! My movements!' The old lady sat up very straight in her chair. 'Upon my word, Mr Busy, you'll be making me think I'm a suspicious character next!'

'Not in the least, madam,' Mallett assured her. 'All that was in my mind was that in that way you might be able to give me some information which would come in useful.'

'I'm to be a nark, that's it! I see!'

'Please, Mrs Large!' said Mallett, shocked almost beyond speech. 'You mustn't say that!'

'A nark!' she repeated triumphantly. 'Don't contradict. That's the word for people who give information to the police. All the books say so. Very well then, I'll nark to you, Mr Busy! Is it a verb as well as a noun?' she asked anxiously.

'I really don't know.'

'You ought to. Well – let me see, Saturday. I was indoors all morning. You can ask the Rector – not that he'll remember much about it. But there I was. There was the laundry to see to, for one thing, and with maids one simply can't trust to do anything by themselves, it needs some seeing to, believe me.

Then no sooner was that done than I had Mrs Bavin on the doorstep to borrow a blanket for her daughter, if you please. I gave her a piece of my mind about the way she'd let her girl misbehave, I can tell you! I thought it my duty to tell her what I thought, though I might as well have been talking to the fish in the Didder for all the good it did. These people have no morals, Mr Busy. I tell the Rector it's his fault. A little good brimstone and damnation from the pulpit is what they want to keep them straight. But he will go on talking to them about the Good Shepherd and His flock. Sheep indeed! They just laugh at him. They know too much about sheep!'

The inspector steered her back to the subject at issue.

'So much for the morning,' he said. 'And what happened next?'

'Let me see. Lunch at twelve o'clock. It always is on Saturdays, so as to give the Rector a long afternoon for his sermon – though as I always tell him, he never has more in his head than he could put on paper in five minutes. But there it is. Then as soon as I had finished, I put on my hat to go out to Runt's farm. Do you know where that is?'

'I think so. It's the other side of the river, isn't it?'

'That's right. I wanted to be there before one o'clock, you see, so as to catch them all at their midday meal. It's the only way to get hold of these village people. I walked up the village street without seeing anyone to speak to, until just where the farm lane turns off the road, I was nearly knocked down by Dr Latymer in his car. He came round the corner at a fearful pace. I only just got into the hedge in time. Going to see the Bavin baby, of course. There's nobody else in the village ill that I know of. It was disgraceful! I suppose even people like that have to be looked after, but that's no excuse. I gave him a piece of my mind – though he was gone and out of sight before I could so much as shake my fist at him – and then I went on. I walked to Runt's farm, and what I said to the girls there about missing Sunday school is nobody's business. I left there a little after one, and I was back again at the river some time after four.'

'After four?' said Mallett in astonishment. 'But surely – '

'After four,' repeated Mrs Large solemnly. 'Three hours in those water-meadows and no alibi. That's serious for me, isn't it? Except', she added, '*Veronica beccabunga* and *Butomus umbellatus.*'

'Veronica – ?'

'Flowers – wild-flowers,' she explained with impatience. 'Bless my soul, but how ignorant you are! Well, there they are – the flowers, I mean, up at the Rectory, if you want to see them, pressed and dried, with the date in the book. And if you want to know why it took me three hours and more to find them, you can go and hunt for them in the water-meadows yourself. There's plenty of the *Veronica* if you know where to look for it, but the *Butomus* takes some finding.'

'I'll take your word for it.'

'Good. Well, I stopped on the bridge for a little – I always do, Mr Busy, it's wonderful how much you can see from there – and I noticed someone right up on the top of Didbury Camp, among the trees – a woman, I think, but I couldn't make out who it was. I must go to Crabhampton to get my glasses changed.' she added. 'This man in Parva is a perfect fool.'

'If you could see anyone on the top of the Camp from the bridge,' said Mallett, 'I don't think you need complain very much of your eyesight.'

'When I first came to the parish', retorted Mrs Large, 'I could have told you the colour of her hair, and whether her skirt was showing more leg than was decent. However, even now there's not much that goes on under my nose that escapes me. Well, that's about all my story, Mr Busy. A little after that Jimmy came along, and you know what I said to him and he said to me. Perhaps you don't know, though, what a state he was in when he left. He was quite white in the face and his hands were shaking. I thought he was going to cry. Funny, wasn't it? I'm afraid you won't think me a very good nark, after all,' she concluded.

'On the contrary, I think you are a very good – I find your account most interesting,' answered Mallett.

'Thank you,' said Mrs Large, deeply gratified. 'Oh, and Mr Busy, I forgot to mention that while I was talking to Jimmy I saw that stupid old Mr Matheson lower down the river, staring up in the sky at something through his field-glasses. I don't know what he was doing there, I'm sure. I remember, I wanted to ask him what to do to keep the bull-finches out of my kitchen-garden. He's supposed to know all about birds, but I don't expect he'd be able to tell me a really useful thing like that. Anyhow, when I'd finished talking to Jimmy he had gone, so I never got the chance. By then I was late for tea already, so I hurried home by the short cut through the larches, and I didn't meet anyone till I got back to the Rectory.'

'You went out by the road, which is the longer way, although you were in a hurry to get to Runt's farm,' Mallett pointed out.

'Tck, tck, Mr Busy, you think of everything! Well, if you must know, there's always a chance of finding *Geranium pyrenaicum* in the bank along the lane. But you must keep it to yourself. There are quite enough collectors about already – not to mention these ignorant hikers, who'll pick anything they see.'

'I will,' the inspector promised. 'Your story is very clear, Mrs Large, and very helpful. Just one more question, though. What time was it when Dr Latymer passed you in the road?'

'The church clock struck the half-hour while I was shaking my fist at him,' said Mrs Large promptly. 'And it's two minutes fast by the wireless.'

'Thank you. Now do you know anything else that might bear on this case – generally, about the people in the village, I mean?'

For the next ten minutes he listened to a rich selection from Mrs Large's lore on the subject of Didford Magna, its feuds and alliances, its hates and loves, lawful and unlawful, with uncensored character sketches of every dweller in, or visitor to, the village. It was an impressive performance, but scarcely germane to the mystery of Sir Peter Packer's death, and therefore not necessary to be chronicled here. At the end of that time, a large, vague cleric with a very limp handshake wandered into the room and the inspector was able to take his leave.

'Good-bye, Mrs Large,' he said in parting. 'And if you hear anything of interest, will you let me know?'

'Mr Busy,' said she with fervour, 'I am your nark from henceforward!'

CHAPTER SIXTEEN
Estimate No. 46802

MALLETT had lunch with Superintendent White in an unpretentious inn close to the riverside – a lunch which made him doubly thankful that he had not experimented with the cakes supplied by the Baghdad tearooms. The proprietor was an old friend of White's, a circumstance which made possible the appearance on the table of a superlative grilled trout. Although the Didder flowed right past the windows of the inn, the fishing rights, as everywhere in Didford Parva, were the jealously preserved property of the Walton club; but as the proprietor had more than once forcibly pointed out, if fish chose to throw themselves right out of the water into his backyard, what was a man to do? And White, who in his time had heard fishing stories at least as tall as this one, swallowed the tale and the trout without complaint.

Over their meal, the inspector related his interview with Mrs Large.

'It's lucky the Chief didn't see you at it,' said White. 'He hates the old lady like poison. I saw you going over to talk to her in the square, and I steered him away. He's up-along in Crabhampton this afternoon, so – '

His face disappeared into a tankard of ale, and the sentence was left incomplete, but its meaning was clear enough.

'I've got something for you,' he went on, wiping his

moustache. 'I was on the telephone to Crabhampton this morning about that matter you asked me to look into, and they've just sent this down.'

He handed a long envelope over the table. Mallett did not look at it until the skeleton of the trout had been removed and a steaming steak and kidney pudding brought in to fill its place. Then he opened it eagerly and drew out two flimsy sheets of typewritten matter, pinned together at one corner. They were headed with the name of a firm of builders and decorators. He read them through slowly and carefully and then, without a word, turned his attention to the food which the superintendent had generously heaped on his plate.

'Have they sent us the wrong one?' White asked. 'This thing didn't seem to me to be hardly what you'd be wanting.'

Mallett, his mouth full, shook his head. When he was able to speak, he replied. 'No, Super, it's the right one all right – Estimate No. 46802. Have you looked at it?'

'Yes. Repairs to a summer-house, or some such, isn't it? I can't see what it's got to do with this case.'

'Neither can I ... and yet ... Super, you've looked at Sir Peter's papers. Would you say that he was a methodical man?'

'No doubt about that. And I've had a word with his solicitor this morning. He tells me that all his affairs were in apple-pie order.'

'Just what I should have thought. Well, all the papers I looked at last night had one thing in common. They were private – private, I mean, in the sense of secret, for one reason or another. The account for this work – repairs to a summer-house in the grounds – was among them. It may be a stray from the place in his papers where it rightly belongs, but I've a strong feeling that Sir Peter's papers didn't stray. He wasn't that sort of man.'

'And so?'

'And so I conclude that there is something private – or secret – about this summer-house that may be worth looking into.'

The superintendent shrugged his shoulders. It was clear that he did not agree, but was too polite to say so.

'When do we go?' he asked.

'I proposed going as soon as I had finished lunch. Are you free to come?'

'Oh, I'll come all right. I shall want to see if there's anything in the place. I noticed there was an item in the estimate for a new lock on the door, by the way,' he added, 'so I reckon I'd best bring Sir Peter's keys along with me.'

'Good. Do you know whereabouts this place is?'

'I never heard tell of it until this moment, but we've only to ask at the Manor – unless,' he added with a touch of malice, 'the whole place is so private and secret they don't know of it.'

The two officers reached the Manor in the early afternoon. The superintendent rang the bell, which was answered by a young footman.

'We want to have a look at the summer-house in the grounds,' said White to him. 'Whereabouts is it?'

'The summer-house, sir?' the lad repeated in obvious surprise.

'That's what I said. Which way is it?'

'Why, over there, sir,' said the footman, pointing across the lawn to a little wooden shelter, open on two sides.

'That's not the one I mean.'

'It's the only one in the place, sir, so far as I know.'

'How long have you been in service here?'

'Six months, sir.' He added: 'Shall I ask Mr Gibbs, the butler, to see if he can help you?'

White nodded, and the footman turned into the house. As he did so, Marian Packer came into the hall from one of the rooms beyond.

'What is it, Thomas?' she asked.

White saluted and came forward. In a few words he explained what had brought them there.

Marian listened to him with a puzzled frown.

'But Thomas is quite right,' she said at last. 'There is no summer-house in the garden, except that little thing out there.'

'Not in the garden, perhaps,' the superintendent persisted. 'But what about the rest of the grounds?'

'No, there's nothing of the kind, except – '

'Yes?'

'I was going to say, except the old pavilion in Owl's Copse. But that has been derelict for years. Nobody ever goes there.'

Mallett spoke for the first time.

'Excuse me,' he said, 'but can you remember if you were here last July?'

'Last July? No, as a matter of fact I was abroad in July and August, staying with relations. I don't quite understand – '

Neither, it was apparent, did the superintendent understand. He glanced at the inspector, who remained silent. Then he said: 'Well, perhaps we had better go and look at this Owl's Copse place. Can anybody show us the way?'

'The butler will direct you,' said Marian.

She rang a bell and the sombre figure of Gibbs, the butler, appeared.

'You rang, my lady?'

'Gibbs, will you take these gentlemen to Owl's Copse? They want to look at the old pavilion.'

'I beg your pardon, my lady?'

'To Owl's Copse, I said. You know where that is, I suppose?'

'Yes, my lady. That is – I think I do.'

'It's close to your cottage, is it not?'

'That is so, your ladyship.'

'Very good. Then take them there.'

'Now, my lady? That is – at once?'

'Certainly.'

'Very good. If your ladyship wishes it. Come this way, please.'

And the man strode out of the house, his lank figure looking black and forbidding against the bright background of lawns and flowers.

The detectives followed him in silence. That he was for some reason uneasy had been apparent from his manner when Lady Packer was speaking to him, and even from behind, the reluctance with which he carried out her orders could be guessed from the slant of his shoulders and his dispirited carriage.

He led them to the back of the house, and then through the kitchen-garden to a neat red-brick dwelling which Mallett presumed to be the butler's cottage. Beyond it a rough path led into a small wood. Owl's Copse had escaped the destruction which had visited the nobler trees by the road corner. By contrast, its thick and unkempt growth seemed to cry out for the hand of the forester to reduce it to order. For a little more than a hundred yards along the path they went, bearing in a direction which the inspector judged would lead them out into the main road again. Then Gibbs stopped, and pointing in front of him said:

'There is the pavilion.'

A short way from them, standing back from the path among the trees, they saw a small wooden house, hardly more than a hut. Its thatched roof was old and decayed, and its general appearance was dilapidated enough to raise a doubt whether any sum could have been spent in repairs upon it for a considerable time.

'There is the pavilion,' Gibbs repeated, and turned about as though to go back the way that he had come. But Mallett checked him.

'I think you had better stay with us for the present,' he said quietly. 'We may need you.'

The butler made a weary gesture of resignation, and walked with them to the pavilion. On closer inspection, it appeared more derelict than ever. The timber of which it was constructed was warped and stained with age, and a strip of carved ornamental woodwork under the eaves seemed on the point of giving way altogether. To reach the entrance it was necessary to walk round the little building to the side farthest from the path. Here they stopped before a door. Mallett gave a grunt of satisfaction when he saw it. In contrast to the rest of the exterior, it was strong, solid, and obviously new. It was fitted with a modern type of lock.

'Have you got the key?' said Mallett to Gibbs.

'The key, sir? I, sir? No!' Gibbs slapped his pockets to give emphasis to his words.

'You mean, perhaps, you left it behind you,' suggested Mallett kindly.

Meanwhile the superintendent was busy with the bunch of keys which he had brought with him. Before long, he found one that fitted. The door opened easily, and the party entered.

They found themselves in a large, light room. It might have been an artist's studio – indeed, had probably originally been built as one, for the windows were set high up in the north wall, incidentally making it impossible for the tallest passer-by to peer inside. It was furnished simply enough with a small table, two arm-chairs and a large couch against one wall. It was provided with electric light, which the inspector tested, and found to be in working order. The room covered the whole ground-plan of the building, except for a small recess at one end, which proved to contain a lavatory basin, fitted with running water, and a large looking-glass.

Mallett looked round him in admiration.

'This has been very cleverly done,' he said to White. 'Do you see? That leaky old roof has been repaired and the walls made watertight – all from the inside. They've left the old shell of the place as shabby as ever, so that you might pass it a dozen times and never guess that it was habitable.'

The superintendent nodded.

'It's stuffy in here,' he remarked. 'Let's have a window open.'

'Wait a bit.' Mallett was sniffing. 'I find the smell here rather suggestive. What do you think?'

'Cigar-smoke, no doubt of it. There's some ash on the table yonder.'

'Yes, that certainly, but something else as well. Don't you get it? What the advertisement writers call "an elusive feminine aura".' He sniffed again. '"Broken Blossoms", I think,' he pronounced. 'But I shouldn't like to swear to it. Something fairly expensive, anyway. All right, let's have some air in now.'

White opened the windows to their full extent.

'We hardly need our noses to tell us what this place was used for,' he said with a chuckle.

'You could tell us all about that, couldn't you?' said the inspector, turning suddenly on Gibbs, who had stood silent by the door since they had entered.

'Well, sir,' Gibbs admitted, 'in a manner of speaking, I could.'

'Then suppose, in a manner of speaking, you did.'

Gibbs coughed, and looked extremely uncomfortable.

'The late Sir Peter, sir,' he said finally, 'was inclined to be a trifle secretive about – about certain matters affecting his private life. Her ladyship – '

'Her ladyship knew nothing about this place, eh?'

'Precisely, sir. The work of repair was done in her absence, last year. It was somewhat of a shock to me when she directed me to take you gentlemen here. But no doubt you had your own sources of information.'

'Never mind about that. Just tell us what you know.'

'I know very little, sir. I – in my position it is sometimes advisable not to know things, if you follow me, sir. During the summer months, when the family was in residence, it was certainly Sir Peter's custom very frequently to go out for a stroll in the evening, and it was my impression, sir, that on such occasions he would from time to time make use of this place for – for his own purposes.'

'Was Susie Bavin one of those purposes?' the superintendent put in.

Gibbs winced at his coarseness.

'There was some gossip concerning the person you mention down in the village,' he admitted. 'Naturally I did not take any part in it.'

'Who else besides Miss Bavin came here?' Mallett asked.

'That I could not say, sir.'

'And how often did you come here yourself?'

'I, sir, Never!'

'Come, come,' said the inspector wearily. 'There's no point in lying about it now. Somebody must have kept this place tidy – aired it and dusted it, and so on. If it wasn't you, who was it?'

The butler bowed his head.

'I did, sir,' he admitted. 'But when I said just now that I had not got the key, I was telling the truth. From time to time Sir Peter would hand me the key, and tell me to put the place in order. It was hardly the type of work for me to do, but Sir Peter was a masterful man, and – and he made it worth my while, sir. Subsequently, I would return him the key, and that was really all I had to do with the matter.'

'I see. And when was the last time that this occurred?'

'Towards the end of last week, sir. I couldn't say exactly.'

'Thank you, Gibbs. I think that's all. You can go now. We'll shut up. And Gibbs!'

'Sir?'

'You will keep your mouth shut about this. Do you understand?'

'Trust me for that, sir.'

After the butler had gone, the two detectives conducted a thorough search of the building. When it was over, they examined their meagre spoils with care.

'What's the colour of Miss Bavin's hair?' Mallett asked, holding two little metal objects in his hand.

'Reddish.'

'And these are black. Is that face powder you've got there?'

'It looks like it.'

'Better have it examined by a chemist. You never know. Well, that's that. Some powder, a brace of hairpins and "Broken Blossoms". You know, White, I've known worse clues to a lady's identity before now.'

Carefully closing the door behind them they left the pavilion in the opposite direction to which they had come. A very short walk brought them to the edge of the wood. Here a quickset hedge was crossed by a low stile, and beyond the stile was the road.

'This path has been used not so very long ago,' the inspector remarked. 'Confound that thunderstorm! It must have washed out a lot of good footprints!'

They crossed the stile and made their way down the road back to the main entrance to the Manor without further incident.

'Well, Super,' said Mallett, as they parted for the night, 'you see that estimate was worth following up after all.'

'We have found out something,' White admitted grudgingly. 'But I don't see yet what it has to do with this case.'

'We shall have to find out a bit more before we know whether it was worth finding out or not. I must say, I'm a bit disappointed with our finds in the pavilion. Any well-conducted woman would have left behind a broken ear-ring, or a fragment of her dress, or something equally unmistakable to identify her by.'

'A well-conducted woman,' said White severely, 'would not have been at the pavilion at all.'

CHAPTER SEVENTEEN

Didbury Camp

WEDNESDAY brought a change in the weather. A harsh, unremitting wind blew from the east, and the sunless sky was a universal grey. It was not a morning to tempt anyone out of doors, one would have thought, but from an early hour the village was astir with crowds of happy sightseers, assembled from near and far for the funeral. Sir Peter had not been noticeably popular in his lifetime, but in his coffin he was certainly the greatest attraction that Didford Magna had ever known.

Mallett, who hated crowds almost as much as he did east

winds, did not attend. He preferred to remain shut up in his room in the 'Polworthy Arms', crouched over a table littered with documents, studying and analysing what he had so far learned. It was not until noon that he emerged. The service had been held early, in a vain attempt to avoid publicity, and by this time the dusty village street was deserted, except for a few belated pleasure-seekers, who still lingered at the church-yard gates. The wind, it was true, remained, but Mallett had already begun to reflect upon the approach of lunch, and de-cided that, whatever the weather, some exercise was essential if he was to do justice to it.

He turned to his left from the inn door and walked quickly past the church in the direction of Didford Parva. A little beyond the church was a row of small cottages, of the type which is the delight of the passing tourist and the despair of the sanitary inspector. From one of these, just before he reached it, he saw Mrs Large emerge. She, too, turned to her left at the door and made off at a smart pace in the same direc-tion, but not before she had thrown a glance towards the in-spector, accompanied by an unobtrusive but unmistakable gesture of invitation.

Mallett followed, keeping at a discreet distance behind her – indeed, at the rate that she was walking it would have been hard to overtake her if he had tried – and presently saw her turn off the road at the point where a narrow track branched steeply up towards the downs on the right. Arrived at the same point, he did the same, and found Mrs Large awaiting him in the shelter of a hedge.

'Well, Mr Busy!' she began at once. 'I was coming to see you this afternoon, but I suppose it's a mistake for narks and busies to be seen about together too much, eh? It puts ideas into people's heads, I mean.'

'I am sure nobody would take you for a – what you mention, ma'am,' said the inspector. 'But what were you coming to see me about?'

'Just this. You saw me coming out of the Bavins' cottage just now – '

'Oh, that is the Bavins' cottage, is it?'

'Bless my soul! You call yourself a busy, and don't know that? I went in to see the baby, of course, and to give Miss Bavin a piece of my mind at the same time. Little wretch! She doesn't seem in the least penitent – I don't wonder young Carter won't have anything more to do with her. It was all I could do to make her agree to have it christened. And the state things were in at the cottage! Her father ran off with a woman from Parva two years ago, the mother is a drunken old wretch, and as for that district nurse, she's no better than a half-wit. It's a fine healthy baby, thank goodness!' She drew breath and then continued: 'However, Mr Busy, I didn't want to talk to you about the baby. It's something I've found out. About Dr Latymer.'

'Indeed?'

'Yes.' She pursed her lips and then said impressively: 'Dr Latymer came to see Susan and her baby late on Saturday evening.'

'Well?'

'And that was the first time he was in there after the baby was born on Friday night.'

'But I thought you told me yesterday – '

'I did, Mr Busy, and I tell you so again. The doctor came careering down the road when I was going up it on Saturday as if Old Nick was after him, and nearly knocked me over. I took it for granted he was on his way to the Bavins'. There was nobody else in the village needing a doctor. That's certain. You can ask – but you needn't ask anybody. I know what's going on in my parish, I hope. So I ask myself, and I ask you, where was the doctor going in the middle of the day on Saturday?'

'Really, Mrs Large, but he might have been doing a dozen different things.'

'Indeed? Well, I should like to hear 'em, that's all. Goodbye, Mr Busy, till we meet again. And think it over.'

Mallett laughed softly to himself as he stared after her retreating figure. There was no doubt that Mrs Large was taking her new-found occupation seriously. But after a moment or two his laughs stopped abruptly. 'By Jove!' he murmured, suddenly serious, 'but just supposing. ... It might explain ...' He sighed. 'This will take a bit of working out.' Then he made his way back to lunch. He had found by experience that things were easier to work out after a square meal.

About three o'clock in the afternoon, although the weather had in no way improved, the inspector again left the 'Polworthy Arms' for a walk. He followed precisely the same route that he had taken earlier in the day, but this time when he reached the track off the road he pursued it up the hill. Ten minutes' steep climbing brought him on to the bare, windswept ridge of the downs. He turned to his right, and set his face towards the tree-crowned summit of Didbury Camp, which filled the centre of the northern horizon. He was walking now on a broad expanse of crisp green turf. To his left the ground sloped away gently to the shallow valley in which ran the 'new road' to Didford Parva. On his other hand the valley of the Didder was for the most part hidden by the shoulder of the hill which he had just climbed. He could distinguish the gleam of the river where it curved to make the road corner. Above that point the reaches of beats three and four were visible, but nothing below it. Save for the plover, wheeling above his head in curves of flight as inconsequent as those of butterflies and more graceful, he was alone. In the east wind the lines of the landscape were hard and clear. The beeches which marked his objective showed almost black against the clear sky.

The hill rose ever higher above him as he approached it. Presently he stood at its foot. To reach the top he could either climb directly up its steep, smooth slope or take a path which led obliquely across the face of the hill left-handed and then serpentined back again above him to the crest. He chose the latter course, and after a few minutes' easy walking reached the top. The Camp, he found, consisted of a simple ring of earthworks, surrounding a space perhaps fifty yards in diameter, now covered with beech-trees of ancient growth. An outer ring of trees grew outside the embankment, but these, more exposed to the winds of centuries, were comparatively sparse and stunted. Mallett walked round its whole circumference. A superb view, of amazing amplitude, opened at every step, but with this he had little concern. He did not pause to test the alleged visibility of Salisbury spire to the west, or the quite authentic vision of Crabhampton tower to the north, nor to lament the eye-sore constituted by the gasworks at Didford Parva in the southerly direction; and when he reached the east, he disregarded the distant prospect before him, but turned his eyes – now tearful from the cutting wind – to what lay immediately beneath him.

He could see at a glance that the superintendent's recollection had been right. The road corner itself was invisible, masked by what remained of the beech copse. The river did not come into view until a point which the inspector judged to be well up-stream of the end of the causeway. Below the road corner, however, he could follow its course to a point well below the farm bridge, which was clearly visible, a small white bar across the shining ribbon of the stream. The road, too, could be seen for about the same distance towards the village, until the flank of the hill cut it off from his view.

Mallett next turned his attention to his immediate surroundings. The Camp was evidently too remote a spot to be a favourite haunt of picknickers. Only a few scraps of greasy paper, cigarette cartons, and broken bottles disfigured the ground. The inspector turned them over meditatively, searching for he knew not what. Then he descended the hill on the side which overlooked the river valley. As he had expected, this path soon led him away from the wide prospect which he had seen from the summit. Its course took him down through a narrow winding gulley, and it was not until he was almost on the road, a little above the corner, that the floor of the valley came into view again. Only once in his descent did he pause. This was when, shortly after he had started to come down, something white, lying under a thorn bush, caught his eye. It proved to be the butt of a common brand of cigarette, and he observed that it was heavily stained with lipstick. As he bent to pick it up, he saw another, a little farther on. This bore no stains. Both had the appearance of having been at some time soaked with water.

Mallett took the short cut back through the larch plantation, automatically counting his paces as he went. Arrived at the inn, he put through a telephone call to the police station at Didford Parva, and asked for Superintendent White.

'Is there a good train to London this evening?' he said.

'The next from here is the seven o'clock,' White told him. 'I wouldn't call it a good train, though. Is it for yourself you're asking?'

'Yes. I think it's about time I tackled this job from the other end.'

If the superintendent felt any surprise, he did not show it.

'Well,' he said, 'if you're in a hurry, you can get the six-twenty from Crabhampton. I can send you a car up straight away. But it will be a bit of a rush.'

'I'd rather not rush if I could help it,' said Mallett.

'I only mentioned it because there's a dining car on the Crabhampton train. Whereas if you waited for the seven o'clock – '

'Send up a car straight away,' said the inspector at once.

CHAPTER EIGHTEEN

Jimmy and the Scotland Yard Person

JIMMY RENDEL was writing a letter. He had written a number of letters in the last few days, but none of them had been posted. This time he was determined to finish the job to his satisfaction. It was not an easy job that he had undertaken. Indeed it was one that might well have taxed the diplomacy of a Talleyrand. Manuals exist which profess to give instructions for the writing of letters on almost every conceivable occasion, but it is questionable whether a satisfactory precedent can be found embodying the sentiments which Jimmy was trying to put upon paper. His was not a very orderly mind, and some of his difficulties probably arose from the fact that he had never squarely faced the problem of deciding exactly what those sentiments were, but if he had done so he might have tabulated them after this fashion:

(*a*) He commiserated very deeply with Marian in her widowhood.

(*b*) At the same time, her husband was a disreputable fellow, and had well deserved to be murdered.

(*c*) He, Jimmy, adored her.

And, as if this were not enough to try his epistolary tact to its utmost the letter would not be complete unless he could contrive to include in it:

(*d*) He fully realized the possibility that she was a murderess, and

(*e*) If so, he was quite prepared to help her in escaping the consequences of that fact.

Finally, Jimmy was acutely conscious of the necessity of conveying this information in a form that would be perfectly clear to its recipient and at the same time be sufficiently veiled to be unintelligible to any detective or other person who might intercept it.

He had begun his task that evening immediately on returning from work to his rooms in Ebury Street, and now, his supper cleared away, he was still sitting at his desk, wasting sheet after sheet of paper in the endeavour to find the magic formula. He was just embarking on his fifth attempt of the evening when his landlady interrupted him. She was a masterful, moustached woman, of whom Jimmy was secretly more than a little afraid.

'There's a man to see you,' she said.

'A man, Mrs Meggs?' Jimmy asked. 'What sort of a man?'

'A big man,' answered Mrs Meggs curtly, and then looking over her shoulder called down the stairs: 'Will you come up, please?'

As Mrs Meggs disappeared from the doorway, Jimmy hastily thrust the draft of his uncompleted letter under a blotter. He turned round a moment later, flushing guiltily, to confront his visitor. His first reflection, when he saw him, was that the big man must have come up the stairs uncommonly quietly, for he had heard nothing of his approach. Then with an unreasoning but ungovernable feeling of alarm he realized that the newcomer was no other than the 'Scotland Yard person' of the inquest. Miserably aware that he was displaying all the symptoms of guilt, he stared at him in silence, his hand still clutching the blotter.

The inspector, however, seemed determined to disregard Jimmy's naïve display of emotion. He appeared to be in high good humour and determined that his host should share it.

'This is a real bit of luck,' he exclaimed with a cheerful smile. 'I'm just off the train, and I thought there might be a chance of having a chat with you this evening. By the way, I haven't introduced myself – do you know who I am?'

Jimmy indicated that he did.

'Well, there are a lot of points in this case that can be more easily cleared up in London than down at Didford and I want your help in doing it.'

'I have given a statement to the police already,' Jimmy ventured.

'Quite right – and not at all a bad statement either, so far as it goes. But I want a bit more, if I can get it. I was reading a highbrow weekly paper in the train just now', Mallett observed unexpectedly, 'which runs a problem competition every week. This week they had what they were pleased to call "a simple problem of elimination". I couldn't have solved it to save my life, but it reminded me of this case – only that isn't so simple either. Anyhow, I want to start eliminating.'

He flung himself back in Jimmy's best arm-chair and filled a large pipe.

'Well, naturally, I want to be eliminated myself,' said Jimmy with a faint smile.

'Of course, that goes without saying. But I think you can

153

go a bit further than that – in eliminating other people, or incriminating them as the case may be.'

'I don't understand.'

'What I mean is this: On Saturday afternoon you met quite a lot of people whose movements may or may not be important. Mr Matheson, to start with, and Mrs Matheson to end with, and in between Mrs Large and Dr Latymer and Lady Packer. Now it occurs to me – '

'But I never said so!' Jimmy interrupted.

'Never said what?'

'That I met Lady Packer! And what's more she never said – '

'No,' said the inspector calmly, 'I know you didn't, and she didn't, but I'm only dealing with the facts now. After all, you weren't on oath, and I don't blame you. As I was saying – '

'But she didn't!'

'Didn't what?' Mallett leaned forward in his chair. The stem of his pipe pointed at Jimmy like an accusing finger. 'Didn't what?'

'She didn't – didn't kill him. She's – she couldn't have – it's not possible!' And Jimmy, to his utter shame, burst into tears.

'My dear fellow!' Mallett was suddenly sympathy itself. 'I'm afraid this is all very distressing for you. Look here, haven't you got any whisky about the place? I thought so ... Yes, thanks, I'll have a spot myself ... That's better. Now look here, don't you think the best thing you can do is to tell me all about it? From the beginning, I mean, starting with your leaving the "Polworthy Arms" that afternoon, right down to the time you got back again. I feel there's such a lot you can say that I haven't heard yet. And after all', he reminded him, 'it's the best thing you can do for either of you – now.'

And suddenly, whether it was the whisky, or the influence of that quiet, compelling voice, Jimmy found that everything had been made perfectly easy for him. With a positive feeling of relief he began to detail once more the events of that fatal Saturday, but this time he omitted nothing. Every incident came back freshly to his mind as he related it – Matheson's foul-hooked trout, the cross-bills in the tree-tops, the conversation with Mrs Large, the encounter at the road corner with Dr Latymer. He did not even falter when he had to recount his meeting with Marian Packer. In a dull, determined voice, as though repeating a lesson learned by heart, he ploughed straight on, sparing himself nothing – since he was betraying her trust, he felt, he might as well do it thoroughly – and even brought himself to describe her well-remembered looks and movements, and how her hand had clutched his arm as the wild duck flew past them. That Rubicon passed, he went on with a lighter heart to complete his story with his return to the inn in the doctor's car and his narrow escape from running down Mrs Matheson on the way.

Mallett heard him out to the end, without adding a word by way of question or comment. When it was all over, he drained his glass and rose to his feet.

'Thank you very much indeed,' he said seriously. 'And now I think it's about time we both went to bed.' He paused at the door. 'Just one thing,' he added. 'I shall have to interview Lady Packer when I get back to Didford Magna. It would be just as well if you didn't write to her between now and then. You see, it would rather destroy the value of her evidence if she knew what you had been telling me.'

'I understand.'

'Good. Shall I see you there next week-end?'

'I don't know. I had meant to come down on Friday night. My office has given me all next Saturday to make up for last. But as it is, I hardly like to – '

'There's no reason why you shouldn't, you know. After all, I think you've earned a day's fishing! Good night!'

When he had gone, Jimmy took from the blotter his half-finished letter and tore it into a great many small pieces. It was at least a satisfaction to know that now it need never be written.

CHAPTER NINETEEN

Smithers and the Hackle Blue

NEXT morning Mallett made the second of the calls which he had proposed for himself in London. This time he did not attempt to drop in unannounced as he had done in Ebury Street. The senior partner of an important firm of solicitors is not to be interviewed without due ceremony by any mere detective, however eminent in his profession, and the inspector had made an appointment. In accordance with that appointment, grudgingly conceded by a preternaturally husky voice on the telephone, eleven o'clock found him walking through the pleasant spaces of New Square, Lincoln's Inn. At No. 46 he sent in his card, asked for Mr Smithers, and was immediately immured by the clerk who received him in a hermetically sealed chamber lined with deed-boxes and furnished with arm-chairs the leather upholstery of which was disintegrating with age. After five minutes or so of this purgatory, he was released by the owner of the husky voice and shown into the senior partner's room.

From behind a vast mahogany desk Smithers' cherubic face confronted him.

'You've come about this Didford affair, I suppose?' said the solicitor.

'Yes.'

'Well, I can give you exactly twenty-five minutes – No, by God, I can't!' he suddenly added violently, at the same time ringing a bell on his desk.

The clerk, who had only that moment left the room, dashed in again at top speed.

'What time is the Jenks appointment?' asked Smithers.

'A quarter to twelve, sir.'

'Then I've just time to get down to Sloman's and back before then. Call me a taxi at once, will you?'

'Very good, sir.'

The clerk disappeared.

'I'm sorry,' said Smithers to the inspector. 'But you see how it is. I had forgotten all about it, till seeing you reminded me. And if I don't do it now, I never shall. It's most important.'

'I have reason to think that my business is important, also,' said Mallett stiffly.

'I dare say you have, but I am a busy man, as you may have gathered, and I can't wait. Also I have to be at a board meeting this afternoon which will last the rest of the day. I cannot allow the police or anyone else to interfere with my arrangements. Now if – '

'The taxi is at the door, sir!' said the clerk, who from his dishevelled state looked as though he had run all the way to the rank and raced the cab home again.

'Good!' Smithers rose to his feet. 'You can come with me if you like,' he remarked to Mallett, as though by an after-thought. 'We can talk on the way down.'

'That will suit me very well,' said Mallett. A moment or two later he found himself beside the solicitor in the taxi, without the smallest idea of where he was going.

'Now,' said Smithers, settling himself comfortably back in his seat, 'what is all this nonsense about? I have already given a full and accurate statement to the country police as to when I last saw Packer, and I can't alter or enlarge on it in any way. Is that understood?'

'Perfectly,' replied Mallett. 'I may say at once that I don't intend to ask you anything on that subject at all.'

'If it's about Lady Packer and young Rendel's rather child-ish love affair with her, I can't help you either. I know no more about it than any policeman who knows his trade could find out in five minutes.'

'The only person I thought you could give me any informa-tion about,' said the inspector, 'was Mr Wrigley-Bell.'

'Oh!' said Smithers violently. 'Oh!'

The taxi proceeded for a full hundred yards before he spoke again.

'There's some hanky-panky been going on in the City in Bell's firm,' he said at last. 'I know that much. I can put you on to Brandish's solicitors if you like.'

'I think I know all I need to about that already,' said Mallett. 'My present concern is with what happened last Saturday?'

'Yes?'

'My information is that Mr Wrigley-Bell had a meeting with Sir Peter very shortly after you did. What I want to know is what he did after that meeting. Now you were fishing the beat immediately above his. I have had a bird's-eye view of all that part of the river from Didbury Camp. It is comparatively open country, and it strikes me that you might have seen something of his movements. At the same time, it occurs to me that after his talk with Sir Peter, Mr Wrigley-Bell might very well be in a mood to ask the advice of a person like yourself.'

Smithers twisted round in his seat to look at the inspector.

'Upon my word, that shows some intelligence,' he exclaimed, in a tone of surprise so sincere that the blow to Mallett's vanity was forgotten in amusement. 'It may be only a lucky guess on your part, of course,' he added at once, 'but as a matter of history I saw a good deal of friend Bell on Saturday – quite as much as I wanted, I may say.'

He was about to say more, when the taxi came to a stop.

'Here we are!' Smithers exclaimed, and jumped out. Mallett followed him into a shop the like of which he had never seen before.

His first impression was one of innumerable straight lines, all parallel, all vertical, stretching from floor to ceiling of the large but overcrowded showroom. It was like a schoolboy's nightmare on the eve of a geometry examination. A second glance showed that the shop approximated more nearly to a schoolboy's Elysium, for every one of those lines was a fishing rod. They were of all sorts and sizes, fragile little feather-weights with top joints tapering off almost into invisibility, stout, blunt-ended weapons for the big game of tropical seas, long two-handed salmon-rods – rods of every kind for every one of the inexhaustible varieties of angling, all glistening in the bravery of paint and varnish, all – and this was to many their chief merit – with the magic name of Sloman engraved on the butt. At one counter, a stout, bald assistant was decorously waving a gigantic split-cane, manfully endeavouring to demonstrate a Spey cast for the benefit of a hesitating prospective purchaser. At another, an elderly customer with weeping moustaches that smothered his utterance was carrying on an interminable argument on the subject of silk backing with a deprecating but determined expert. Over all hung a hushed religious atmosphere, and the inspector felt as though he had intruded into a cathedral where a service was in progress, of infinite solemnity indeed, but conducted with rites of which he was entirely ignorant.

Smithers walked briskly to the farther end of the shop, where a high priest welcomed him with an expression of grave joy. At this counter were multitudes of little cardboard boxes, labelled with names of allurement: Wickham's Fancy, Greenwell's Glory, Rough Olive, Pale Watery Dun.

'I want,' said Smithers in a brusque tone that sounded positively blasphemous in those surroundings, 'a dozen of your small hackle blue fly. I don't know its name, but it has been taking fish on the Didder lately.'

'The small hackle blue, sir? Exactly. A very killing fly, this season.' A deft hand seized one of the cardboard boxes and opened for inspection. 'Tied on OO hooks, sir. We find the smaller sizes the more successful.'

Smithers turned them over with a stumpy forefinger. He grunted crossly.

'This is the wrong fly,' he pronounced.

'Sir?' There was a world of pained surprise in the intonation.

'The pattern I want is tied on a quill body, and the hackle's quite short – not a great whiskery affair like this. I haven't one to show you, but Mr Wrigley-Bell described it to me exactly.'

'Mr Wrigley-Bell, sir? His fly is a variant of this. As you

say, it has a quill body, and the hackle is not quite so – h'm – abundant. We tied a few to his instructions as a special order. But you will find this answers the purpose very well.'

'Kindly give me a dozen of the pattern which you supplied to Mr Wrigley-Bell,' said Smithers in a voice that made the shop assistant start.

'Certainly, sir. That is – I'll see if I have a few in stock,' he bleated and hastened away.

Smithers turned to the inspector.

'Now you see why I have to leave my practice to come down here, if I'm to get what I want,' he said. 'These people are all out to rob you if they can.'

His last words were not lost on the assistant, who returned at that moment with a box in his hand.

'I think this is the article you require,' he said severely, emptying it out on to the counter. 'But you will understand of course, sir, that we do not guarantee them in any way.'

'I have yet to hear of any fly that was guaranteed,' retorted Smithers.

But the assistant had the last word.

'By the way,' Smithers asked, as the tiny parcel was being wrapped up, 'have you a name for this pattern?'

'We are thinking, sir, of naming it the Caveat Emptor.'

Smithers grunted, and then barked out an order for a special brand of tapered gut casts that sent the assistant scurrying away once more.

'It will make Bell sit up to find that I've got some of these,' he said with satisfaction to Mallett. 'He is the meanest devil alive when it comes to sharing a good thing.'

'They are his speciality, I take it?' Mallett asked.

'Yes. Nobody else in the syndicate had them last week-end, at any rate, and Bell left his last in a fish at the road corner on Friday evening.'

'You're sure of that? Mr Matheson, for instance, hadn't any of them?'

'Quite sure. I looked through Matheson's box on Friday night, to see what he had got, and I know. Matheson asked him for one that evening, I remember, but he had none to give. Why this sudden interest in flies, may I ask?'

'There may be nothing in it, of course, but from Mr Rendel's account to me last night, Mr Matheson was using a fly remarkably like it on Saturday afternoon.'

'Then the boy is wrong,' said the solicitor positively, just as the assistant returned to the counter. 'In any case one fly is just like another to people who don't know what they are looking at. That's why this fellow' – he glared at the hapless man – 'tried to fob me off with the wrong pattern just now. How can you positively guarantee that this gut will –'

He turned at once to a technical discussion with the salesman which was utterly above the inspector's head.

The purchase was completed and they were about to leave the shop when Mallett had a sudden inspiration.

'I should like one of those flies,' he said.

His intervention was greeted with the surprise that attends the bid of an amateur in an auction-room full of dealers.

'*One*, sir?' said the man. 'Just so – one. Which pattern would you be requiring – the original or the variant?'

'Perhaps one of each would be best.'

'Very good, sir. Let me see, I don't think you have an account with us, have you?'

'No.'

'At the desk, please. Miss Goodson, *two* dry flies.'

The inspector, as he paid, was astonished to find these sacred articles were after all quite cheap.

'As I was saying,' said Smithers, taking up the conversation where he had left off as soon as they were back in the cab again, 'Bell made a positive nuisance of himself to me on Saturday. He came up behind me first while I was watching a fish near the bottom of my beat –'.

'About what time would that be?' the inspector put in.

'About twelve, I should think. Not much before, anyhow. It was certainly before twelve-twenty, because that was the time when I finally killed the fish, and he was still with me then. In fact, he helped me land it. I always note the time when fish are caught,' he explained. 'I'm rather interested in the sol-lunar theory of the feeding of trout. I don't expect you know what that means. It doesn't matter. It has nothing to do with this case. To continue: I asked him why he wasn't fishing, and he said that there didn't seem to be anything doing on his beat – which I knew to be a damned lie anyway, because I had marked down three rising fish on my way up, and in any case if you want to catch trout you have to be on the water, whether they are rising or not. Then he said he couldn't do any good because he had run out of hackle blues – these flies which I've got here. In the first place, that was a wholly inconsistent reason with the one he'd given first, and in the second it was all nonsense. They are good flies, of course, but not indispensable – no fly is.'

'Nonetheless, it is important sometimes to have a particular fly?'

'Obviously. That is why people like Sloman's exist, and pay substantial dividends too. May I ask, Inspector, whether you are thinking of going in for that trade when you retire from the C.I.D.?'

'No, no. I was just wondering whether – But you were telling me about Mr Wrigley-Bell.'

'I was – until you interrupted me. I formed the impression that he was in that nervous state when people can't bear to be alone, and as to me the principal charm of fishing is that one is alone, I was moderately rude to him. Finally he went off a little way downstream and sat on a seat on the bank, pretending to look at the water. When there was a rise just above him he started to fish it, but even from where I was, a couple of hundred yards away, I could see that he was making the most horrible mess of it – which was unlike him, I must admit. Then he sat down again, and I moved on up, but whenever I looked back he was still there. About two o'clock, I decided to have lunch, and I had no sooner started than he appeared again and asked if he could eat his lunch with me. I couldn't very well refuse. He ate next to nothing but drank quite a good-sized flask of whisky. There was obviously something on his mind, but I wasn't going to help him out. Finally he said that he would like to ask my advice. I asked him whether he meant professional advice. He said yes. I told him that I never gave professional advice except at Lincoln's Inn, and that whatever trouble he was in would get no worse over the week-end. That shut him up. It was confoundedly hot in the afternoon, and he said he thought he would lie down in the shade. I wasn't surprised after all that whisky. He went up to the hut at the top of the water, and I was free of him for the rest of the afternoon. About five o'clock he came down again, and I think he did contrive to get a little fishing between then and when the rain began, when I picked him up and made him drive me home. That's all.'

Smithers had timed his recital neatly. As he finished it, the taxi drew up outside his office. The husky-voiced clerk had evidently been looking out for it, for he came running down the steps and flung open the door.

'Mr Jenks is here, sir,' he croaked.

'Right. Pay the cab, will you?' said Smithers and walked briskly inside.

As he was about to disappear, Mallett called after him.

'Shall I see you at Didford over the week-end, Mr. Smithers?'

The solicitor turned in the doorway and barked: 'What the blazes do you imagine I bought these things for today, you – you fatuous person?'

'Mr Smithers is in a very good mood today, sir,' the clerk observed. 'He never calls anybody *that* unless he's feeling very friendly indeed, sir.'

He went into the office, leaving the fatuous person thoughtfully considering two little grey-blue objects, each adorned with a tiny but purposeful hook.

'I'm no fisherman,' was his unspoken comment, 'but perhaps I shall catch something with these!'

CHAPTER TWENTY

Conversation in Kensington

MALLETT looked at his watch. He had planned his afternoon carefully, but he was no slave to the time-table, and after what he had learned in the last half-hour, he felt at liberty to make an alteration in his arrangements. His next move was to have been to the City. Instead, he stopped just short of Temple Bar, and turned into a chop house off the Strand, on the borders of the precincts of the Middle Temple.

It was a favourite haunt of his, and he was a favoured customer. Lunching early, he had leisure to select his steak with care, to see it placed upon the grill, and to watch its gradual progress to perfection from where he sat at table. Outside, the sun beat down fiercely on the narrow courts and alleys, and the pavements were hot to the feet. A foreigner would have marvelled that anyone could prefer on such a day to choose such food and to eat it in a stuffy room, with a fierce open grill to raise the temperature yet still higher. But the inspector was a true Cockney, and he regarded with scorn those weaklings who succumbed in warm weather to fish salads, iced water, and other such American innovations. Even in these degenerate days, he was far from being alone in his belief, and before he had finished his meal the place was fairly full.

Most of the customers were connected with the law in some way or other, for the situation of the house made it a regular port of call to solicitors' and barristers' clerks. It was one of these latter who presently joined Mallett at his table. He was in the service of a leader on the circuit in which Didford was situated, and he numbered the inspector in the enormous circle of acquaintance that every competent barrister's clerk possesses.

'You're on this Didford murder, I'm told, old man,' he said.

The inspector admitted that he was.

'Well, between ourselves, old chap, as man to man – d'you think there's likely to be anything for us at the next assizes out of that affair?'

'I think,' said Mallett deliberately, 'that there is likely to be something for somebody at the next assizes.'

'The term's getting on, y'know,' the clerk observed. 'If you don't get somebody committed soon, it'll throw the case over the long vacation.'

'That is so, of course.'

'We don't go circuit as much as we used, but we'd always be prepared to accept an Attorney-General's nomination in a case like this. The Attorney has a pretty high opinion of us, I can tell you.'

'I can well believe it.'

'Unless,' said the clerk confidentially, 'unless it's the woman that's done it. Now that's the kind of defence we like to do. Sentimental appeal – you follow me? You couldn't give me a line on whether it's likely to be the woman or not, between ourselves, old man, could you?'

'I'm afraid not,' said Mallett, and rose to go.

'Well, so long, old man, and you'll bear in mind what I said about the long vacation, won't you? 'Smatter o'fact, next term may not see us here at all. To be perfectly frank, the work's getting a bit too much for us, and I shouldn't wonder if we was to find ourselves on the bench any time now.'

'I shall look forward to it,' answered the inspector gravely. 'Good day.'

Mallett walked along the south side of the Strand as far as Somerset House. As he came abreast of the entrance, a slim, well-dressed young man came out of it just in front of him. Leaning forward, Mallett tapped him on the shoulder.

'Well, Frant?' he said. 'Have you got all you want there?'

Sergeant Frant fell into step with him and they walked on together.

'I didn't expect to see you here,' he said. 'I thought you were going to the City.'

'I was, but I've changed my mind. Suppose we walk a little. I can get the Underground from Westminster – that is, if you've got what I'm looking for.'

'I've got all there is to find, at all events,' said Frant. A little packet of papers changed hands. 'Here you are: Copy Marriage Certificate of John Richard Sneyd, Captain in His Majesty's Army, to Laura Lydia O'Shea, spinster, thirteenth April, nineteen oh one; Copy Birth Certificate of Mary Euphemia Sneyd, daughter of the above, born in London on the fourth September, nineteen oh two; ditto of Hilary Montague Sneyd, son of the above, born at Aldershot on the twenty-fourth March, nineteen oh seven; Copy Marriage Certificate of Robert Matheson, widower, to the said Mary Euphemia Sneyd, spinster, ninth June –'

'Thanks,' said the inspector, stuffing the papers away in his pocket. 'I think that's all I need. There's no doubt that Hilary Montague is our Hilary, I suppose?'

'Not the least doubt. I've checked him up from the records and it's the same fellow all right.'

'That's splendid!' said Mallett. 'But how very odd!'

'What is odd?'

'That Matheson should have got married like that, right in the middle of the fishing season!'

Then to the obvious disappointment of his colleague, he changed the subject, and insisted on discussing other matters all the way back to New Scotland Yard.

At three o'clock precisely, Mr Matheson closed the door of his Kensington house behind him and walked briskly away, intent upon the happy prospect of a quiet afternoon at the Rod and Line Club. At 3.1, as he left the square by its northern exit, Mallett entered it from the south. Exactly how this delicate feat of synchronization was achieved would take too long to relate in detail, but it may be stated that it depended in part upon the unconscious collaboration of Matheson's parlourmaid and the porter at the Rod and Line, both expansive individuals with a weakness for conversation with amiable strangers. Regularity of habit is a disease that grows with old age, and it is one that makes the patient particularly vulnerable to the attentions of those whose plans depend on their being in or out of the way at a given moment.

'Inspector Mallett's compliments, m'm, and can he see you for a moment or two?' said the parlour-maid to her mistress about the time that Mr Matheson was contentedly climbing into his taxi.

Euphemia Matheson was looking particularly fetching that afternoon – as fetching as only a woman of mature years can look after a morning spent at Madame Jeannot's beauty establishment in Bond Street. It was all the more unfortunate therefore that she permitted herself to greet the maid's announcement with a heavy frown, restoring at one blow the wrinkles which an expert had laboured a full hour to remove.

'Ask him to come in,' she said to the servant. 'Damn! Damn!' she said aloud to herself as she looked into the mirror above the mantelpiece. Whether the exclamation was inspired merely by the spectacle of a ruined forehead or by some preoccupation that lay deeper than wrinkles remained obscure.

As the maid was leaving the room she called to her over her shoulder.

'Oh, Barber, just a moment!'

'Yes, m'm?'

'If anybody calls while I'm engaged, will you show him – show whoever it is into the library and ask him to wait?'

Barber greeted this apparently innocent order with pursed lips and lowered eyes.

'Yes, m'm,' she said in a tone which conveyed, and was meant to convey, that she knew perfectly well who it was that she was expected to show into the library and that she heartily disapproved of such goings on.

A moment later Mallett entered the room. Mrs Matheson's frown had utterly disappeared, and she greeted him with as much cordiality as if he had been an old and valued friend.

'Come in, come in, Inspector!' she cried. 'Sit down, and make yourself comfortable. That chair over there is a good one. I shall sit here, facing the window. You'd prefer that, wouldn't you? You see, I read all the detective stories and I know what is expected of me!'

Her warm smiles played around him. A delicate scent pervaded the air. Mallett, as he lowered himself into a comfortable arm-chair, sniffed appreciatively. 'Broken Blossoms,' he told himself.

'I am so sorry you've missed my husband,' Euphemia went on. 'He has only just this minute gone to his club.'

'I am sorry, too,' said Mallett unblushingly, 'but in point of fact it was you I came to see.'

'Yes?' The wrinkles on her brow seemed for an instant to become more noticeable.

'Yes. It's a rather delicate matter, Mrs Matheson. Perhaps I may say that it is a matter which is best discussed in the absence of your husband.'

'Oh!' said Mrs Matheson.

She sat upright in her chair, regarding him intently, her lips slightly parted.

'Oh!' she said again. Then she went on in a lighter tone: 'There are so many things that are best discussed in the absence of one's husband, aren't there? For instance, if you wanted to ask a wife about – about – just give me an example, Inspector?'

'About another man,' said Mallett bluntly.

Mrs Matheson's expression became suddenly serious. Her eyes seemed to contract until they were like two very bright small stones.

'Another man,' she repeated softly. 'You speak in riddles, Inspector, and I don't like riddles. Who are you talking about?'

'I am inquiring into the death of Sir Peter Packer,' said Mallett.

'Well?' she said defiantly. 'I have told the police already that I know nothing about that.'

'Nonetheless,' answered Mallett, 'there are some questions that I must ask you about yourself and Sir Peter.'

'I see. This is to be an inquisition into my private affairs, is it?'

'I am afraid so. You are not bound to answer any questions, unless you wish, of course, but in the exercise of my duty I must ask them. And if I cannot get the information in one way, I must seek it in another.'

'It will be no use asking my husband,' she put in quickly. 'He knows nothing – nothing!'

'That will be for me to find out – if necessary,' said the inspector drily. 'Meanwhile, you will observe that I have given you the opportunity of speaking to me in his absence.'

'That is very kind of you,' she retorted bitterly. She reflected for a moment, and then said: 'Very well, I give in. Yes, it's quite true about – about Peter and me. I have been his – we have been lovers now for quite a little time, off and on. I know there were plenty of people who said hard things about him' – her words began to come in a quick, breathless rush – 'and his character wasn't very attractive in a lot of ways, but there was something about him, all the same ... Women are like that, you know, Inspector.' She looked up at him inquiringly. 'Am I shocking you very much?' she asked.

'I'm not here to be shocked,' said Mallett.

'You see,' she was speaking slowly now, apparently addressing her forefinger, which was describing little circles on the top of a small table beside her, 'I am very, *very* fond of my husband. I married him fifteen years ago for love, and I have never regretted it – not for an instant. But' – she gave vent to a little laugh that did not ring quite true – 'after all, I am a young woman, and he is an old man, and I like my little bit of fun, and why not? That's what I say.' She took a deep breath, and looked up again. 'So that's how it was, Inspector,' she concluded.

Mallett waited a moment to see if she had anything to add, and then asked:

'When did you last see Sir Peter?'

'The evening before – before it happened. We met at a little summer-house near the road.'

'I know the place.'

'You know a terrible lot, don't you, Inspector?' she said with a rueful smile. 'Yet we'd been pretty careful, I thought. I *had* to be careful,' she added with emphasis. 'My husband didn't know – and he *mustn't* know.'

She paused for the inspector to reply, but he said nothing.

'Well,' she said at last, in a tone of forced cheerfulness. 'The skeleton is out of the cupboard now with a vengeance! Is there anything else you want to know?'

'Yes,' Mallett replied. 'I want you to tell me the truth, Mrs Matheson.'

She turned to him a face that had suddenly gone quite white.

'I – what do you mean?' she said in a voice only just above a whisper.

'I mean that you have not told me the truth about your relations with Sir Peter Packer. Oh' – he waved her protestations aside – 'I don't mean what you told me just now about the summer-house and so on. I accept that. For that matter, I knew it already. What you have not told me is the real reason why you ever went there.'

'I don't understand you. I have told you already –'

'Yes, and I do not believe it. Consider: you are a woman, happily married, to a man much older than yourself, I agree, but to a man who loves you and whom you love. And you are a woman of taste and intelligence. Are you asking me to believe that if you must be unfaithful to your husband you would of your own free will choose a man like Sir Peter?'

'Inspector,' she said with a fine show of dignity, 'this subject is very distasteful to me, and I cannot pursue it any longer. I have told you what I did – something that, looking back on it, I am fairly ashamed of. But it is a thing that people do every day, as a man in your position ought to know very well, and for no better reason than I had. Why you should suggest some hidden motive, I can't for the life of me imagine. Do men and women want motives for that kind of thing, do you think? I simply don't know what you are talking about.'

'Mrs Matheson,' said the inspector, 'must I remind you that you have a brother?'

She turned on him in a flash.

'Oh, so you've been asking Hilary questions, have you?' she cried.

'Never mind where I have my information from. The point is that I know. Your brother Hilary was in a position in which Sir Peter could have had him sent to prison if he wished. He refrained from doing so, and my suggestion is that the price of his forbearance was –'

But Mrs Matheson was crying.

'Oh, what's the good of pretending any longer!' she sobbed. 'Yes, it's true! I never loved that beast – I hated him – hated him! But when he came to me and said that for my sake he'd let Hilary go, what was there to do? He knew there was nothing I wouldn't do rather than let them take him to prison. And I never dreamed how awful it would be! I told him that I couldn't go on with it, and then he threatened to tell my husband. He'd have done it, too, just for the fun of the thing. He knew how I hated him all the time and that was what he really enjoyed – seeing me suffer. That was the kind of man he was.' She dabbed her eyes, blew her nose, and added in a calmer tone: 'It's been a bit of a nightmare, the last two years, really.'

'How was it,' asked Mallett, 'that you never asked your husband for help – in your brother's affairs, I mean?'

She shook her head.

'I couldn't,' she said. 'I'd tried once before, when he was in trouble, but it was no good. My husband was always very unfair to Hilary. He won't even let me see him now. You see, Hilary once did something rather stupid about one of Robert's cheques, and he is fearfully strict about that sort of thing.'

She fumbled in her bag for a powder-puff, and going to the mirror over the fireplace, began to powder her face with a hand that trembled. Then, turning to the inspector, she said in a voice surprisingly calm: 'That's all. And now will you please, *please* go away?'

But Mallett had not yet finished with an interview that had begun to be almost as painful to him as it was to her.

'There is still another question I must ask you,' he said, in his gentlest tones.

'Oh God!' she cried impatiently. 'Haven't I told you enough? What else is there to tell? Go away, I say!'

But the inspector stood his ground.

'You have told me so much that in your own interests I must give you an opportunity of explaining one other thing,' he said. 'You said to the police at Didford that on Saturday you spent the afternoon at Didbury Camp and went straight home from there by the downs. I have reason to think that that is untrue, and that in fact you were seen in the lane, close to the road corner, a few minutes after Sir Peter's body was found. From what I now know –'

She interrupted him.

'Do you think that if I had had the courage to kill that man, I shouldn't have done it months before?' she said, a terrible bitterness in her voice.

'Then you do admit that you were there?' he persisted.

'Oh, yes, yes, I suppose so,' she said wearily. 'What does it matter? If you say so, I was.'

'How did you come to be there?'

She gave him a long look before replying.

'I had just got out of Dr Latymer's car.'

It needed all Mallett's training to conceal the surprise which he felt.

'Dr Latymer's car?' he repeated.

'Yes, I got out of it when I heard him tell Mr Rendel to drive down to the village in it. I think he was speaking specially loudly on purpose for me to hear.'

Mallett reflected for a moment before he spoke again.

'We know something of the movements of that car,' he said. 'Dr Latymer had only driven up in it a short while before. Were you in it with him then?'

'Yes – no, I mean,' she corrected herself hurriedly. 'I have said already, I was on the downs all day. I don't know anything about where the car had been.'

'Do you mean that you found the car there when you came down from the hill, and got into it?'

'Yes, that's exactly what I do mean.'

'Why did you get into it, then?'

'Dr Latymer asked me to. I had just come down into the road when I met him. He was getting out of his car in the gateway at the corner. He asked me to wait for him while he went to see a patient at the cottage, and then he was going to drive me home. That is all.' She contrived to smile. 'There's nothing in it, really, you see, Inspector.'

'But I still don't understand why you left the car as soon as Mr Rendel came along.'

'I just didn't particularly care to be seen with Dr Latymer at that moment, that's why.'

'Was that because you were afraid of your husband getting to know?'

'That's enough about my husband!' she exclaimed in a sudden fury, and before Mallett could speak again, had pushed past him and run from the room.

A moment later Mallett left the house. Upstairs in her bedroom Euphemia was crying once more, while Barber had the malicious pleasure of telling Mr Sneyd, when he called shortly afterwards, that his sister would not, after all, be able to see him that afternoon.

CHAPTER TWENTY-ONE

Conference at Crabhampton

ON Thursday morning Mallett returned to Didford Parva. He was met at the station by White.

'Glad to see you back, Inspector,' said the latter. 'Was your trip to London a success?'

'It was quite useful,' Mallett admitted. 'Now the next thing I want to do –'

'It isn't what you want that matters,' said the superintendent with a grin. 'The next thing you're to do is to come along to headquarters at Crabhampton. The Chief has called a conference.'

'What for?' asked Mallett.

'Just an idea of his.'

'And who are to be there?'

'Just you and me and him – and Dr Latymer wants to be there, too, I think. I hope you don't object to that?'

'On the contrary,' said the inspector, tugging thoughtfully at his moustache. 'Quite the contrary, in fact. I shall be very glad to meet him. But why Crabhampton, White? Why not here? It's much handier for all concerned.'

'Orders is orders,' White answered, in a resigned tone. 'As you'll find out pretty soon when you've known the Chief a bit longer. Conferences happen at headquarters in Crabhampton. Don't ask me why. It's just a notion he's got. I reckon he gets some sort of a kick out of calling people from all over the county to his office, when it would be much less trouble to everyone if he went to see them himself. He said something to me once about a prophet and a mountain, but I never could make out what he was after.'

'What time are we due there?'

'Eleven-thirty sharp. We shall have to hurry if we're not to be late.'

The two men climbed into the waiting police car.

'I had almost forgotten,' said Mallett, as they were about to drive off. 'I want to stop at the chemist's on the way. Where is it?'

'There's old Wood's shop on the Magna road,' the superintendent told him. 'and a branch of Sandal's in the High Street. Sandal's is the best, I think. Wood is getting very out of date.'

'I think Wood sounds more likely to have what I want, all the same. We'll stop there, if you don't mind. We can always go back to Sandal's if necessary.'

Somewhat surprised, the superintendent gave the order to the driver, and the car passed the ornate plate glass windows of the great multiple chemist, to stop farther on outside a little old-fashioned shop, with three coloured jars displayed behind its small square panes. Mallett went in, and emerged after a few minutes carrying a small package.

'Right first time,' he announced in a satisfied tone.

White lifted his eyebrows but said nothing as they drove away. After they had gone a mile, he turned to the inspector and said: 'Anything important?'

'I don't know. Probably not. It's just a little hole that wants stopping.'

'Sounds as if it was a dentist you were needing, instead of a chemist,' White observed. Then, as the other still remained obstinately uncommunicative, he could not prevent himself from asking: 'What exactly is in that parcel?'

'I've no idea,' said Mallett happily. 'It feels like a bottle, but I haven't opened it yet.'

After that, there were no more words spoken between them until they reached Crabhampton.

Having summoned his conference with all due pomp and ceremony, Major Strode, it was soon apparent, was somewhat at a loss as to what form the proceedings should take. He sat impressively behind his massive flat-topped desk and glared across it at White and Mallett, perched on rather uncomfortable chairs opposite him. Dr Latymer, sitting on the end of a sofa to one side of the desk, seemed like an interested but detached spectator in the wings.

'Well!' said Major Strode, in an important voice. 'Well, we are all here, I think.' There being no answer to this statement, he cleared his throat and continued: 'Just so! I thought it would be useful to get together and see how we stand over this affair. Time's getting on, you know, and scent's getting cold. No use lifting hounds at a check unnecessarily – likely to do more harm than good, I know that – but all the same, I mean, where are we?'

There was a pause. Dr Latymer looked at the major with

a quizzical expression of almost professional interest, the major looked at the superintendent, the superintendent looked at the inspector and the inspector gazed thoughtfully at the ceiling. Someone had to break the silence, and in the end it was Mallett who did so.

'I have been in London,' he said quietly, almost apologetically, 'since I last saw you, sir. I have interviewed there Mr Rendel, Mr Smithers, and Mrs Matheson.'

'*Mrs* Matheson?' said Strode in surprise.

'Yes, sir.'

'I should have thought ... However, you know your own business best, I suppose. Carry on, Inspector.'

'I will, sir.'

'I mean – dash it – haven't you anything to tell us now? Isn't there anything we can do here, now?'

'Yes, sir, I think there is. That is, if Dr Latymer doesn't mind answering a few questions.'

'Dr Latymer? Humph! Ha!' said Strode, while the doctor said smoothly: 'Of course I don't mind. I take it that that is what I am here for.'

'Very well. Then first I should like to know where you were going in your car about half past twelve on Saturday.'

'That is very easily answered. I wasn't.'

'Wasn't what?' snapped the major.

'Wasn't in my car at half past twelve on Saturday. In point of fact I was never in my car at all between ten minutes to twelve and the time when I drove away in it to go to Parva for the post mortem.'

'Mrs Large tells me that she saw your car in the lane going towards Didford Magna just before twelve-thirty,' said Mallett.

Strode broke in before he could answer.

'Didn't you tell me that evening that you drove up to the road corner just before young Rendel got there?' he asked.

'To answer the second question first,' said the doctor equably, 'I never told you anything of the sort.'

'You did, sir! How dare you deny it?' said the major, turning an angry red.

'Pardon me, but I did not. You told me – and Superintendent White will bear me out – that you knew I had driven up
to the road corner just at that moment, and I did not contradict you. You will agree that that is quite a different thing.'

The chief constable rounded on White.

'What is all this nonsense?' he asked in a furious tone.

The superintendent, however, gave him no support.

'What the doctor says is correct, sir, I must admit,' he said
deprecatingly. 'So far as my recollection goes, the doctor told
us that he was at the road corner at five o'clock. You then – er
– suggested to him that he need not waste time on the point
because Mr Rendel had already told us that the car had driven
up about that moment.'

'Oh, I did, did I?'

'Yes, sir. But I am bound to add, that you went on to ask
the doctor if Mr Rendel's statement was correct, and he said
that it was.'

'There you are then! You were lying, Dr Latymer, or as
good as lying.'

'Well, well,' replied the doctor with an unperturbed smile,
'I will admit to a certain *suggestio falsi*, if you like. But after
all, Major, you put the words into my mouth and as I didn't
see – don't see now, in fact – that it mattered two straws what
I did with my car on Saturday afternoon, I concluded that it
was better not to waste your time correcting you. You were in
rather a hurry that evening, you may remember,' he added
maliciously.

'You tell me now that you didn't drive up to the road
corner at five o'clock?' said Strode.

'That precisely is what I am endeavouring to indicate.'

'How did you get there then?'

'At five o'clock? On my feet.'

'But young Rendel says –'

'Forgive me, Major, but I am not in the least concerned
with what young Rendel says or does not say.'

'Let me tell you,' shouted the major, 'that you are putting
yourself in a position of great danger in the way that you are

177

treating this matter – in a position of very great danger indeed! Here's a man found murdered –'

'That, at least, is not exactly news to me.'

'How dare you, sir!' Major Strode banged his fist with violence on the desk before him.

In the silence that followed this outburst, Mallett said quietly, 'If I might be allowed to make a suggestion, sir, I think it would help to clear matters up if Dr Latymer were to tell us exactly what his movements were on the day in question.'

'I should be delighted to do so,' said the doctor, without giving Strode time to reply. 'And in so doing, I shall be able to indicate why in my interview with our excellent chief constable the other day I exercised what one of our judges once happily described as a certain economy of truth. It was quite natural in the circumstances, though as I see now it has had unfortunate results.'

'Say what you've got to say and don't waste time,' grumbled Major Strode.

'You must allow me to say it in my own way, please. You will recollect the unfortunate consequences of trying to cut me short on the last occasion. But my story can be put quite succinctly, in its essentials at any rate. On Saturday morning, I left my house at Collington by car at approximately half past eleven. I drove to the spot which we have agreed to call the road corner, and left my car just off the road there at exactly ten minutes to twelve. I looked at my watch at the time, and you may take it that my watch was right. It always is. I returned to that place – and to my car – at round about five o'clock, when I climbed the gate into the path in order to visit a patient at the cottage. That was the precise moment when I met young Rendel.'

'But Rendel says he heard your car drive up,' the major objected.

'He may say so, but how anybody could hear anything, even a noisy old machine like mine, with that infernal sawmill functioning, I do not understand.'

'But Mrs Large saw you in the lane at half past twelve,' put in White.

'As to Mrs Large, she is a patient of mine, and I know her pretty well. She has excellent eyesight and a capacious memory. At the same time she has a very lively imagination.'

'You mean she's a liar,' said Strode.

'I mean nothing of the sort.'

'I think,' said Mallett, 'that what Dr Latymer means is that the lady, seeing a car which she recognized as his – and which nearly knocked her down, she tells me – not unnaturally jumped to the conclusion that the doctor was inside it.'

'You have hit it exactly.'

'So far as Mr Rendel was concerned, he may very well have heard a car being driven up and, seeing you immediately afterwards, have thought that you had driven up in it.'

'That had not occurred to me, but of course it is possible.'

'It might have been taken away from where you had left it, in your absence, and then returned to the same place without your seeing it just a moment or two before you came back from – where had you been all this time, Doctor?'

'You seem to have studied this matter very thoroughly. Where do you think I was?'

'I should say that you were somewhere in the neighbourhood of Didbury Camp,' said Mallett.

'Be careful!' exclaimed Strode. 'There you go, putting words into his mouth!'

'Quite right, Major,' returned Latymer. 'He is – and I was. Actually in the Camp, in fact, from twelve o'clock midday until I came down again to pay my very overdue call on my patient at the cottages.'

'So you say,' said Strode.

'So I say. And it will not perhaps surprise you to hear that for almost the whole of that time I was not alone. Inspector, you said just now that you interviewed Euphemia Matheson in London.'

'I did. But I must tell you that although Mrs Matheson also appears to have chosen to spend a good deal of Saturday on Didbury Camp, she did not mention having met you there.'

'That is just what I might have expected of Euphemia. Moreover, I have little doubt that she will continue to deny it, if pressed on the matter, for a number of excellent reasons of her own. It is unfortunate, but there it is.'

'You say that you met her at the Camp?' the inspector pursued.

'Yes. I was there at about 12.0 midday, and she arrived a quarter of an hour later.'

'Was that by appointment?'

'That is rather a difficult question to answer in one word. Let me put it this way – I was there in pursuance of an appointment which I had made, or thought I had made, with her. When she arrived, I discovered, to my deep disgust, that her appearance on the spot was pure coincidence, and had nothing to do with me at all. My disgust may be gauged from the fact that I had asked her to bring sandwiches for two, and in the result we had to share the supply she had intended for herself alone. And Euphemia,' added Dr Latymer regretfully, 'is a hearty eater.'

'I don't in the least understand what you were talking about,' grumbled the major.

'No? Well, in plain words, then. I wrote her a note on Friday evening at that dingy little pub at Didford Magna, asking her to meet me for a quiet chat on the downs next day. I handed it to her – somewhat ingeniously, I thought – along with a prescription which I had just prepared for that rather pathetic senile husband of hers. It turned out when I met her that the stupid creature had failed to understand my simple little ruse, and had handed over both documents without reading them to the chemist next morning. What sort of nostrum he compounded from them I can't imagine.'

'Perhaps I can settle that point,' said Mallett, fumbling in his pocket. He pulled out the small packet which he had brought from Wood's shop, and broke the seals that held it together. 'Would this be the medicine?' he asked, extending a small bottle of greenish fluid, labelled, '*The Mixture. To be taken three times a day after meals.*'

Latymer drew the cork and sniffed the contents.

'That seems right,' he observed. 'An ordinary little strychnine tonic, quite harmless and possibly even beneficial. Inspector, you are a positive conjurer! Have you any more white rabbits up your sleeve?'

'I have the prescription, at all events,' said Mallett, opening an envelope in his hands. 'And,' he added, 'there seems to be another document attached to it.'

He picked out two sheets of paper, pinned together, detached one of them, carefully smoothed out its creases and laid it on the desk in front of the chief constable.

'*I must have a talk with you. Meet me at the Camp tomorrow; noon, and we will have lunch together and clear up this ridiculous misunderstanding,*' read the major slowly. 'And it's signed: "*P.P.L.*".'

'Philip Pauncefort Latymer,' observed the doctor. 'I think that Euphemia is almost the only person alive to know the secret of my second name. Inspector, I am full of curiosity. How on earth did you lay your hand on this?'

'It was quite simple. Mrs Matheson's statement clearly says that she left the prescription at the chemist's to be made up. She never mentions anywhere that she went back for it. By way of checking up, I thought it desirable to call at the chemist's to substantiate the truth of that part of her story. That she had left your note along with the prescription was, of course, just a piece of luck.'

Latymer nodded appreciatively.

'Well, gentlemen,' he said, 'are you satisfied now? Is the mystery of my whereabouts sufficiently explained?'

'This note doesn't say anything about her bringing sandwiches for two,' Major Strode objected with great seriousness.

'Most excellent Major, it does not,' replied Latymer, who was by now in almost boisterous good humour. 'It does not, and thereby the whole of my carefully concocted story falls to the ground! I can see suspicion rising in your sleuth-like eye! But if –'

'I wish you wouldn't talk such nonsense,' said Strode curtly. 'I was only pointing out, what was perfectly obvious, that this *billy doo*, or whatever you like to call it' – the major spoke the word in a manner that showed a glorious contempt for the habits, morals, and pronunciation of foreign races – 'does not contain any reference to sandwiches. That's all.'

'And I was only going to say that if by some means – preferably torture – the charming Euphemia could be induced to speak the truth, it would be found that in all our *al fresco* meals together she had supplied the sandwiches and I the whisky. It was not, therefore, necessary to mention them in this – ah – *billy doo*.'

'Humph! Well, Inspector, I think that clears up that point pretty well. I think the only other question for Dr Latymer is precisely what he was doing all the afternoon at Didbury Camp with Mrs Matheson, eh?'

'Come, come!' said the doctor. 'And precisely what does one do all an afternoon with a pretty woman, at Didbury Camp or anywhere else?'

In the shocked silence with which the chief constable greeted this remark, White interposed: 'The question I should like to see answered, sir, is – who was driving the doctor's car when it nearly knocked into the Rector's wife? When we've answered that, we shall know a whole lot about this case, or so it seems to me.'

'I agree,' said Mallett. 'And it's a question that I hope to answer in a very short time.'

'Glad to hear it,' said Strode. 'Well, this conference has certainly helped in clearing the air a little. Dr Latymer, you've behaved very badly – very badly indeed. I wonder you have the face to show yourself here at all. I really do.'

'As the meeting seems to be about to break up,' said Latymer, quite unabashed, 'perhaps it would be as well to remind you that I came to it to give some information to the inspector – information, I mean, apart from the sordid story of my amours which has so unexpectedly occupied us.'

'God bless my soul! I quite forgot!' exclaimed Strode,

dropping back into the chair from which he had half-risen. 'Dr Latymer, gentlemen, has something further to tell us – though what else he can have to confess, I've no idea.'

'Don't be alarmed,' said the doctor. 'There are no more skeletons in my cupboard. Dropping the role of suspect which I have been unwittingly supporting all this time, I want to say a few words in my proper character of a medical man. When you first came on the scene, Superintendent, I am afraid I disappointed you by my vagueness in answering your very natural question as to the approximate time at which the deceased had died. Quite frankly, murder is not in my line – this county has been laudably deficient in homicides lately – and I was only able to give a very rough guess. Since then, however, I have had the opportunity of consulting the latest works on forensic medicine and talking the matter over with some of my colleagues. I have gone over the evidence again in my mind, and I think I am now in a position to answer the question fairly accurately – within limits, of course.'

'And the answer is?' said Mallett eagerly.

'In my opinion, Sir Peter must have been dead for from three to five hours at the time he was found.'

'I am very much obliged,' said Mallett. 'That is obviously of great importance.'

The meeting broke up. Latymer left the room first, the superintendent followed him, and Mallett came behind. In the passage outside, White suddenly felt a hand gripping his shoulder. He turned round to see the inspector, looking, for him, unusually excited, and even agitated.

'What's up?' asked White.

'Good Lord!' Mallett said softly. 'Good Lord ' His strong fingers dug deeply into the other's flesh. 'I clean forgot! What an ass I've been, Super! What a kettle-rendered, double-distilled ass! Why, it's as plain as – Here, wait a minute!'

He hurried back into the chief constable's room. Major Strode, who had barely had time to remove his feet from the top of his desk at the sound of Mallett's entrance, and no time at all to conceal the newspaper which he had opened at the sporting page as soon as he found himself alone, regarded him sourly.

'What is it now?' he asked.

'I am sorry to trouble you again, sir,' said Mallett, 'but I shall be going back to Didford Magna this afternoon, and I wondered whether you could let me have a revolver to take with me.'

'A how much?'

'A revolver, sir.'

'What on earth for? You don't imagine there's any danger, do you?'

'Not at all, sir. It's just a little experiment I wanted to try there, that's all.'

'An experiment – ha! I don't know what you're talking about. I don't like experiments with firearms – they're too dangerous.'

'It's not a dangerous experiment at all, sir,' said the inspector mildly. 'It's only – only that I *should* like the loan of a revolver for this afternoon, sir.' He might have been a small boy begging for a second helping of cake.

'Well, I suppose you know your own business best,' said Major Strode in a tone that indicated that he did not really think so for a moment. He pulled open a drawer of his desk. 'I've got a little automatic here. Will that do?'

'That will suit me excellently, sir. Thank you.'

'Don't go shooting anybody with it, that's all. Good day. Oh, Inspector?'

'Sir?'

'When do you think you will be in a position to make an arrest in this case?'

'Will tomorrow suit you, sir? Or the next day?'

'Dammit, Inspector, don't laugh at me!' stormed the major. But when he looked at Mallett's face he saw that he was perfectly serious.

CHAPTER TWENTY-TWO

At the 'Tump' Again

AFTER lunch, White and Mallett drove back the way they had come. At the crossroads where the 'new road' to Didford Parva diverged from the old road through Didford Magna, they took the latter. Stopping the car at the road corner, they alighted. The sawmill was deserted. Since the death of the man responsible for it, it had ceased its assaults on the quiet of the river valley. The two men conferred together for a while, and then White made his way to the mill. Mallett waited until he had had time to get into position and then walked quickly up the river bank and round the bend to the little grassy knoll where the body of Sir Peter had been found. Save for a water-rat, which dived into the stream at the sound of his approach, the place was deserted.

From his pocket the inspector pulled the pistol which the chief constable had lent him. Pointing its muzzle a few inches from the green turf of the "tump", he pulled the trigger. After a pause, he stepped back a few paces, and fired again, in the same direction. Then after a similar pause he fired once more, this time into the air. After the third shot, he opened the weapon, unloaded the cartridges that remained, and put it back into his pocket. This done, he sat down on the 'tump' and lit a pipe.

'What are you doing here?' said a woman's voice.

The inspector started to his feet, and his pipe nearly dropped from his mouth. Marian Packer had come quietly round the bend in the bank and now stood before him, annoyance and anxiety in her face.

'Upon my word,' said Mallett, 'but that's what I should like to ask you!'

'I have a right to be here, I suppose?'

'Yes – of course. I only meant I did not expect you to be here.'

'Somebody was shooting – I came to see what it was.'

'I was responsible for that. You heard it?'

'Of course. I was in the cottage, visiting the man who was injured. I don't understand. Why –'

The superintendent came into view.

'Three shots,' he said. 'I heard them all distinctly.' Then, catching sight of Marian, he exclaimed: 'Oh! I didn't know –'

'Neither did I,' said Mallett. 'Lady Packer was in the cottage, and came out because she heard them. I think that proves my point even better than I hoped.'

'Of course,' said White, 'we can't be sure that it was the same kind of gun.'

'Lady Packer,' said the inspector, 'I wish you could tell me, just what sort of pistol was your husband's?'

He drew from his pocket, as he spoke, the pistol which he had just used, and held it so that she could see it. Marian's eyes grew wide with fear and surprise.

'Why,' she exclaimed, 'but that *is* my husband's pistol!'

'Come, come!' said Mallett. 'We have to be careful in these things, you know. Just take it, Lady Packer, and look at it carefully. Was there any particular mark on your husband's pistol which you recognize?'

Very gingerly, with the tips of her fingers, she took the weapon from where it lay in the inspector's palm. She glanced at it hastily, turned it over once or twice and then returned it.

'No,' she said. 'There were no particular marks that I know of. I only meant that it was just the same size and shape as this one – that's all. It was silly of me to say what I did. I couldn't be in the least sure, really, whether it is the same or not.'

'Did you ever examine your husband's pistol at all closely?'

'No, never.'

'But you had seen it, more than once?'

'Oh, yes.' She raised her chin, and added in a low, clear voice: 'He had threatened me with it once or twice.'

'Well,' said Mallett in an unexpectedly loud and hearty voice, as if to demonstrate that the point was definitely and finally disposed of, 'I think that that answers your objection,

Super. We have got the right type of pistol, so we have reproduced the conditions as far as possible. Are you going back to Parva now?'

'Yes. There's plenty for me to do there.'

'I'll find my own way back. The walk will do me good. Till tomorrow, then!'

White walked away in the direction of the road. Turning round, Mallett was just in time to see Marian disappearing in the opposite direction. He walked after her and came up with her at the head of the causeway.

'Can you spare me a few minutes?' he said.

She made a gesture of helplessness.

'What do you want?' she asked wearily.

'Only to ask a few questions. I had intended to call at your house this afternoon, but if you can spare the time now, this is perhaps as good a place as any. The best place, perhaps, for what I have to say.'

She walked on for a few paces in silence, then stopped at a rough little seat which the fishing syndicate had set up on the bank, and sat down.

'Go on,' she said.

The inspector stood in front of her, hesitating for a moment how to begin. There was something daunting in her frozen immobility.

'Please sit down,' she said with a sudden smile. 'There is room for us both.'

And sitting side by side with her on the verge of the quiet stream, Mallett began his questions.

'You gave Major Strode some account of your movements on Saturday afternoon,' he began.

'Yes. I repeated it afterwards to the other officer who was here just now.'

'We have some reason to think that your account was not quite complete.'

She remained silent for a moment, her gaze bent upon the river. Then raising her eyes to his, she said: 'Yes?'

'Dr Latymer tells us that –'

187

'Oh, Dr Latymer!' she interrupted him quickly. 'How foolish of me to have forgotten him! I might have known that he must have seen ... Tell me, is this going to go very hard with Jimmy – with Mr Rendel, I mean?'

The inspector did not answer her question.

'Do I understand that you now agree that your statement was not the whole truth?' he said.

She nodded.

'Lady Packer,' Mallett went on earnestly, 'in your own interests, as well as those of – of other people, I must beg you now to tell me everything that happened.'

'Everything? About – about Jimmy, do you mean?'

'I said everything, and I meant everything,' said Mallett impatiently. 'In as much detail as you can remember.'

She smiled. 'Oh, I can remember all the details! One isn't likely to forget! There wasn't so very much that was untrue in what I told Major Strode. Where shall I begin?'

'You told Major Strode,' he reminded her, 'that you had walked down from the house to the river.'

'That is quite true. I came down that path behind us – but I will show you.'

She rose and went to the point where the path joined the bank.

'I could see from here that my husband was not at the mill,' she explained. 'Then I went on down the bank to about this point.' She stopped a yard or two beyond the end of the causeway. 'You see, Inspector, it is impossible to see from here round the corner to where – where he was. I went no farther. Inspector, you believe that, don't you? You must believe that!'

'I do not believe it,' said Mallett quietly. 'Do you notice that stick in the ground near where you are standing? That marks the farthest spot from which it was possible to see your husband as he lay. You are a good two feet beyond it. What have you to say to that, Lady Packer?'

She stared at him miserably, her large eyes filling with tears.

'I – I – I – ' she said, and then the sobs began.

Mallett, without a word, went to her, and, putting his arm in hers, helped her back to the seat. Presently her tears ceased and she began to speak again.

'I have tried to tell the truth,' she said.

'Suppose you try again,' suggested the inspector drily.

'But when the truth's so horrible! Listen, Inspector. I was speaking truthfully when I said just now that I went no farther. It – it was because I knew that my husband was there that I stopped.'

'Yes?'

'I could only see the tips of his shoes – '

'Of course,' murmured Mallett, 'the superintendent is a taller man. I had forgotten.'

'What are you saying?'

'Nothing. Go on.'

'I knew that he was prone to an attack of sunstroke. I thought that he had had another. I – I wanted him to die. So I came away. If you knew what my life had been, you wouldn't condemn me. Can you understand?'

Mallett made no answer. She went on:

'Just then, someone came quickly up the causeway and nearly ran into me. It was Mr Rendel. He – do you want to know what he looked like, Inspector?'

'You had better tell me.'

'He seemed flushed and angry about something. At first he hardly seemed to know who I was. We walked together upstream to near where you are standing now – talking. Then, as we stood there, the mill was started up and it was almost impossible to say anything. But I thought I heard someone calling – I thought for a moment it might be my husband – '

'Did he hear it?'

'No, he thought I was startled because a bird flew past at that moment.'

'Did a bird fly past, in fact?'

'Oh, yes. A wild duck. It got up out of the water near the bank below there and came close to us. A moment later we both heard the voice. It was Dr Latymer calling Mr Rendel's name. I stayed where I was while he went back. The doctor came round the corner, and when the mill had quieted down for a moment, I heard him say: "Sir Peter is dead." Then I turned round and came home.'

'Why?' asked the inspector.

'I didn't want anybody to see how happy I was.'

It was impossible to doubt the tragic sincerity with which she spoke these words.

After a long silence she added: 'You must remember, Inspector, that he said: "Sir Peter is dead," not: "He has been murdered." I never guessed the truth until Major Strode told me.'

Mallett seemed suddenly to have lost interest in her narrative.

'Quite,' he said absently, kicking at the grass with his toe. Then he roused himself abruptly, and taking off his hat, extended his hand to her.

'Good-bye, Lady Packer,' he said. 'And thank you for your assistance. I must tell you that it is a great pity for all concerned that you were not more frank in the first place.'

'There is one question that you have not asked me,' she said.

'What is that?'

'I should like to explain why I said what I did in the first place.'

'As you say, I haven't asked you that – perhaps because I know the answer. I think it is a matter which you and Mr Rendel can best settle between yourselves. He tells me that he is to be here this week-end.'

Without more, he turned away and walked down the causeway. Marian Packer watched his broad back recede into the distance, anxiety and bewilderment upon her face.

Arrived at the end of the causeway, the inspector was surprised to see that White had not after all gone back to Didford Parva. He was standing by the gate that led into the road, in earnest conversation with a black-browed, middle-aged man, dressed as for fishing.

'This is Inspector Mallett of Scotland Yard,' said White to the newcomer. 'This gentleman, Inspector, is Mr Wrigley-Bell. You will remember his name, no doubt. We happened to meet here just as I was leaving, and in view of the statement which the lad Carter made to us the other day, I thought it was a good opportunity to put a few questions to him. Mr Wrigley-Bell now tells me that he would like to make some alterations to the story he told me last Saturday – quite considerable alterations, in fact.'

Mallett could not but smile. Everybody seemed to be amending their statements that day!

'I have the new statement here in my book,' the superintendent went on, 'and Mr Wrigley-Bell has signed it.'

He held out his note-book to Mallett, who put it in his pocket without looking at it.

'Where are you fishing today?' asked the inspector suddenly, turning to Wrigley-Bell.

'Beat four,' was the reply. 'The top beat of all.'

For a man who had just endured a cross-examination, and been compelled to confess to having told several untruths in a serious matter, he seemed unexpectedly at ease. While the detectives were talking he had been engaged in selecting a fly from his case and tying it on to a cast, and Mallett had observed that his fingers did not once tremble during the delicate operation.

'I wish you luck,' sad the inspector amiably. 'You are certainly luckier than most people, in being able to take a holiday in the middle of the week.'

Wrigley-Bell frowned expressively.

'It is not my usual habit,' he protested. 'Indeed, Inspector, I should say that few men have worked harder or taken shorter holidays than I. But it so happens that I am at leisure at the present moment.'

'Indeed? I thought your appointment continued until the first of January next?'

'It did,' answered Wrigley-Bell with a grimace, 'it did. But my directors were good enough to allow me to anticipate the time by a few months, and as I do not take up my new position until the beginning of July –'

'You have a new position, then?'

'Oh, certainly, certainly.'

'Might I know what it is?'

'By all means. I have been appointed managing director of Packer's, Limited. You see, the sudden death of Sir Peter left matters in a somewhat confused state there, and the board felt that it was advisable to select a strong man from outside with a thorough experience of the trade. And I think,' said Mr Wrigley-Bell modestly, 'that I answered the description.'

'You seem to have come out of this affair very well,' observed Mallett.

Wrigley-Bell smirked in a self-satisfied way.

'Matters have certainly turned out better than I could have hoped,' he said. 'And now, if you will excuse me, but the afternoon is getting on –'

'I hope that you won't leave your fly in a fish this time,' said Mallett, stepping aside to let him pass.

'Yes, indeed! That was shocking bad luck! You are a fisherman too, I suppose, Inspector?'

'Not exactly, but I'm interested. Where exactly did the fish lie that did the damage?'

'I can show you.' Wrigley-Bell led him to the bank. 'Here is the place,' he said, indicating a point just below the elbow formed by the road corner. 'He rose between the bank and that reed there sticking up in the water. A very tricky place to cover. I hope I'll get him yet.'

'You think the fish is still there, then?'

'Certain to be,' said Wrigley-Bell with confidence. 'These big fish don't often shift their position. I'm prepared to bet that he's still there.'

'You lost your last fishing bet, didn't you, Mr Wrigley-Bell?'

'That's true,' said the other with an ugly grin, and then, as if the recollection was painful to him, walked quickly away.

'Super,' said Mallett, 'I think I'll change my mind about walking home. I feel I need my tea, so I'll take a lift back with you. I don't know what you think, but I'm quite sorry for the board of Packer's, Limited.'

CHAPTER TWENTY-THREE

Setting the Stage

THE superintendent called early next morning at the 'Polworthy Arms'. He found Mallett taking his ease in the parlour after breakfast, his feet on the mantelpiece, his pipe in his mouth, deeply absorbed in a crossword puzzle. It was the first time that he had ever seen his colleague engaged on any occupation other than the matter that had brought him to Didford, and his face showed his surprise and disapproval clearly enough. But Mallett was in no way abashed.

'Good morning,' he said cheerfully. 'Have you seen this one, Super?'

'I have not,' said White severely. 'I hardly ever look at the things.'

'It's wonderful what these fellows think of,' the inspector went on. 'Just listen to this: "Did Hamlet think they had only hash?" Five letters, beginning with T. Can you imagine what that is?'

'No, I can't. And if you ask me, these puzzles are no more than a sinful waste of time.'

'Got it!' cried Mallett triumphantly. 'You've given me the word, Super. "Times." D'you see? "The times are out of joint." That's why they only had hash! Now I call that ingenious.'

Superintendent White was a mild-mannered man, but for once he came near to losing his temper.

'I thought you came down here to solve a case of murder and not a blasted newspaper puzzle,' he said roughly.

But the inspector only grinned at him.

'I did, Super, I did,' he admitted. 'But all the same, I can tell you these puzzles are a rare refreshment to a man's mind when he's finished his work.'

'When he's *finished* his work – I dare say!' said the superintendent with heavy irony.

'When he's finished, I said, and meant. And that, Super, is why you find me doing a crossword puzzle this morning.'

White sat down at the table and looked hard at Mallett.

'Now what exactly,' he said, 'might you be getting at?'

Before answering, Mallett rose and went to the door. He opened it, looked out, closed it and returned.

'We shan't be disturbed,' White reassured him. 'There's nobody about. As for Wrigley-Bell, I saw him just now going down to the ford with his fishing-rod.'

'Did you? He brought home two beauties last night. I had part of one of them for breakfast, but it wasn't a patch on the one you gave me on Tuesday at Parva. I dare say it wasn't cooked right. Tell me, d'you think they're better boiled or grilled?'

The superintendent groaned.

'You and your stomach!' he said. 'Dang it, Inspector, won't you talk some sense for once?'

'Right,' answered Mallett, 'I will.'

He pulled another chair to the table and reached for the case in which his papers were kept. From it he extracted a large sheet in his own handwriting, which he handed to White.

'A time-table,' he explained. 'Just look at it carefully, Super. Some of the times are only approximate, and for a good many of them we only have the word of the particular witness involved, but I think all the same it tells us a lot.'

White read:

10.15. a.m. Smithers leaves the inn on foot to go to beat four.
A little before 11.0. Sir Peter leaves the Manor to go to the road corner.
Approximately 11.0. Smithers meets Sir Peter at the road corner.
About the same time. Wrigley-Bell leaves the inn by car to go to beat three.

Shortly after 11.0. Mrs Matheson leaves the inn on foot to walk on the downs.

11.10. (about). Wrigley-Bell arrives at the road corner. (N.B. Smithers has by this time finished his argument with Sir Peter and walked on.)

11.15 (about). Matheson leaves the inn on foot to fish beat one.

11.50. Latymer leaves his car at the road corner.

12.0 noon. Latymer reaches the top of Didbury Camp.

Between 12.0 and 12.20 p.m. Wrigley-Bell helps Smithers to land a fish on beat four.

12.15 (about). Mrs Matheson reaches the top of Didbury Camp and meets Latymer there.

12.30 p.m. Mrs Large sees Latymer's car in the lane.

Nearly 3.0 p.m. Rendel arrives at the hotel.

Some time between 3.15 and 4.0. Rendel meets Matheson on beat one and they walk together to the bottom of beat two.

After 4.0. Mrs Large arrives at the farm bridge, sees somebody at the Camp, and meets Rendel.

4.30 (about). Lady Packer finds that Sir Peter has not come in to tea, and goes out to look for him, say at 4.45.

Shortly before 5.0. Rendel finds Sir Peter on the bank.

Just before 5.0. Latymer's car is driven up to the road corner.

About 5.0. Latymer and Mrs Matheson come down to the road from the Camp. Mrs Matheson gets into the car and Latymer meets Rendel at the bottom of the causeway.

Just after 5.0. Rendel meets Lady Packer at the top of the causeway.

At almost the same time. Latymer finds Sir Peter's body.

The superintendent studied the documents for a long time in silence.

'Well,' Mallett asked: 'What do you make of it?'

'The first thing that strikes me,' was the reply, 'is that there's a very big gap in it – from 12.30 to 3.0, in fact.'

'That true, but it's not so serious as it looks at first sight. We know that Wrigley-Bell and Smithers were lunching together at the top of the water during most of that time, Matheson was seen by the landlady here on beat one at intervals between 12.45 and 2.30, Mrs Matheson and the doctor were at the Camp together and Lady Packer didn't leave the Manor till tea-time.'

'In any case,' said the superintendent, 'from what the doctor now tells us, we needn't bother much about what happened after 2.0, since Sir Peter must have been dead by then.'

'Agreed. But all the same, Super, you are right in saying that there is something missing from our table.'

'You mean Phil Carter's movements?'

'As to Carter, his times coincide with Smithers' and Wrigley-Bell's. I'm not worrying about *him*. No, there's something else which we've left out. Something important.'

'And that is – ?'

Mallett told him.

'But I don't see what that's got to do with it.'

'Don't you? Well, this is how I look at this case – '

And then the inspector began to talk in good earnest. For something over half an hour he spoke, emphasizing a point now and then by reference to one or other of his documents. During that time, White did not once interrupt him, and even when the recital had ended, he sat for some time in silence.

'Well?' said Mallett. 'Am I right?'

'Well!' said the superintendent. He pressed his iron-grey hair yet closer to his skull. 'This takes a bit of thinking about!'

'Am I right?' repeated the inspector inexorably.

'It doesn't hardly seem possible!'

'Am I right?'

'Well – '

'Or have you any other explanation that fits in with the facts?'

'No,' the superintendent admitted, 'I haven't. But all the same,' he added, 'it isn't exactly what I was expecting.'

Mallett smiled. 'Well, after all, if it had been, it would hardly have been worth while calling me in, would it?'

After a pause, White said: 'And what do we do next? This looks like a case for another conference.'

The inspector shook his head.

'I'm not ready for that yet,' he said. 'There's still one little missing link in this case, and I can't supply that before this evening. You must ask the chief to come over here after his dinner. Remind him of my promise to him yesterday, and he'll come quick enough.'

'And meanwhile?'

'Meanwhile – I'm going to try and finish this crossword puzzle.'

The mid-week quiet of the 'Polworthy Arms' was at an end. Wrigley-Bell came in from the home beat for a hasty lunch and went out again. During the afternoon the Mathesons first, and then Smithers arrived by car, and picked up their fishing gear and departed to their respective beats. It was Matheson's turn to fish the top of the water, and his wife went with him, contrary to her usual custom. She seemed to Mallett, watching unobserved from his bedroom window, more attentive than ever to her husband. Jimmy Rendel was the last to arrive. Having no car of his own, he drove up in the station cab, and kept it waiting while he changed. He was just pulling on a disreputable pair of patched plus-fours when the inspector walked into his room.

'Good evening!' he said. 'Where are you fishing today?'

'Beat three,' answered Jimmy, hopping on one leg. 'I've got the car waiting to take me up to the road corner, and – '

'And you're in a hurry, I suppose. Well, I won't keep you. What flies are you going to use?'

'Can't tell that until you see what's on the water. The guv'nor – Mr Matheson – wants me to try a new invention of his, a Coachman tied a new way. It ought to be useful for the evening rise.'

'Would this be any good to you?' Mallett asked.

Jimmy looked in surprise at what Mallett held out to him.

'Hullo! Where did you get that?' he asked.

'Have you seen it before?'

'Yes, it's — No it isn't, though. It's rather like, but it's not the same.'

'Not the same as what?'

'I was going to say, the same fly which the guv'nor caught that foul-hooked fish on. But it isn't.'

Mallett put away the Hackle Blue and produced the Caveat Emptor.

'And this?' he asked.

'That is the fly,' said Jimmy positively.

'Certain?'

'Absolutely certain. I say, do you think you could let me have it this evening? I should be awfully grateful.'

'I'm afraid not. You'll have to do the best you can with Mr Matheson's Coachman. Now I won't keep you any longer. Good-bye, and – what is it fishermen say? – tight lines!'

Apart from a telephone call which he put through in the course of the afternoon, Mallett did nothing worthy of note until late that evening. Time hung heavy on his hands. He was conscious of a feeling of suppressed excitement which was unusual to him. For all the indifference which he had assumed before White, he felt in reality intensely anxious, not on the score of the accuracy of his own reasoning – he was entirely confident that he was right in his reading of the case – but as to his ability to carry conviction of his rightness in the proper quarter. But it was too late now to change his arrangements. He had decided on his plan of action and must carry it through as best he could. There was considerable comfort in feeling that he had made an irrevocable decision.

About half past nine, Major Strode arrived at the inn. He sailed into the parlour with the purposeful air of a warship with its decks cleared for action. The superintendent was with him.

'White has just told me a very extraordinary story,' he said.

'It is an extraordinary story, sir,' Mallett admitted. 'But I am prepared to stake my reputation that it is true.'

'Humph! Well, it's your responsibility, you know, Inspector.'

'Forgive me, sir, but as the chief officer of police in this county, you are responsible. If you are in any way dissatisfied with me, I must, of course, retire from the case.'

'No, no, hang it, Inspector, I didn't mean that! I mean, I'm giving you a free hand, that's all. Now the only question is, how do we act now?'

'The first thing to do, I think, sir, is to leave this room. The fishing people will start coming in at any time now. I have asked the landlady to let us have the use of her room for the evening.'

In the little room behind the bar Mallett explained what he intended to do. As he had expected, the chief constable raised objections.

'It all seems to me very melodramatic,' he grumbled.

'I'm afraid it is,' said Mallett apologetically. 'I don't care for melodrama myself. I only suggest it because I feel that it is the best way of arriving at the truth. And now, sir, it seems that there is nothing for us to do but wait until everybody is assembled in the parlour. I will ask Superintendent White to keep observation and let us know when it is time to act.'

A lady's bicycle of antique design was slowly ascending the rise from the road corner in the direction of Crabhampton. It stopped at the lodge gates of the Manor, which had been kept closed ever since the day of Sir Peter's death. The lodge-keeper, as soon as he recognized the rider, made haste to let it through, and it passed quickly round the curve of the drive to the entrance of the house. Gibbs, who opened the door, was made of sterner stuff than his colleague, and told the visitor respectfully but inexorably that his mistress was at home to no one. Having delivered this pronouncement with all the melancholy dignity that only a butler in a house of mourning can command, he was preparing to close the door when he found that the intruder had already slipped past him and was marching with purposeful footsteps to the drawing-room. Only by the utmost agility was he able to prevent the disaster of allowing her to walk in unannounced. As it was, by the time he had reached the door it was too late to do more than regularize the position as best he could. He flung it open just in advance of the invader, and in a tone which he strove to make as deprecatory as possible exclaimed: 'Mrs Large, my lady!' before flying to the butler's pantry for restoratives.

Marian Packer looked up in astonishment from the book which she had been holding open at the same two pages for the last hour, and opened her mouth to protest. But Mrs Large was too quick for her.

'How de do, dear?' she said, and the next moment Marian found herself being kissed with a clumsiness that seemed to show that the giver of the kiss was not used to endearments, but with a warmth that was quite unmistakable.

'I've come up,' Mrs Large went on, somewhat unnecessarily. 'That Gibbs of yours tried to stop me, but I've come. I dare say it's the Rector's place to comfort the sorrowful, but you and I know, dear, how much good the Rector is. Besides, it's another woman you want. I can't bear to think of you all alone here. Why on earth didn't you go and stay with your cousins when they asked you to?'

'But who told you that my cousins had asked me to stay?' Marian managed to get out.

'Mrs Jenkinson at the post office, of course! That woman is a perfect gas-bag – she oughtn't to be where she is! But what can you expect when people will send telegrams in a country place? It's a funny thing,' said Mrs Large reminiscently, 'but sudden deaths and telegrams always seem to go together. I remember it was just the same when my father died. (That was a weak heart – though none of his children inherited it, thank goodness!) It must have been quite a boon to the post office, all the telegrams that kept coming. There weren't so many telephones in those days, though, so there was some excuse.'

She drew breath for a moment, and Marian had the opportunity to say: 'It's very, *very* kind of you to come, Mrs Large, but really – '

'But really it's a dreadful hour of the night to be coming to see anyone, you were going to say,' Mrs Large finished for her. 'Fiddlesticks, my dear! You're not going to get past me with that! If I'd come here at midnight, I shouldn't have

found you in bed, and if I had it would have made no difference. Why, you haven't had so much as a wink of sleep the
last three nights, to my knowledge!'

'But my dear Mrs Large, how could you possibly have told
that?' Marian asked in bewilderment.

'Because I can see your windows from my bedroom at the
Rectory, of course. That's what comes of living on the top
of a hill. There's something about that in the Bible, isn't
there?'

'You mean that you've been waking and watching every
night to see if I – But Mrs Large, what about your own
sleep?' Marian's hand sought and found her visitor's and
clutched it tightly.

'Pooh!' said Mrs Large, going rather red. 'When you're
as old as I am, you don't need to sleep!' Her tone was rough,
but she made no attempt to disengage her hand.

'I – I never thought that there was anyone near me who
cared whether I slept or not,' murmured Marian, her eyes
beginning to fill with tears.

'That's quite enough of that!' said Mrs Large, thoroughly
alarmed by this display of emotion. She snatched her hand
away and went on briskly: 'What we've got to do now is to
put our heads together.'

'I don't understand.'

'You will when I've finished with you. Now listen to me,
Marian Packer. I don't care whether you killed your husband
or not – '

'Mrs Large, how can you – !'

'That's a matter between you and the Almighty. But I'm
not going to see the wrong person accused of doing it, if I can
help it. I've been thinking this matter over ever since I talked
to that Mr Busy from Scotland Yard the day of the inquest.
I let my tongue run away with me then, and I dare say I'm
responsible. But it's my belief that he's going to arrest Jimmy
Rendel.'

'Jimmy!' cried Marian, starting up. 'Oh, that's not possible! They couldn't – they mustn't!'

'Quite right, my dear, they mustn't. I've got quite other plans in my head for you and Jimmy. As soon as this business is over you and he are going away together and getting married – '

'No, no! I tell you, Mrs Large, I don't want to marry Jimmy – or anyone else – ever again!'

'H'm!' said Mrs Large. 'You disappoint me. However, that's a side issue, as the Rector always says when I put him right about anything. The point is, do you want Jimmy to be hanged?'

'No!' wailed Marian.

'So I thought. And that, my dear, is what I've come about. We've got to stop it, and stop it tonight!'

'Stop it? How can we? And why tonight?'

'Tonight,' repeated Mrs Large firmly, 'or it will be too late. That Busy is at the "Polworthy Arms" now, simply waiting for Jimmy to come in from his fishing to pounce on him. The superintendent has gone over to fetch the chief constable – that odious, conceited little man – and they may be there by now. Bowyer, the village policeman, told my Annie and that's what brought me up. There's no time to lose.'

'But what can we do?' Marian asked, her head spinning.

'Do?' said Mrs Large. 'If you and I can't stop a pack of men making fools of themselves, things have come to a pretty pass! Come along now, we've wasted enough time talking already. Have you got a bicycle?'

'No.'

'A pity. Mine's at the door. You can ride on the step, though.'

'I can drive you down in my car,' suggested Marian, by now completely under the spell of the stronger personality.

'Splendid! I'll leave my bicycle here, and the Rector can walk up for it in the morning. The exercise will do him good. Come along!'

And before she was well aware what she was about, Marian found herself driving out of her garage, with Mrs Large sitting bolt upright beside her.

While the two officers sat in tense expectation in the land-lady's room, the members of the syndicate were dropping in one by one to their late supper in the parlour. The evening rise had been short but fruitful, even beat one yielding one sizable fish to Wrigley-Bell's rod, and an air of good humour and contentment prevailed. Jimmy was able to report a success with Matheson's patent version of the Coachman, without thinking it necessary to mention that he had left two specimens of that precious fly in the thorn bushes which were the bane of beat three. Wrigley-Bell and Matheson chatted together in perfect amity, while Euphemia, more silent than usual, listened with a contented smile. Even Smithers seemed affected by the prevailing good fellowship.

'This is really remarkably pleasant,' he remarked, in a tone which sounded all the more sincere because he seemed to grudge making the admission. 'This time last week, everything seemed to be at sixes and sevens. This evening, I hardly know you all, you seem so good-natured. Yet apart from Rendel, whom I congratulate on having landed a fish at last, we are the same party as last Friday. It must be the disappearance of Packer that has put us all in such good spirits.'

At that moment, as if to emphasize the parallel which Smithers had drawn with the scene of the week before, Dr Latymer put his head in at the door.

'Latymer!' cried the solicitor. 'This is positively uncanny! What are you having – whisky and soda? Don't tell me that there is another illegitimate birth in the village!'

'Smithkins, be quiet!' said Euphemia from her corner on the sofa. 'This is getting too much like a Priestley play, altogether.'

The doctor meanwhile helped himself to a drink.

'No,' he said, 'there are no more erring village maidens in need of my help that I know of. I just happened to be passing and thought I'd look in.' He looked at Mrs Matheson as he spoke, as though expecting a clue. Her face was entirely blank. He went on: 'How are you feeling, Matheson? Not had any recurrence of that trouble?'

'I'm perfectly well,' answered the old man, with a trace of defiance. 'Never felt better in my life.'

'That's good,' said Latymer. Nonetheless, he was frowning and there was perplexity and uneasiness in his face as he carried his drink to a chair at the other side of the room.

A sudden constraint seemed to have fallen over the party. Jimmy, who was by a good many years the youngest, felt it the least, and his voice was the next to be heard.

'I say, sir,' he said to Smithers, 'can you tell me whether – '

He broke off abruptly as the chief constable, looking preternaturally solemn, entered the room, followed by Mallett and White.

'Keep your seats, all of you!' he exclaimed, though nobody had shewn the least disposition to move.

'And who may you be?' inquired Smithers.

'I am the chief constable of this county. This is Inspector Mallett of Scotland Yard. He has something to say that is of importance to everyone in this room.'

So called upon, Mallett stepped forward and, standing with his back to the empty fireplace, looked round at the ring of faces turned with eager inquiry towards his own.

It was an anxious moment. Mallett cleared his throat self-consciously, but before he could speak, there was an interruption. A sound of scuffling was heard outside the door, and Police Constable Bowyer's voice protesting: 'No, indeed, ma'am! Really, my lady, but you can't!' drowned by a feminine voice saying: 'Stuff and nonsense, my good man!' and then the door was thrown open by Mrs Large, dragging Marian Packer in her wake.

'Ha!' exclaimed the Rector's wife. 'Just in time, I fancy!'

'How dare you, madam!' stormed Major Strode. 'Lady Packer, I must beg you to go. You have no business here.'

'Our business,' said Mrs Large firmly, 'is to see that you people don't make idiots of yourselves. This is a public room in a public house, and we shall stay.'

Strode looked round helplessly.

'White, can't you put these people out?' he said.

But Mallett intervened.

'With your permission, sir, I think these ladies had better remain,' he said. 'At least, I should like Lady Packer to remain, as she is one of the people most concerned in the matter I am about to discuss. And I dare say she would like Mrs Large to stay too, to support her.'

'I should think so, indeed!' said Mrs Large. 'Marian dear, there's room for you on the sofa next to Jimmy. Major, I'll trouble you to tell Bowyer to get me a chair.'

When they were all settled, the chief constable said: 'Now, Inspector, after that interruption, perhaps you will say what you have to say.'

'And don't forget, Mr Busy, I have my eye on you,' interjected Mrs Large.

CHAPTER TWENTY-FOUR

Solution

WHATEVER diffidence he felt in facing his audience, thus unexpectedly increased, Mallett showed none. Certainly no speaker ever addressed a gathering more keenly attuned to listen. The atmosphere of the little room was electric with varied emotions. It was impossible not to feel that within the narrow compass of those four walls the spirits of curiosity, anxiety, fear and guilt were alive and active. The only person who seemed entirely uninfluenced by their presence was the speaker himself, who began his exposition in the quiet, balanced tones of a lecturer.

'I have been inquiring into the circumstances of the death of Sir Peter Packer,' he said, 'and as it is a matter which in one way or another more or less intimately concerns everybody present, I thought it advisable to take this opportunity of giving you the results of my investigations. I must begin with an apology – to Dr Latymer, who has been brought here by something very like false pretences. But his presence here was necessary, as I shall show in a minute or two, and I thought myself justified in using the most persuasive arguments I could find to bring him here. He will forgive me for saying so, but I thought that the prospect of a patient was more likely to bring him out late at night than an appeal to his duty to assist the police.

'Sir Peter Packer, as you all know, was found by the river bank last Saturday afternoon, shot dead, apparently by a pistol of small calibre. Dr Latymer has had some difficulty in establishing the time of death, but he now fixes it as at about three to five hours before the discovery of the body. I have accordingly had to concentrate in this inquiry particularly on the hours between twelve noon and two o'clock in the afternoon. Now this is the first point on which I require your assistance, doctor. May I take it that the period you have given can be extended half an hour each way?'

The doctor nodded.

'Let us say between half-past eleven and half-past two, then. Those are the hours between which I have been at some pains to trace the movements of every person in this room – a task which has not been made easier by reason of the fact that a number of the statements originally made to the police proved to be more or less untrue. But I think that I have at last succeeded in my task. Before I go on to deal with that aspect of the case, however, there are two important questions which I must answer.

'The first is: How did Sir Peter come to be in the place where he was killed? There is no difficulty in answering that. He was there by appointment, and his appointment was with Mr Wrigley-Bell. Mr Wrigley-Bell had written to Sir Peter demanding an interview, and suggesting that what he had to say would be of particular concern to Mr Cawston, the secretary of the company with which Mr Wrigley-Bell was associated. Now it so happened (as I think Mr Wrigley-Bell was aware), that Mr Cawston was actually due at the Manor during the week-end, to discuss matters of business with Sir Peter. Sir Peter was evidently determined that if this interview was to take place, it should not be in the presence of Mr Cawston. He therefore telephoned to Mr Wrigley-Bell and insisted on making the appointment for the next morning, not at the Manor but at the waterside. Perhaps Mr Wrigley-Bell's position was not quite so strong as he had represented it to be – at all events, he found it wise to fall in with the suggestion and agree to meet Sir Peter at the point indicated. But he was in this difficulty: the spot agreed on for the meeting – the only part of the water where Sir Peter's property runs down to the bank – was on beat two, where Mr Matheson would in the ordinary course be fishing that day. However much he might have desired the presence of Mr Cawston, he was not anxious for any outsiders to overhear what he and Sir Peter had to say. By some means or other, he had to secure that beat two was deserted at eleven o'clock that morning. What did he do? With considerable presence of mind, as soon as he had finished his telephone conversation, he came back into this room, and there and then picked a quarrel with Mr Matheson, induced him to bet on his capacity to catch fish on the lowest beat of the water and so arranged that the place of the meeting would be free from interruption, at all events until the afternoon, when Mr Rendel was due to arrive.'

'Oh, Wriggles!' exclaimed Euphemia in a tone of deep reproach. Wrigley-Bell flushed a deep red, and his gums bared in a nervous grin. Nobody else spoke. Mallett went on:

'The second question is this: Why was Sir Peter, when he was found, lying in his shirtsleeves on top of his coat? That is a question which raises a number of others. I am assured by those who saw the body at the time that there was no sign of its having been brought to the place after death. I therefore conclude that he was shot on the same spot, sitting on the bank in his shirtsleeves. Now there is every reason to think that the weapon which killed Sir Peter was his own revolver, and that he had that revolver on his person when he went to keep his appointment with Mr Wrigley-Bell. What does that imply? That the murderer took the weapon from him while he sat or lay there – took it either from his hand, or, as seems more probable, from his pocket. Now, Dr Latymer, this is where I need your assistance again. I understand that the deceased was liable to attacks of sunstroke?'

'That is quite correct,' said the doctor.

'Being so liable, if he sat in the sun without a hat, would it take long for such an attack to develop?'

'No. It might come on within a few minutes.'

'What form would it take?'

'Unconsciousness, more or less complete.'

'Have you considered the possibility of someone finding him in this state, removing the pistol from his coat without disturbing, him and then shooting him, still unconscious?'

'Certainly. My opinion has not hitherto been asked on the point, but I have always considered it the most likely theory of how this crime came to be committed.'

'I am much obliged. But that does not quite dispose of all the difficulties. It is clear that on the assumption, the murderer must have known that he would find the pistol in Sir Peter's pocket, or at least have had a reason for searching him, and a motive for using the pistol when he found it. I can point to one person only who might have possessed that knowledge – Lady Packer.'

'Now look here, sir –!' exclaimed Jimmy, starting up at the mention of the name.

'Silence!' roared Major Strode.

Mallett went on imperturbably.

'But need the pistol have been in Sir Peter's pocket?' he continued. 'Is it even likely, on the balance of probabilities, that it was? Let us reconstruct Sir Peter's movements on that morning. He received at breakfast a threatening letter from the lad Carter. We do not know the terms of it because it has been destroyed, but it was in sufficiently strong language for him to consider it wise to go about armed. With the weapon in his pocket, he went down to the riverside to keep his appointment with Mr Wrigley-Bell. He went to the bottom of the causeway and awaited him there, but the first person he met was Mr Smithers, on his way to beat four at the top of the water. According to Mr Smithers' account – which is here borne out by the evidence of Carter – there were some angry words between them on the subject of rights of way, which ended in Sir Peter, who no doubt at this moment saw Mr Wrigley-Bell approaching, allowing him to pass, and Mr Smithers proceeded on his way up the river. There is no evidence that Mr Smithers returned that way until the late evening, and it is beyond question that he left Sir Peter alive and well. There then followed the interview between Sir Peter and Mr Wrigley-Bell. It appears to have been an interview in which both parties lost their tempers, and I have evidence that during the course of it Mr Wrigley-Bell went so far as to threaten Sir Peter. On the other hand, Carter's statement makes it clear that the deceased was then fully dressed and in complete possession of his faculties. Mr Wrigley-Bell, therefore, had no opportunity of committing the crime in the way in which it must have been committed, at that time.

'What follows? The interview is over, and Sir Peter is alone. It is a warm day, and after two violent scenes he is feeling flushed and exhausted. He decides to sit down on the bank for a while and rest, and since it is hot, he takes off his coat and sits upon that. But the revolver is in his coat pocket. It is an uncomfortably hard thing to sit upon. So he takes it out, and lays it beside him on the grass, until such time as he shall feel sufficiently rested to get up and go home. That time never comes. Before long, unconsciousness descends on him, and Sir Peter is lying there, helpless, the weapon beside him, ready to the hand of the murderer.'

Mallett paused for a moment. Everybody was regarding him fixedly, as though afraid of shifting their gaze for a moment, lest by looking round the room they might read suspicion in one another's eyes. Only Mrs Large seemed immune from the spell, darting bird-like glances in every direction.

'I have already dealt with Mr Smithers,' Mallett continued. 'As to Mr Wrigley-Bell, I have shown that up to the time that he left Sir Peter his innocence is established. The only way in which he could have done this crime, therefore, was by returning later on. Yet the evidence of Mr Smithers seems to me to establish conclusively that he came straight from the scene of the interview to the upper part of the water, and remained within observation there until after the murder was in fact discovered. I therefore dismiss him from the case.

'The next person actually at or near the scene of the crime, as we now know, was Dr Latymer himself. According to his account, he arrived at the road corner at 11.50, and was on the top of Didbury Hill ten minutes later, where he was shortly afterwards joined by Mrs Matheson.'

There was a furious 'Oh!' from Euphemia. Her husband said nothing, but continued to sit, grey-faced, staring straight in front of him. Mallett continued calmly:

'That account appears to be correct. Police officers have checked the time when the doctor left his house that morning and it seems clear that even if he had had the desire to do so, he would not have had the time to walk to where Sir Peter was and reach the top of the hill when he did, that is, even supposing that he had the means of knowing where to find Sir Peter. So much for Dr Latymer, and so much also for Mrs Matheson, who at all material times was with him.'

'But Inspector, if I was, that doesn't mean –' Mrs Matheson began, but her husband interrupted her.

'Be quiet, Phemy,' he said wearily. 'I know all about it.'

'I can deal shortly with Philip Carter,' the inspector continued, 'by saying that I have satisfied myself that from the position in which he was, he never had the opportunity to kill Sir Peter. But there are two other persons who undoubtedly had – I mean Mr Rendel and Lady Packer.'

'Ha!' interjected Mrs Large suddenly. 'Now, Mr Busy, you had best be careful!'

'Silence, woman!' barked the chief constable.

'I will not silence! I want to tell this man here, before he goes any further, that he's not to believe a word I said about Jimmy. He and Marian are –'

'Please, please, Mrs Large!' Lady Packer begged her.

'Please be quiet! Don't you see how important this is for me? I must hear what he has to say. You can say what you like afterwards, if – if it becomes necessary.'

'Well, go on, then, Mr Busy! And don't forget I've still got my eye on you.'

'Mr Rendel,' Mallett proceeded, 'arrived at the scene of the crime from the direction of the village. Lady Packer came to it from the Manor. It seems that they must have been there at about the same time. It is quite certain that they were together just after the fact of the murder was discovered. Now it is perfectly true that, at the earliest, they were there long after the times with which I have been so far dealing. If Dr Latymer is correct in his estimation of the time when death took place, neither of them could be guilty; but the doctor will forgive me for saying that he may be wrong. It is all the more fortunate for them, therefore, that there is another piece of evidence which altogether exculpates them. Each of them when interviewed separately and spontaneously said that at the moment when Dr Latymer approached the place where the deceased was a wild duck rose from the water and flew past them. Did you notice the wild duck, Dr Latymer?'

'I'm afraid I can't remember,' was the reply. 'It is highly unlikely that I should notice such a thing at such a time.'

'Very true. But it is still more unlikely that both Mr Rendel and Lady Packer should have invented it independently. If then the passage of Dr Latymer up the bank should have disturbed a bird at or near the scene of the murder, how could it not have been disturbed by either Mr Rendel or Lady Packer or the report of a pistol, a few moments before? Mr Matheson, you are an expert on bird-life. Am I right in my deduction?'

Matheson roused himself from the lethargy into which he had fallen to say: 'Yes.'

'I am obliged to you,' said Mallett. 'That appears to dispose of the case so far as Mr Rendel and Lady Packer are concerned.'

'I should think so!' put in Mrs Large. 'Mr Busy, I apologize. You've got more wits than I gave you credit for. Go on. This is interesting.'

'I have now dealt with all the possible suspects in this case,' said Mallett slowly, 'with the exception of one individual only.' He paused, looked around him, and said: 'That individual is Robert Matheson.'

There was a sudden quickening of interest in the inspector's audience. The emotional tension of the little gathering seemed all at once to be strung to a higher pitch. Nobody stirred, but everyone's breath came a little faster as if at the approach of some long-awaited climax. Only Matheson was to all appearances untouched by the prevailing atmosphere of expectation. He might have been a figure of wood as the inspector continued to address him.

'Your case is particularly interesting. You are the only person who has a complete alibi in this matter. Thanks to the ingenuity of Mr Wrigley-Bell, you were fishing on the lowest beat of the river. It is known that you left the hotel at 11.15 on Saturday morning. You were seen by the landlady engaged in fishing an hour and a half later and again more than once up to half past two. At three o'clock, or not very long after, Mr Rendel met you, still on the same beat, and you had by then caught two fish, and were actually engaged in catching another. As you were at pains to point out to Superintendent White at the outset, you are not a fast walker, and it was physically impossible for you to walk from the hotel to the spot where Sir Peter was found and back again, let alone catch the fish that you did, within the time in which you were not under observation. I have been over the ground myself, and I agree. It is not physically possible. Yet you did it, Mr Matheson, or how was it that when Mr Rendel arrived, you were fishing with a fly the only specimen of which had been left fast in a trout at the road corner the night before?

'Let me explain how it was done.

'When you left the hotel, you did not begin fishing on the bottom beat. Instead, you walked directly up to the road corner, taking the path through the larch copse, which screened you from observation. You walked as fast as you could. I think you were there well before twelve. Mr Wrigley-Bell had disappointed you by starting late, but you were there in time, I think, to see Dr Latymer drive up in his car and begin to make his way to the top of Didbury Camp. You were there, at all events, in time to see through your glasses Mrs Matheson on the crest of the downs approaching the same spot. That was what you had come for – to establish the fact that they were meeting there, in pursuance of the letter which Dr Latymer had handed your wife overnight, along with the prescription, and which you had read while she was out of the bedroom fetching her bag from downstairs. And you had to go all the way to the road corner to do it, because only from there could you see the whole range of the downs, as distinct from the Camp itself. But that done, there was still something else to occupy you. Before all else, you are an angler, and you had your reputation at stake and a wager to win. So you set to work to fish the pool where you found yourself – the best pool in all the water, where you were morally certain of catching at least one fish to vindicate yourself. You were doubly lucky, for not only did you find a rising fish at once, but when you caught it, it proved to be the one that Mr Wrigley-Bell had lost, with his fly still in its mouth – the same fly which you were to use with such effect later on. And there you were, Mr Matheson, within a few yards of the spot where Sir Peter was lying helpless, a revolver by his side! It was jealousy of Dr Latymer that had brought you to the road corner, but the elderly husband of an attractive wife may have reason to be jealous of more persons than one, and of the two it was Sir Peter who had given you the greater cause to hate him.

'The time came for you to leave the road corner. Your design was to get back to your own water – beat one – before half past twelve, when Mr Rendel was expected, so that he would be in a position to establish that you were keeping the conditions of your bet and to prevent your wife from knowing that you had been spying on her. Dr Latymer's car was ready to your hand. You took it, drove as fast as you could down the lane, nearly knocking down Mrs Large on the way, ran the car into the gateway at the bottom of the larch copse, made your way to the river again, and there you were, ready for Mr Rendel, on the water where you were supposed to have been all the morning.

'That was the point at which your plan went wrong. It was essential for its success that you should return the car to its place before your wife and Dr Latymer left the Camp. But Mr Rendel was delayed, and for nearly three mortal hours you had to stay there, occupying yourself fishing, at the mercy of anyone who happened to come up the lane and notice the car, at the mercy of the doctor, if he should return and find it gone. I envy your nerve, Mr Matheson, to be able to fish in such circumstances. During all this time you could not tell, you were only able to hope, that the doctor and your wife were still on Didbury Camp. At last Mr Rendel arrived, just as you were playing your third fish. You found an excuse to go with him up the river to a point from which you could see that the couple had not yet left the Camp, and that your theft of the car had not yet been discovered by them. That was what you were looking at through your glasses – not cross-bills! Luck was with you. A moment or two later they moved out of view. In fact they were coming down the hill by the path on the farther side. You just had time to do what was necessary. You hurried back to the car, drove it to the road corner and left it in its place. On the foot-brake also you unwittingly left the piece of water-weed which Mr Rendel was to find later. Then you slipped away just before Dr Latymer and your wife came off the hill into the road. After that you simply walked back to your beat through the copse again and the trick was done.

'Mr Matheson, you alone, of all the persons concerned, had the means and opportunity to kill Sir Peter Packer at the very time when we were assured it is most likely that the murder took place. As to motive, you and Mrs Matheson know best that that was not lacking. The case against you seems complete.'

CHAPTER TWENTY-FIVE

Conclusion

THERE was utter silence in the room as the inspector ceased his recital. Then Smithers spoke:

'*Seems*, Inspector?' he said. '*Seems* complete?'

Mallett looked round once more at his audience before he answered.

'Yes,' he said slowly. 'I used the word advisedly. The case against Mr Matheson is a strong one, but it is not complete. It fails to answer one essential question. How is it that nobody heard the shot that killed Sir Peter? The people at the cottage – the men at the sawmill – not one of them heard it, and yet I have proved that they were within easy earshot of the place where the pistol was fired. Why not? There is only one explanation – that at the moment when it was fired some louder sound drowned the report – a sound which did not itself attract attention. I know of nothing that could have produced such a sound except the sawmill itself. But the mill did not start work on Saturday until half past twelve. Sir Peter himself had seen to that, so that his interview with Mr Wrigley-Bell should not be disturbed. And before half past twelve Mr Matheson had already left the spot and was passing Mrs Large on the road, travelling away from it. Therefore, I am forced to the conclusion that it is impossible for him to have fired the shot. The case against him breaks down, just as the case against all the others breaks down. I have failed to find a single person who could fulfil all the conditions necessary to commit this crime in the way in which it apparently must have been committed.'

He paused. Dr Latymer expelled a deep breath from his lungs, as though he had been holding it for an unnaturally long time.

'Well, in that case I take it that we may as well go to bed,' he said. 'I don't see why – '

'In that case,' Mallett went on without giving him time to finish, 'we must start our inquiry all over again, and see whether we have not all along been working on a wrong assumption. We have assumed, Dr Latymer, that Sir Peter was dead at least two and a half hours before he was found. Suppose that assumption is wrong – radically wrong? We have assumed, further, that when Mr Rendel caught sight of Sir Peter's legs projecting on to the bank he was looking at a dead man. Suppose that assumption is also wrong – that the man he saw was not dead, but only unconscious through sunstroke? Suppose – '

'What the hell d'you mean?' Latymer had sprung to his feet, his countenance livid and distorted almost beyond recognition.

Mallett turned suddenly to Euphemia.

'Mrs Matheson,' he said, 'Major Strode asked Dr Latymer yesterday what you and he were doing on Saturday afternoon at Didbury Camp. He did not answer directly. Are you prepared to do so now?'

She turned very pale, but answered in a firm voice.

'Yes, I am.

'I have been friendly with Dr Latymer for some time, until lately when I found that friendship was not enough to satisfy him. I told him again and again that it was no use, but he wouldn't believe me. When I met him, quite by chance, on Saturday, he thought I had come there to make love, and when I refused he was furious. Then he began to ask questions about me and Sir Peter – I don't know how he had guessed anything, but he seemed to know. I was miserably unhappy, and I felt the strain of keeping up pretences was more than I could bear. I had to confide in somebody, and I told him – everything.'

She bit her lower lip and bowed her head.

'And then?' Mallett asked.

'Then he suddenly became quite calm, said he understood perfectly, and wanted only to befriend me. He promised that this should be a secret between us, that he would never ask anything from me again, that – '

'You bitch!' roared Latymer. 'You brought me into this!'

He made a rush across the room, but White was quick to intervene.

'Dr Latymer,' said Mallett, 'you killed Sir Peter Packer.'

'Of course I did!' shouted the doctor, beside himself. 'He took my woman – mine – yes, I say *mine*, you impotent old dotard!' he snarled at Matheson.

'When you were told that he was lying on the bank, you went there not to help him, but in the hope that you would find him dead. He was still alive. At that time of the afternoon his head was in the shade of the rushes behind him. He was beginning to recover consciousness. You took your opportunity. You found the pistol lying on the grass beside him – '

'I did not! He had it in his hand! Oh, God!'

Major Strode stepped forward.

'That will do,' he said. 'White, take this man outside.'

The superintendent touched Latymer on the arm. For a moment he braced himself as if to resist. Then his muscles slackened, and he allowed himself to be led away without resistance.

After his departure the first to speak was Wrigley-Bell.

'I'll thank you for the return of that five pounds,' he said to Matheson.

'Melodrama – yes,' said Mallett afterwards. 'But you see, Super, if it hadn't been for the melodrama, we should never have got the confession. And without the confession, the evidence simply wasn't there. I had to play upon his nerves until they broke. Were you watching his face while I was speaking? Did you notice his look of relief when I dismissed him and Mrs Matheson from the case, and the look of pure devilish exultation when I exposed poor old Matheson's alibi? It was hard on the old man, I admit, but I had to make Latymer feel he was perfectly safe, and then let him down with a bump at the end. It was a risk, but it came off.'

'I reckon the man was mad,' said White.

'Mad? Yes, if sheer, unadulterated vanity is madness, I think that living alone here in the country so long, cock of his own little walk, he had begun to think nothing impossible for him, and he simply couldn't credit the idea that a woman could refuse him. The sight of the man who had succeeded where he had failed was too much for his self-control. When he heard her declare publicly that she had never cared for him he broke down altogether, as you saw.'

The superintendent shuddered.

'It's not a sight I want to see the likes of again,' he said. 'But there, Inspector, when all's said and done, murder isn't a nice thing to have to do with.'

The major's comment was: 'I'm glad it wasn't one of the fishing crowd that did it. I'm not in the least surprised. After all, it was a damned unsporting murder.'

Mrs Large and Marian had left the inn together. Exactly how he did not know, Jimmy found himself with them outside the door. A brilliant moon flooded the village street and in its light Marian's white skin shone like alabaster.

'I shall walk home from here,' said Mrs Large. 'Good night, dear.' She pecked at Marian's cheek, then turned to Jimmy and to his complete astonishment pecked him too. 'Be a man now, Jimmy,' she said, and disappeared.

They stood together in the moonlight. Jimmy strove to speak but could find no words. After what seemed a long time, Marian broke the silence.

'Jimmy?' she said.

'Yes – Marian,' he croaked.

'Jimmy, this is awfully difficult for me to say – but do you want to marry me?'

With an effort he managed to get out: 'Yes – oh, yes!'

'I was afraid so. Mrs Large seems to want it too. But' – she shook her head slowly – 'it's no good, Jimmy. I've turned it over and over in my mind and it won't do. You're young, and you're alive, and I'm only the shell of a woman. The real me died a long time ago. We'd simply have to spend our days pretending – pretending that the youth hadn't been killed out of me before we ever met – pretending that there was ever anything in common between us except the common dislike of a man who isn't there any more. So it's good-bye now, Jimmy, for good. I'm going away tomorrow for a long time, and perhaps, when I come back, we'll meet again, and you won't be feeling quite so badly about things as you are now.'

He felt her lips upon his for the first and last time and then she was gone.

Jimmy was heart-broken for two full days, and when they were over began to feel greatly relieved, and greatly ashamed of himself for so doing. His fishing has improved considerably lately, and he is now the secretary of the syndicate. Matheson has given up the Didder altogether. He and his wife have taken up rock gardening together. They are a devoted pair.

THE PERENNIAL LIBRARY MYSTERY SERIES

E. C. Bentley

TRENT'S LAST CASE
"One of the three best detective stories ever written."

—Agatha Christie

TRENT'S OWN CASE
"I won't waste time saying that the plot is sound and the detection satisfying. Trent has not altered a scrap and reappears with all his old humor and charm."

—Dorothy L. Sayers

Gavin Black

A DRAGON FOR CHRISTMAS
"Potent excitement!"

—New York Herald Tribune

THE EYES AROUND ME
"I stayed up until all hours last night reading *The Eyes Around Me,* which is something I do not do very often, but I was so intrigued by the ingeniousness of Mr. Black's plotting and the witty way in which he spins his mystery. I can only say that I enjoyed the book enormously."

—F. van Wyck Mason

YOU WANT TO DIE, JOHNNY?
"Gavin Black doesn't just develop a pressure plot in suspense, he adds uninfected wit, character, charm, and sharp knowledge of the Far East to make rereading as keen as the first race-through." —*Book Week*

Nicholas Blake

THE BEAST MUST DIE
"It remains one more proof that in the hands of a really first-class writer the detective novel can safely challenge comparison with any other variety of fiction." —*The Manchester Guardian*

THE CORPSE IN THE SNOWMAN
"If there is a distinction between the novel and the detective story (which we do not admit), then this book deserves a high place in both categories." —*The New York Times*

THE DREADFUL HOLLOW
"Pace unhurried, characters excellent, reasoning solid."

—San Francisco Chronicle

END OF CHAPTER

". . . admirably solid . . . an adroit formal detective puzzle backed up by firm characterization and a knowing picture of London publishing."
—*The New York Times*

HEAD OF A TRAVELER

"Another grade A detective story of the right old jigsaw persuasion."
—*New York Herald Tribune Book Review*

MINUTE FOR MURDER

"An outstanding mystery novel. Mr. Blake's writing is a delight in itself."
—*The New York Times*

THE MORNING AFTER DEATH

"One of Blake's best."
—Rex Warner

A PENKNIFE IN MY HEART

"Style brilliant . . . and suspenseful."
—*San Francisco Chronicle*

THE PRIVATE WOUND

[Blake's] best novel in a dozen years . . . . An intensely penetrating study of sexual passion . . . . A powerful story of murder and its aftermath."
—Anthony Boucher, *The New York Times*

A QUESTION OF PROOF

"The characters in this story are unusually well drawn, and the suspense is well sustained."
—*The New York Times*

THE SAD VARIETY

"It is a stunner. I read it instead of eating, instead of sleeping."
—Dorothy Salisbury Davis

THOU SHELL OF DEATH

"It has all the virtues of culture, intelligence and sensibility that the most exacting connoisseur could ask of detective fiction."
—*The Times* [London] *Literary Supplement*

THE WHISPER IN THE GLOOM

"One of the most entertaining suspense-pursuit novels in many seasons."
—*The New York Times*

THE WIDOW'S CRUISE

"A stirring suspense. . . . The thrilling tale leaves nothing to be desired."
—*Springfield Republican*

Nicholas Blake *(cont'd)*

THE WORM OF DEATH

"It [The Worm of Death] is one of Blake's very best—and his best is better than almost anyone's."　　　　　　　　—Louis Untermeyer

Christianna Brand

GREEN FOR DANGER

"You have to reach for the greatest of Great Names (Christie, Carr, Queen . . .) to find Brand's rivals in the devious subtleties of the trade."
　　　　　　　　—Anthony Boucher

Marjorie Carleton

VANISHED

"Exceptional . . . a minor triumph."
—Jacques Barzun and Wendell Hertig Taylor, *A Catalogue of Crime*

George Harmon Coxe

MURDER WITH PICTURES

"[Coxe] has hit the bull's-eye with his first shot."
　　　　　　　　—*The New York Times*

Edmund Crispin

BURIED FOR PLEASURE

"Absolute and unalloyed delight."
　　　　　　　　—Anthony Boucher, *The New York Times*

D. M. Devine

MY BROTHER'S KILLER

"A most enjoyable crime story which I enjoyed reading down to the last moment."　　　　　　　　—Agatha Christie

Kenneth Fearing

THE BIG CLOCK

"It will be some time before chill-hungry clients meet again so rare a compound of irony, satire, and icy-fingered narrative. *The Big Clock* is . . . a psychothriller you won't put down."　　　—*Weekly Book Review*

Andrew Garve

THE ASHES OF LODA

"Garve . . . embellishes a fine fast adventure story with a more credible picture of the U.S.S.R. than is offered in most thrillers."

—*The New York Times Book Review*

THE CUCKOO LINE AFFAIR

". . . an agreeable and ingenious piece of work."   —*The New Yorker*

A HERO FOR LEANDA

"One can trust Mr. Garve to put a fresh twist to any situation, and the ending is really a lovely surprise."   —*The Manchester Guardian*

MURDER THROUGH THE LOOKING GLASS

". . . refreshingly out-of-the-way and enjoyable . . . highly recommended to all comers."   —*Saturday Review*

NO TEARS FOR HILDA

"It starts fine and finishes finer. I got behind on breathing watching Max get not only his man but his woman, too."   —Rex Stout

THE RIDDLE OF SAMSON

"The story is an excellent one, the people are quite likable, and the writing is superior."   —*Springfield Republican*

Michael Gilbert

BLOOD AND JUDGMENT

"Gilbert readers need scarcely be told that the characters all come alive at first sight, and that his surpassing talent for narration enhances any plot. . . . Don't miss."   —*San Francisco Chronicle*

THE BODY OF A GIRL

"Does what a good mystery should do: open up into all kinds of ramifications, with untold menace behind the action. At the end, there is a bang-up climax, and it is a pleasure to see how skilfully Gilbert wraps everything up."   —*The New York Times Book Review*

THE DANGER WITHIN

"Michael Gilbert has nicely combined some elements of the straight detective story with plenty of action, suspense, and adventure, to produce a superior thriller."   —*Saturday Review*

DEATH HAS DEEP ROOTS

"Trial scenes superb; prowl along Loire vivid chase stuff; funny in right places; a fine performance throughout."   —*Saturday Review*

Cyril Hare (cont'd)

WITH A BARE BODKIN
"One of the best detective stories published for a long time."
—*The Spectator*

Robert Harling

THE ENORMOUS SHADOW
"In some ways the best spy story of the modern period. . . . The writing is terse and vivid . . . the ending full of action . . . altogether first-rate."
—Jacques Barzun and Wendell Hertig Taylor, *A Catalogue of Crime*

Matthew Head

THE CABINDA AFFAIR
"An absorbing whodunit and a distinguished novel of atmosphere."
—Anthony Boucher, *The New York Times*

MURDER AT THE FLEA CLUB
"The true delight is in Head's style, its limpid ease combined with humor and an awesome precision of phrase."   —*San Francisco Chronicle*

M. V. Heberden

ENGAGED TO MURDER
"Smooth plotting."   —*The New York Times*

James Hilton

WAS IT MURDER?
"The story is well planned and well written."
—*The New York Times*

Elspeth Huxley

THE AFRICAN POISON MURDERS
"Obscure venom, manical mutilations, deadly bush fire, thrilling climax compose major opus.... Top-flight."
—*Saturday Review of Literature*

Francis Iles

BEFORE THE FACT
"Not many 'serious' novelists have produced character studies to compare with Iles's internally terrifying portrait of the murderer in *Before the Fact,* his masterpiece and a work truly deserving the appellation of unique and beyond price."   —Howard Haycraft

Julian Symons (cont'd)

BLAND BEGINNING
"Mr. Symons displays a deft storytelling skill, a quiet and literate wit, a nice feeling for character, and detective ingenuity of a high order."
—Anthony Boucher, *The New York Times*

BOGUE'S FORTUNE
"There's a touch of the old sardonic humour, and more than a touch of style."
—*The Spectator*

THE BROKEN PENNY
"The most exciting, astonishing and believable spy story to appear in years.
—Anthony Boucher, *The New York Times Book Review*

THE COLOR OF MURDER
"A singularly unostentatious and memorably brilliant detective story."
—*New York Herald Tribune Book Review*

THE 31ST OF FEBRUARY
"Nobody has painted a more gruesome picture of the advertising business since Dorothy Sayers wrote 'Murder Must Advertise', and very few people have written a more entertaining or dramatic mystery story."
—*The New Yorker*

Dorothy Stockbridge Tillet
(John Stephen Strange)

THE MAN WHO KILLED FORTESCUE
"Better than average."
—*Saturday Review of Literature*

Simon Troy

SWIFT TO ITS CLOSE
"A nicely literate British mystery . . . the atmosphere and the plot are exceptionally well wrought, the dialogue excellent."
—*Best Sellers*

Henry Wade

A DYING FALL
"One of those expert British suspense jobs . . . it crackles with undercurrents of blackmail, violent passion and murder. Topnotch in its class."
—*Time*

THE HANGING CAPTAIN
"This is a detective story for connoisseurs, for those who value clear thinking and good writing above mere ingenuity and easy thrills."
—*Times Literary Supplement*

Hillary Waugh

LAST SEEN WEARING . . .
"A brilliant tour de force."   —Julian Symons

THE MISSING MAN
"The quiet detailed police work of Chief Fred C. Fellows, Stockford, Conn., is at its best in *The Missing Man* . . . one of the Chief's toughest cases and one of the best handled."
                    —Anthony Boucher, *The New York Times Book Review*

Henry Kitchell Webster

WHO IS THE NEXT?
"A double murder, private-plane piloting, a neat impersonation, and a delicate courtship are adroitly combined by a writer who knows how to use the language."   —Jacques Barzun and Wendell Hertig Taylor

Anna Mary Wells

MURDERER'S CHOICE
"Good writing, ample action, and excellent character work."
                              —*Saturday Review of Literature*

A TALENT FOR MURDER
"The discovery of the villain is a decided shock."   —*Books*

Edward Young

THE FIFTH PASSENGER
"Clever and adroit . . . excellent thriller"   —*Library Journal*

**If you enjoyed this book you'll want to know about
THE PERENNIAL LIBRARY MYSTERY SERIES**

Nicholas Blake

☐	P 456	THE BEAST MUST DIE	$1.95
☐	P 427	THE CORPSE IN THE SNOWMAN	$1.95
☐	P 493	THE DREADFUL HOLLOW	$1.95
☐	P 397	END OF CHAPTER	$1.95
☐	P 398	HEAD OF A TRAVELER	$2.25
☐	P 419	MINUTE FOR MURDER	$1.95
☐	P 520	THE MORNING AFTER DEATH	$1.95
☐	P 521	A PENKNIFE IN MY HEART	$2.25
☐	P 531	THE PRIVATE WOUND	$2.25
☐	P 494	A QUESTION OF PROOF	$1.95
☐	P 495	THE SAD VARIETY	$2.25
☐	P 428	THOU SHELL OF DEATH	$1.95
☐	P 418	THE WHISPER IN THE GLOOM	$1.95
☐	P 399	THE WIDOW'S CRUISE	$2.25
☐	P 400	THE WORM OF DEATH	$2.25

E. C. Bentley

☐	P 440	TRENT'S LAST CASE	$2.50
☐	P 516	TRENT'S OWN CASE	$2.25

Buy them at your local bookstore or use this coupon for ordering:

**HARPER & ROW, Mail Order Dept. #PMS, 10 East 53rd St.,
New York, N.Y. 10022.**

Please send me the books I have checked above. I am enclosing $ _____
which includes a postage and handling charge of $1.00 for the first book and
25¢ for each additional book. Send check or money order. No cash or
C.O.D.'s please.

Name _____

Address _____

City _____ State _____ Zip _____
Please allow 4 weeks for delivery. USA and Canada only. This offer expires
10/1/82. Please add applicable sales tax.

Gavin Black

☐ P 473 A DRAGON FOR CHRISTMAS $1.95
☐ P 485 THE EYES AROUND ME $1.95
☐ P 472 YOU WANT TO DIE, JOHNNY? $1.95

Christianna Brand

☐ P 551 GREEN FOR DANGER $2.50

Marjorie Carleton

☐ P 559 VANISHED $2.50

George Harmon Coxe

☐ P 527 MURDER WITH PICTURES $2.25

Edmund Crispin

☐ P 506 BURIED FOR PLEASURE $1.95

D. M. Devine

☐ P 558 MY BROTHER'S KILLER

    $2.50

Kenneth Fearing

☐ P 500 THE BIG CLOCK $1.95

Buy them at your local bookstore or use this coupon for ordering:

HARPER & ROW, Mail Order Dept. #PMS, 10 East 53rd St., New York, N.Y. 10022.
Please send me the books I have checked above. I am enclosing $ _____ which includes a postage and handling charge of $1.00 for the first book and 25¢ for each additional book. Send check or money order. No cash or C.O.D.'s please.

Name _____

Address _____

City _____ State _____ Zip _____
Please allow 4 weeks for delivery. USA and Canada only. This offer expires 10/1/82. Please add applicable sales tax.

Andrew Garve

☐	P 430	THE ASHES OF LODA	$1.50
☐	P 451	THE CUCKOO LINE AFFAIR	$1.95
☐	P 429	A HERO FOR LEANDA	$1.50
☐	P 449	MURDER THROUGH THE LOOKING GLASS	$1.95
☐	P 441	NO TEARS FOR HILDA	$1.95
☐	P 450	THE RIDDLE OF SAMSON	$1.95

Michael Gilbert

☐	P 446	BLOOD AND JUDGMENT	$1.95
☐	P 459	THE BODY OF A GIRL	$1.95
☐	P 448	THE DANGER WITHIN	$1.95
☐	P 447	DEATH HAS DEEP ROOTS	$1.95
☐	P 458	FEAR TO TREAD	$1.95

C. W. Grafton

☐	P 519	BEYOND A REASONABLE DOUBT	$1.95

Edward Grierson

☐	P 528	THE SECOND MAN	$2.25

Buy them at your local bookstore or use this coupon for ordering:

HARPER & ROW, Mail Order Dept. #PMS, 10 East 53rd St., New York, N.Y. 10022.
Please send me the books I have checked above. I am enclosing $ _____ which includes a postage and handling charge of $1.00 for the first book and 25¢ for each additional book. Send check or money order. No cash or C.O.D.'s please.

Name _____

Address _____

City _____ State _____ Zip _____
Please allow 4 weeks for delivery. USA and Canada only. This offer expires 10/1/82. Please add applicable sales tax.

Cyril Hare

Francis Iles

☐ P 517 BEFORE THE FACT $1.95
☐ P 532 MALICE AFORETHOUGHT $1.95

Lange Lewis

☐ P 518 THE BIRTHDAY MURDER $1.95

Arthur Maling

☐ P 482 LUCKY DEVIL $1.95
☐ P 483 RIPOFF $1.95
☐ P 484 SCHROEDER'S GAME $1.95

Austin Ripley

☐ P 387 MINUTE MYSTERIES $1.95

Thomas Sterling

☐ P 529 THE EVIL OF THE DAY $2.25

Julian Symons

☐ P 468 THE BELTING INHERITANCE $1.95
☐ P 469 BLAND BEGINNING $1.95
☐ P 481 BOGUE'S FORTUNE $1.95
☐ P 480 THE BROKEN PENNY $1.95
☐ P 461 THE COLOR OF MURDER $1.95
☐ P 460 THE 31ST OF FEBRUARY $1.95

Buy them at your local bookstore or use this coupon for ordering:

HARPER & ROW, Mail Order Dept. #PMS, 10 East 53rd St., New York, N.Y. 10022.
Please send me the books I have checked above. I am enclosing $ _____
which includes a postage and handling charge of $1.00 for the first book and
25¢ for each additional book. Send check or money order. No cash or
C.O.D.'s please.

Name _____

Address _____

City _____ State _____ Zip _____
Please allow 4 weeks for delivery. USA and Canada only. This offer expires
10/1/82. Please add applicable sales tax.

Dorothy Stockbridge Tillet
(John Stephen Strange)

☐ P 536 THE MAN WHO KILLED FORTESCUE $2.25

Simon Troy

☐ P 546 SWIFT TO ITS CLOSE $2.50

Henry Wade

☐ P 543 A DYING FALL $2.25
☐ P 548 THE HANGING CAPTAIN $2.25

Hillary Waugh

☐ P 552 LAST SEEN WEARING . . . $2.50
☐ P 553 THE MISSING MAN $2.50

Henry Kitchell Webster

☐ P 539 WHO IS THE NEXT? $2.25

Anna Mary Wells

☐ P 534 MURDERER'S CHOICE $2.25
☐ P 535 A TALENT FOR MURDER $2.25

Edward Young

☐ P 544 THE FIFTH PASSENGER $2.25

Buy them at your local bookstore or use this coupon for ordering:

HARPER & ROW, Mail Order Dept. #PMS, 10 East 53rd St., New York, N.Y. 10022.
Please send me the books I have checked above. I am enclosing $ _____ which includes a postage and handling charge of $1.00 for the first book and 25¢ for each additional book. Send check or money order. No cash or C.O.D.'s please.

Name _____

Address _____

City _____ State _____ Zip _____
Please allow 4 weeks for delivery. USA and Canada only. This offer expires 10/1/82. Please add applicable sales tax.